Merlin's Trials

Also by J. A. Thornbury

Merlin: The Prophet of Britain

Book I
Merlin's Sister

Merlin: The Prophet of Britain
Book II

Merlin's Trials

J. A. Thornbury

Gavia Press

For Robert and Donna

BRITANNIA c. 500
ROADS AND PLACES
ANTONINE WALL
DIN EIDYN
CATHURES
LOTHIAN
CALEDONIA
ARFDERYDD
RHEGED
HADRIAN'S WALL
LARK'S FORT
LUGUVALIUM
DERVENTIO
BROCAVUM
ITUNA ESTUARY
CUMBRIA
HIBERNIA
GLANNOVENTA
EBORACUM
IRISH SEA
BRIGANTIA
LINDUM
DEVA
SEGONTIUM
DINAS EMRYS
VIROCONIUM
CAMBRIA
SAXON LANDS
SAXON LANDS
DYFED
MORIDUNUM
VENTA SILURUM
GLEVUM
VERULAMIUM
BURRIUM
ISCA
LONDINIUM
SABRINA ESTUARY
AQUAE SULIS
CALLEVA
GIANTS' RING
DUMNONIA
CAMALAT
SAXON LANDS
CLAUSENTUM
ANDERIDA
ISCA DUMNONIORUM
TINTAGEL
VECTIS INSULA
BRITISH SEA
ALETH
MOUNT TOMBE
ARMORICA
CONDATE RIEDONUM
DARIORITUM

Places

<table>
<tr><td>Aleth</td><td>St-Malo, France</td></tr>
<tr><td>Anderida</td><td>Pevensey, England</td></tr>
<tr><td>Aquae Sulis</td><td>Bath, England</td></tr>
<tr><td>Arfderydd</td><td>Arthuret, England</td></tr>
<tr><td>Armorica</td><td>Brittany, France</td></tr>
<tr><td>Brocavum</td><td>Penrith, England</td></tr>
<tr><td>Burrium</td><td>Usk, Wales</td></tr>
<tr><td>Caledonia</td><td>Scotland</td></tr>
<tr><td>Calleva</td><td>Silchester, England</td></tr>
<tr><td>Camalat</td><td>South Cadbury, England</td></tr>
<tr><td>Cambria</td><td>Wales</td></tr>
<tr><td>Cathures</td><td>Glasgow, Scotland</td></tr>
<tr><td>Clausentum</td><td>Bitterne, England</td></tr>
<tr><td>Condate Riedonum</td><td>Rennes, France</td></tr>
<tr><td>Darioritum</td><td>Vannes, France</td></tr>
<tr><td>Derventio</td><td>Cockermouth, England</td></tr>
<tr><td>Deva</td><td>Chester, England</td></tr>
<tr><td>Din Eidyn</td><td>Edinburgh, Scotland</td></tr>
<tr><td>Dinas Emrys</td><td>Fort near Yr Wyddfa (Snowdon) in Wales</td></tr>
<tr><td>Eboracum</td><td>York, England</td></tr>
<tr><td>Giants' Ring</td><td>Stonehenge</td></tr>
<tr><td>Glannoventa</td><td>Ravenglass, England</td></tr>
<tr><td>Glevum</td><td>Gloucester, England</td></tr>
<tr><td>Hibernia</td><td>Ireland</td></tr>
<tr><td>Isca</td><td>Caerleon, Wales</td></tr>
<tr><td>Isca Dumnoniorum</td><td>Exeter, England</td></tr>
<tr><td>Lark's Fort</td><td>Caerlaverock, Scotland</td></tr>
<tr><td>Lindum</td><td>Lincoln, England</td></tr>
<tr><td>Londinium</td><td>London, England</td></tr>
<tr><td>Luguvalium</td><td>Carlisle, England</td></tr>
<tr><td>Moridunum</td><td>Caerfyrddin, Wales</td></tr>
<tr><td>Mount Tombe</td><td>Le Mont-St-Michel, France</td></tr>
<tr><td>Segontium</td><td>Caernarfon, Wales</td></tr>
<tr><td>Tintagel</td><td>Tintagel, Cornwall</td></tr>
<tr><td>Vectis Insula</td><td>Isle of Wight</td></tr>
<tr><td>Venta Silurum</td><td>Caerwent, Wales</td></tr>
<tr><td>Verulamium</td><td>St. Albans, England</td></tr>
<tr><td>Viroconium</td><td>Wroxeter, England</td></tr>
</table>

Characters

Aled	Second son of Prince Constantine and Princess Elen
Alys	Wife of Lord Cei
Ana	Sister of Uther Pendragon, later wife of King Budicius of Armorica and mother of King Hoel
Anna	Queen of Lothian, daughter of Queen Igraine and King Gorlois, half sister of King Arthur
Annwr	Wife of Bedwyr
Arthur	High King of Britain, son of Queen Igraine and High King Uther Pendragon
Arwel	Eldest son of Prince Constantine and Princess Elen
Barinthus	A mariner
Bedwyr	Cupbearer and friend of King Arthur
Budoc	An officer in the King's Harriers
Cadog	Friend of Dinabutius
Cador	King of Dumnonia, brother of Queen Igraine
Cei	Seneschal and foster brother of King Arthur, son of Lord Ector and Lady Drusilla
Cerdic	A Saxon king
Conanus	Son of Lord Efan
Constantine	Prince of Dumnonia, son of King Cador
Dafydd	A stablehand
Delwyn	Eldest son of Alys and Lord Cei

Dinabutius	A bully
Drusilla	Wife of Lord Ector, foster mother of King Arthur
Drustan	Commander of the Sea Hawks
Ector	A lord of Cumbria, father of Cei, foster father of King Arthur
Efan	A lord of Dumnonia, brother of Princess Elen
Elen	Princess of Dumnonia, wife of Prince Constantine
Galfridus	A monk
Gallus	A fisherman
Ganieda	Queen of Cumbria, twin sister of Merlin, wife of King Rodarch
Gawain	Prince of Lothian, eldest son of Queen Anna and King Lot
Gerin	Armorican military commander, husband of Helena
Giraldus	A monk
Guendoloena	Queen of Dyfed, wife of Merlin
Gwasawg	Steward of King Rodarch
Gwenddolau	A marauding warlord who was defeated and slain during the battle of Arfderydd
Gwenhwyfar	Queen of Britain, wife of King Arthur
Gwyn	Prince of Cumbria, son of Queen Ganieda and King Rodarch
Helena	Sister of King Hoel, wife of Lord Gerin

Helena the Younger	Daughter of Helena and Lord Gerin, niece of King Hoel
Hen	A farmer
Hermogenes	Queen Ganieda's agent
Hoel	King of Armorica, cousin of King Arthur
Igraine	Queen of Britain, wife of High King Uther Pendragon, mother of King Arthur and Queen Anna
Judoc	An Armorican farmer
Kentigern	Bishop of Cathures
Llew	Brother of Bedwyr
Lucius	Captain of the Sea Hawks
Machaon	A doctor
Madoc	A blacksmith
Madog	A friend of Merlin
Marin	King of Brigantia
Meleri	Eldest daughter of Annwr and Bedwyr
Meliot	An officer in the King's Harriers, son of King Marin
Merlin	King of Dyfed, The Prophet of Britain
Mordred	Second son of Queen Anna and King Lot
Morgen	The Lady of Avalon
Mori	A fisherman

Morken	King of Alclud
Morwen	Merlin's former lover
Nimue	Chief Advisor to King Arthur, cousin of Meliot
Olwen	Princess of Cumbria, daughter of Queen Ganieda and King Rodarch
Pelleas	Commander of the King's Eagles, husband of Nimue
Peredur	King of Rheged
Rhiwallon	A lord of Cumbria, father of Guendoloena
Rodarch	King of Cumbria, husband of Queen Ganieda
Stater	A chieftain of Dyfed
Taliesin	A bard
Tomos	Friend of Dinabutius
Ulfin	Chamberlain to King Arthur
Uther Pendragon	High King of Britain, father of King Arthur
Winoc	An Armorican scout
Yanig	An Armorican farmer

Contents

Part I

Part II

Part I

Prologue

Ganieda, the Queen of Cumbria, was walking down a dimly lit hallway when she paused to peer through a narrow window. It was still pouring rain. Turning away with a little sigh, she continued along the corridor. Reaching an oaken door at the end, she pushed it open and entered into a dark and cavernous room. Running down the middle of the room for much of its length was a long table with benches on either side. At the far end of the chamber stood a smaller table, elevated on a raised platform, with its chairs arranged along one side so that its occupants could look out over the feasting hall. In the open hearth between the two tables, a fire had been allowed to burn down to feebly glowing embers. The gloomy hall was deserted save for a single woman who had remained seated at the table on the dais long after the midday meal was finished. She seemed to be studying the tabletop but looked up at the other woman's approach. Some twenty years younger than Ganieda, she, too, was a queen. With hazel eyes, curling, honey-colored hair and attractive features, she would have been considered beautiful if not for a careworn expression which pinched her face like an extended illness.

The woman was Merlin's wife.

Ganieda sat beside her, gently touching her arm. "I'm afraid the rain's not letting up, Guen. Shall we postpone our walk until tomorrow?"

Guendoloena nodded mutely in answer, looking as cheerless and miserable as the weather. Ever since her husband's disappearance, now over eight months ago, the once irrepressible and vivacious newlywed had become a shadow of her former self. On only one occasion since the fateful battle of Arfderydd had Guendoloena's face been lit by its former radiance. On that day, when Ganieda had seen in a vision that her brother still lived, the two women had hugged and kissed and cried for joy, expecting that Merlin would soon be found. Since that time, now over six weeks ago, Guendoloena's initial hope and optimism had faded into her present state of perennial melancholy.

The previous summer, the marauding northern warlord Gwenddolau had been defeated in battle by three allied British kings near Arfderydd, some ten miles north of Luguvalium and the great Roman wall which stretched from coast to coast across northern Britain. Although they had defeated their enemy, the kings' victory had been a Pyrrhic one. Ganieda's husband Rodarch had lost nearly a third of his forces during the bitter internecine conflict, while his staunch ally to the north, King Peredur of Rheged, had lost an even greater number of men. Additionally, Peredur had suffered a most grievous personal loss when all three of his brothers were killed on the field of battle. The third king, Merlinus Ambrosius of Dyfed, the brilliant scholar and former chief advisor to Arthur, High King of Britain, had also suffered a most grievous personal loss – he had lost his mind.

When Peredur's two younger brothers had defied orders and impetuously charged into battle, Merlin had tried, but failed, to save their lives and the life of the third brother. Then, on the heels of that catastrophe, Merlin had suddenly and inexplicably fallen during the battle, writhing on the ground in excruciating pain. Only later had his twin sister Ganieda been able to deduce that her brother had been given poison, guilefully slipped into his wine flask by a vengeful former lover. Although the poison was meant to kill him, Merlin had survived, but its effect on his mind had been devastating. Rendering him unable to speak, he had fled soon after the battle into the vast forests of Caledonia, where he now lived as a wild man of the woods, fearing men and their ways but communing as one with the animals of the forest. Although search parties had been sent to find him and restore him to his family, Merlin had eluded them for months. Even Merlin's loving wife Guendoloena had met with no better success as she continued the search for her husband long after all others had given up the attempt as hopeless. Concerned for Guendoloena's welfare and safety, Ganieda had managed to convince her sister-in-law to return with her to Brocavum, Cumbria's capital. There, waiting for news of her husband, Guendoloena had fretted like a caged animal while Ganieda's agent Hermogenes continued the search.

Then, in late winter, human remains were discovered not far from Arfderydd. Thought to be those of Merlin, they were brought to Brocavum in a solemn funeral cortege. But Ganieda had not been so certain. By examining the skull and noting the perfect front teeth, she had proven that the remains could not have been those of her brother whose left front tooth had been chipped in childhood. Then, shortly after that discovery, a jubilant Ganieda had seen in a vision that her brother still lived. Amid optimism that he would soon be found, Ganieda's agent had set out once again. So far, however, his search had proven fruitless.

Since the rainy weather precluded their walk, Ganieda was trying to distract Guendoloena by proposing a game of chess when there was a knock at the door, and a tall, bearded man wearing a rain-soaked traveling cloak entered the room. Ganieda recognized him as one of Peredur's couriers from Rheged. Walking across the hall, he bowed and presented Ganieda with a letter. Seeing her agent's handwriting on the outside of the folded parchment, she thanked the messenger and asked him to wait outside in the hallway until she knew if an immediate reply were required. Bowing to the two queens, he left the room.

With equal amounts of hope and apprehension, Ganieda broke the wax seal and began to read aloud. Anxiously, Guendoloena listened to the words that would bring her either joy, disappointment, or sorrow.

Chapter 1

The Stray

The morning began like all others when Hen and his wife rose at dawn to start another day. With a storm still raging from the night before, there was barely enough light inside the ramshackle cottage by which to see. Making her way to the hearth, Hen's wife rekindled a fire from smoldering embers and set a battered pot over the flames. While she stirred the porridge left over from their previous night's supper, Hen threw some cold water on his face from a bucket and dressed. Neither spoke while they ate at a small wooden table. Quickly finishing his porridge, he pushed away the bowl and told his wife that he was going to check on the ewes. She nodded and put a chunk of day-old barley bread into a bag. Tying the bag to his belt, he slipped a woolen cloak over his head, picked up his shepherd's crook and whistled to a dog that was curled up in the corner of the room. With an eager yelp, the dog ran to Hen and squirmed happily as his tail beat against his master's leg.

As soon as Hen opened the door, his face was stung by cold rain driven by a lashing wind blowing out of the northeast. Holding down the hood of his cloak with his free hand and hunching his shoulders, he trudged across a muddy stubble field and up the hill toward the higher ground of the pasture.

Surrounded on three sides by wild and desolate mountains, his farm was hardly a choice piece of property, but it was all he had been able to afford. Every single one of his neighbors was better off than he, with better land, better animals, and a wife who had given her husband three or four or more children. His wife had given him none. So while everyone else had helping hands, he had to do all the work by himself, on a farm from which he could barely scrape a living.

When he reached the dry stone enclosure, he cursed his bad luck; a section of the wall had tumbled down during the night. Climbing over the rubble, he entered the fold and counted the ewes, now big with the lambs they were carrying. Three were missing. Climbing out again, he began searching and found two of them a short distance up a path. With the help of his dog, he soon had them inside the fold again and did a quick repair, restacking the stones to fill the gap. When he straightened himself, he looked back up the path apprehensively. He never liked to go very far that way even on a bright summer day. The valley it led to was remote and bleak, and the high surrounding mountains seemed to glower down menacingly. He could hardly afford to lose a single ewe, however, and that was most likely where she had strayed. So, calling the dog to his side, Hen set off, striding briskly along the path.

After entering the woods, the path dwindled to a rough game trail and soon disappeared altogether, but Hen continued, keeping the vigorously flowing stream to his right. All around him the trees were sighing mournfully as their trunks swayed and creaked in the blustery wind, while overhead their still-bare branches clattered like skeletal fingers as they were tossed about by the gusts. Shivering, Hen turned his eyes back to the ground and resolutely strode on in the face of the driving rain.

Where a tributary came tumbling down from the left to join the main stream, he paused for a moment to listen. Hearing a faint bleat coming from far-off on that side, he cursed under his breath. Just his luck that the ewe had wandered into that awful place. He had entered that deep ravine only once before. Vividly, he remembered how the steep-sided gorge had been filled with spires of blackened rocks that looked as if they had been scorched by flame. Other rocks were weirdly shaped and contorted, like otherworldly demons frozen into stone. Once, when he turned back quickly to look, he was sure he caught one of the stones moving toward him before it abruptly stopped again. Breathlessly reaching his pasture, he had sworn he would never return. The sheep bleated again. Cursing the bad fortune that followed him like a cloud, he called his dog to his side and entered the gorge, walking alongside the quickening stream.

As he was passing a rocky outcrop on his left, he noticed how it was so deeply undercut that it formed an overhang large enough to shelter a man. He was more than a little unnerved to see a thick layer of dry bracken inside, as if someone had placed it there. Just then, he heard another bleat and looked up to find the ewe calmly cropping some grass. As he was walking toward the silly beast, he heard another sound – a sound that chilled his blood – a long, wavering and mournful wail that dissolved into piteous sobs and then silence.

Hen's first impulse had been to turn and run, but seeing his dog looking attentive rather than afraid, he paused. The dog invariably bristled at danger. Observing the dog's calm reaction and his own curiosity being slightly greater than his fear, he stealthily advanced toward the place from which the sound had come and hid behind a rock. Then, gripping his crook tightly, he slowly raised his head to see who or what had made that dreadful noise.

Hen was surprised to find a barefooted man sitting on his haunches by the side of a spring, his long arms clasped around his bony knees. Water was dripping from the ends of his straggly gray hair and beard, and the tattered garment he was wearing afforded scant protection from the cold wind and driving rain. Rocking back and forth, the huddled man was muttering doleful and incomprehensible groans and sighs. Hen had never seen a more pitiable and abject sight in his life. By the look of him, he was some harmless and unfortunate halfwit. A thought suddenly struck Hen. Maybe, in exchange for a little food and a place to sleep in the barn, the fellow could be taught to do tasks around the farm. The idea pleased Hen – having someone around even worse off than himself somehow made him feel better. Fishing around in his bag, he pulled out the chunk of slightly sodden bread. Holding it on the palm of his out-stretched hand, he slowly emerged from behind the rock.

The man tensed when he saw Hen, but seeing the friendly gesture and catching sight of the proffered bread, he did not flee. Emboldened, Hen eagerly took a few steps closer, and the man, who had been eyeing the bread, suddenly gave a cry of fear. Nimble as a goat, he sprang up, clinging onto the sheer rock wall of the gorge. Then he began to climb. Within seconds he had disappeared up into the wooded flanks of the looming mountain. Hen was terrified. No mortal man could have ascended those steep rocky slopes with such ease. Stumbling out of the gorge as fast as he could, Hen paused just long enough to send the dog to retrieve the sheep, but only after he had reached his own pasture again did he feel safe enough to steal a fearful glance back toward the mountains whose tops were now quite hidden in the swirling mist.

Shifting uncomfortably on his saddle, Hermogenes pulled down the hood of his cloak, trying to keep the cold rain from pelting his face. Having spent months crisscrossing the vast wooded stretches of southern Caledonia, even the usually optimistic Hermogenes was finally beginning to admit to himself the virtual impossibility of the task that he had set out to accomplish. He now realized that he might as well be looking for a coin dropped somewhere between Luguvalium and Cathures or a mouse set loose in a meadow. Last autumn, he had at least been rewarded with tales of people who had caught glimpses of the wild man. Now, with no new sightings to report, he was fearing the worse. No one, not even Merlin himself, was likely to have survived the winter alone and without any resources. Shivering with the thought, he urged his tired mount to a trot.

It was late afternoon, and the rain was finally abating when he rode into the village where he was planning to stay for the night. The inn, he remembered, was a one-room hovel, but the thought of the warm fire in the hearth was cheering, and the loft in the stable was not the worst place he had ever had to spend a night.

After bespeaking a place for himself and his mount, Hermogenes returned from the stable and put down a coin to pay for a cup of beer and a bowl of watery stew. He took both to a table near the hearth and gratefully sat on a bench with his back to the crackling fire. A few regulars were there, talking among themselves when the door opened, and a short, undernourished-looking man came in. From the mockery in the voices that greeted him, Hermogenes easily recognized the type; the fellow was the town butt. Among other taunts Hermogenes heard one of them say, "Seen any more wild men today?" as everyone hooted with laughter. The man was so used to their scorn that he merely bore it. He wanted to put a cup of beer on account, but the innkeeper shook his head. Just as he was turning to leave, Hermogenes intervened, showing a copper. Grunting, the innkeeper took the coin and put a cup in the little man's hands. Bobbing his head, the fellow thanked the stranger gratefully. He was looking around for a place to sit when Hermogenes waved him over and said, "There's room here, friend."

With a flash of triumph at his neighbors, he sat at the table opposite Hermogenes. Raising his cup toward his benefactor, he took a long appreciative pull. After learning the stranger's name, he introduced himself as Hen.

"So, Hen, what's all this about a wild man?"

Hen immediately became defensive, suspecting he was about to be subjected to more ridicule, but Hermogenes quickly put him at ease. "I meant no harm in the question, friend." Then, lowering his voice in a confiding manner, he added, "To tell you the truth, I am actually looking for just such an unfortunate. Indeed, the man whom you saw may very well be the man whom I seek."

Gratified that someone was finally taking him seriously, Hen replied, "I see you're an educated man. Unlike these neighbors of mine who'd rather have a laugh than believe the truth," he added, with a jerk of his head toward his tormentors.

Signaling to the innkeeper to refill their cups, Hermogenes gave Hen his full attention. Feeling self-important for a change, Hen glanced around to see if his neighbors were listening. Satisfied that they were, he began to tell his tale. When he reached the part where the wild man climbed up the sheer walls of the gorge, he hesitated, but Hermogenes urged him to omit nothing. Since the other man was listening so intently and, Hen thought, so intelligently, he told the whole story. He was gratified that the stranger received the information eagerly.

"How long ago was this?" Hermogenes asked.

"Yesterday morning."

"Yesterday morning!"

Hen was pleased to see the effect this bit of news had. "That's right," he affirmed, nodding. "About two hours after sunrise, yesterday morning."

"This man you saw, what did he look like?"

"Very tall and thin with long gray hair and beard."

"What was he wearing?"

"Just rags. Looked like old, torn blankets."

"Anything else about him? Any distinguishing marks?"

Hen's face screwed up in thought. "A scar," he said finally. "He had a scar on his left cheek. But it was mostly covered by his beard."

Hermogenes asked, "Would it be possible to reach this gorge before dark tonight?"

"It might," Hen replied slowly.

"I'd like you to take me there."

Hen, looking at the stranger appraisingly, did not reply.

Seeing his hesitation, Hermogenes said, "I assure you that I have nothing but good intentions for this man. I have actually been sent by his sister to find him, so that he may be restored to his loving and anxiously awaiting family. They are all very concerned about him."

When he saw that Hen was still hesitating, Hermogenes smiled knowingly. Reaching into his bag, he handed Hen a coin. The farmer stared speechlessly at the piece of silver in his hand.

"I'd like to be off as soon as possible, if you don't mind."

"No, sir, not at all," Hen replied, quickly draining his cup.

As Hen was following Hermogenes to the door, he could see that every eye in the room was riveted upon him. Jauntily flipping the coin into the air with his thumb and deftly catching it, he slipped it into the bag on his belt and exited the inn with a triumphant flourish.

After mounting his horse, Hermogenes pulled the little man up behind him. With Hen clasping him rather tightly around the waist, he set off at a canter down an overgrown lane. Following the farmer's direction, he turned his horse from the lane when they came to a track that led toward the distant mountains to the north. Upon reaching the edge of the wooded valley, they dismounted, and Hermogenes tied his horse so it could graze. Then, with Hen in the lead, they made their way into the forest.

They had entered the narrow gorge and were walking alongside the vigorously flowing stream when Hen pointed out the rock shelter with the dried bracken inside. Hermogenes nodded silently. Moving stealthily, they advanced to a large boulder and crouched behind it. Having heard nothing after listening for several minutes, Hermogenes slowly raised his head. He could see the spring that Hen had described but was disappointed to find no one around it. He lowered his head again, and the two continued to wait. The sun had set, and it was rapidly growing dark before Hermogenes finally abandoned their hiding place to examine the area around the spring. Hen was concerned that Hermogenes might demand to have his coin back and was greatly relieved that the impressions of large, bare feet in the orange-colored mud seemed to satisfy him.

By the time they returned to the horse, it was quite dark, and Hermogenes readily accepted Hen's offer of a place to sleep for the night. As Hen led the way to his farm, he was now quite certain that his luck had finally changed for the better as he listened to two silver coins clinking together in his bag.

Hen's guest spent all of the next two days in the gorge with the same disappointing results. On the morning of the third day, however, Hermogenes returned to the house unexpectedly early, excited to have seen fresh tracks in the mud obviously made the previous night. Having decided to return to Brocavum with the news, he instructed the farmer not to enter the gorge in his absence. Hen was more than happy to comply with that request. After promising Hen that he would be well rewarded for his trouble, Hermogenes vaulted into his saddle and set off down the lane, urging his horse to a gallop. Waving, the farmer smiled as he listened to five coins clinking in his bag, the latest one gold.

Chapter 2

Reunion

Ganieda was reading in the room that she used as her study when a guard entered to inform her that Hermogenes had returned. After waiting several anxious minutes, she relaxed as he entered, and she saw the pleased look on his face. Eagerly, she listened to his report. When he finished, she waved away his apology that he had hoped to have brought Merlin himself rather than mere news about him and assured her agent that he had done very well indeed.

"How would you wish me to proceed, My Queen? Do you think additional men…?"

Ganieda shook her head. "No, I think not. That course of action has already proven unsuccessful. More men will simply frighten my brother away. I do have an idea, however. Taliesin is still at King Peredur's court in Luguvalium, is he not?"

"Yes, I believe he'll be there until the end of the month."

"Good. I plan on going back with you to this spring that you've described. When we reach Luguvalium, I'll ask Taliesin to accompany us there. I'm sure he'll be happy to help an old friend. I feel certain that if anyone can reach my brother's troubled mind, it is he."

Hen was quite beside himself with excitement at the unbelievable turn of events. Not only had Hermogenes returned, but with him were none other than Ganieda, the Queen of Cumbria, and Taliesin, the most famous bard in all Britannia. Then, with his head still spinning over that development, he learned to his utter amazement that his resident wild man was none other than Merlin himself. Had King Arthur and Queen Gwenhwyfar shown up next, he would scarcely have been surprised.

Queen Ganieda graciously thanked Hen and his wife for their help and cooperation, pressing a gold coin into the hand of each. Hen's wife, looking stunned and a little frightened, attempted a curtsy as her husband performed an elaborate bow. Then, with Hermogenes leading the way, Ganieda and Taliesin immediately set off for the spring.

Reaching the edge of the wooded valley, they dismounted and continued through the forest on foot. They entered the gorge and were in a little clearing just short of the spring when Hermogenes stopped and silently pointed to a large stone ahead. Ganieda nodded. Then, in accordance with their previously discussed plan, he bowed to his queen and turned back to wait by the horses.

Looking around the pleasant glade, Ganieda chose a seat on the gnarled root of an ancient oak while Taliesin perched on the trunk of a fallen tree opposite her. Shafts of light streaming through the trees from a bright noonday sun were illuminating the many varied and interesting black and ochre-colored rock formations that filled the narrow valley. All around, budding branches were murmuring softly as they swayed gently in the warm breeze. Amidst the branches' fresh golden-green foliage, birds, welcoming spring and the fair weather, were filling the air with exuberant song.

Taliesin removed the leather case slung over his shoulder and set it beside him on the log. He lifted out an exquisitely crafted maple lyre, decorated with gilt escutcheons ornamented with garnets, and held the instrument lovingly as he tuned it. Plucking the strings above the handsomely carved amber bridge, he then tightened or loosened them by turning the bone pegs on the yoke. The birds, attracted by new and unfamiliar notes, were gathering around the bard curiously as they chirruped and hopped from branch to branch. When he was finally satisfied, Taliesin cradled the lyre in his arms and began playing a melody with long graceful fingers. Then he added his own pure and clarion voice to the varied sounds of nature.

The song he sang was about a boy – a gifted boy who had outwitted priests and soothsayers by knowing why a tower would not stand, who summoned dragons and prophesied to kings, who rebuilt the circle of stones put into place by giants and who plunged the Sword of Avalon into solid rock – King Arthur's wise advisor, Dyfed's just king, Britain's own prophet – Merlin.

As the last note faded, Taliesin scanned the woods hopefully. Seeing no one, he looked disappointed as he turned to Ganieda. She nodded encouragingly. Once again the bard raised his voice in song.

He sang a song about another gifted boy – a boy called Gwion Bach. Spellbound by a witch named Ceridwen, the little boy had been forced by her to stir a brew intended to endow her undistinguished son Morfran with wisdom. Every day, Gwion had labored, stirring the witch's brew in a cauldron over the fire. After exactly one year and one day, the potion was finally ready. While Morfran stood by, waiting for the gift to be bestowed upon him, the three precious drops of distilled wisdom leapt out of the cauldron and flew toward him. Shrewdly, Gwion shoved Morfran aside, so the drops would fall upon him instead. When the burning drops landed on his fingers, he instinctively sucked them off, thus gaining the wisdom meant for the witch's son. In a towering fury, Ceridwen lunged at Gwion, intending to kill him, but the now gifted boy escaped by changing into a hare. The witch quickly answered by transforming herself into a greyhound. When the hare was blocked by a river, he jumped into the water and turned into a trout, but Ceridwen followed closely behind him by changing into an otter. Leaping from the river, Gwion took to the air as a sparrow, but the witch stooped upon him as a sparhawk. Hard-pressed, Gwion flew into a barn where wheat was being winnowed and turned into one of the grains. Triumphantly, the witch turned herself into a hen and swallowed him up into her belly. There, she carried him for nine months until she had deliverance of him. With him finally at her mercy, she was about to kill the baby when she gazed upon his radiant face and found herself unable to do him harm. The reborn babe was renamed – Taliesin.

The bard stopped singing and looked around hopefully. Silently, Ganieda shook her head. Taliesin paused to re-tune the lyre. Then, plucking out the notes of a sad lament, he began to sing:

> O sorrowful the doleful sighs of Guendoloena!
> O pitiful the wretched tears of Guendoloena!
> Beyond the fragrant rose,
> Beyond the lily in the field,
> Beyond goddesses is the beauty of Guendoloena!
> Like twin stars sparkle her two bright eyes,
> Like lustrous gold shimmers her hair!
> But the bloom on her cheeks is now faded,
> For she knows not where her dear love has flown,
> And if he is still with the living,
> Or if with the dead he has gone.
> At her side Ganieda is weeping,
> In sadness their tears are conjoined,
> In sorrow their tears flow together,
> For a brother or husband they mourn.

Their two tortured hearts torn asunder,
Time passes in dolor and woe,
Time passes so slowly in sadness,
Grief and sorrow now all they can know.

As the last note faded, the only sounds to be heard were the babbling of the brook and the murmur of the wind in the branches overhead. Quietly, a man stepped out from behind an oak tree and stood beside it. Ganieda and Taliesin held their breath, afraid that any word or the slightest movement might frighten him away, but entranced by the music, he merely put up a hand to wipe way his tears. When he lowered it again, he seemed transformed, his dark brown eyes once again clear and blue. He was smiling at them with recognition. Softly he said, "I feel quite overcome by that sad lament which has so touched my heart, my dear Taliesin."

Ganieda, hearing her brother speak, leapt to her feet with joy and ran to embrace him. Happily, Merlin embraced her in turn. When she finally released him, however, he seemed confused. Seeing his bare feet and the torn and ragged garment he was wearing and feeling his bearded face, he said, "I do not seem to be myself, Ganieda. What has happened to me?"

Ganieda replied, "You have not been well, my dear. You were lost to us for a while, but everything is fine again. Everything is very fine indeed."

"Lost? I have no memory of it. For how long have I been lost?"

Ganieda hesitated, not sure what his reaction would be. "You have been gone for nearly nine months," she replied softly.

Merlin looked shocked. "Nine months? Nine months have passed of which I have no recollection? What have I been doing in all that time?"

She shook her head. Gently, she asked, "What is the last thing that you do remember, Merlin?"

"Ah!" he exclaimed, staggering, his mind suddenly flooded with unpleasant memories. "Peredur's brothers are dead! Eridur, Iugenius, and Gwyrgi have been killed in battle. And the five brave soldiers who were with me trying to save them are dead. Even Blackthorn, my noble horse Blackthorn, is dead. All are dead because of me."

"No, no, my dear brother, not because of you," Ganieda said comfortingly as she laid her hand on his arm. "You are not to blame. No one blames you for what happened on the battlefield. Peredur himself, seeing how you courageously tried to save his brothers, has only commended you for your brave actions at Arfderydd."

"Arfderydd?" Bewildered, Merlin looked around. "This is not Arfderydd. Where are we, Ganieda?"

"We are in Caledonia, my dear, about fifty miles north of Arfderydd. Can you recall nothing after the battle?"

"Pain!" he exclaimed suddenly. "Searing, agonizing pain! I was bound and carried into a building, a horrible place that smelt of burning and filth and of blood. All around me soldiers were screaming. A man approached me with a knife. I was hoping he was coming to put me out of my misery, but he merely cut my bonds, his touch that of a skilled doctor. Then Rodarch, dear Rodarch, looking so worried gave me water to drink and even washed my feet. It touched my heart. After being in agony for what seemed an eternity, the pain finally began to lessen. But as the pain dissipated, so did everything else. My memories, my knowledge, my self-awareness – my very mind. The harder I tried to stop it, the quicker everything drained away, like water poured into a basket."

He gasped in horror. "Like it is doing now! My mind is slipping away again!" He turned to Ganieda, his eyes wide with fear. "Now I know what is wrong," he cried despairingly, "I have gone mad. Tell me, sister. Tell me the truth!"

"No, Merlin," Ganieda asserted, "You did not lose your mind. You were poisoned. Poisoned by Morwen, that evil woman who once before tried to kill you. By devious means, she gained access to the kitchens at Brocavum and guilefully slipped poison into your wine flask. Her insane jealousy was re-kindled when she learned of your marriage."

"Guendoloena!" Merlin suddenly cried. "Ah, my poor Guendoloena! What misery I have brought to my dear wife. How selfish I was to have married her, knowing full well that I had chosen for myself the path of pain. To give myself a few months of pleasure, I have given my wife a lifetime of sorrow."

"Merlin, brother, nothing has changed," she assured him. "All of Guendoloena's sorrow will disappear as soon as you return to her."

"Nothing has changed?" Merlin repeated incredulously. "Do you not see me, Ganieda? See what I have become?" He struck his chest with his fist. "Soon, I shall be nothing more than a beast, unable to speak, unable to reason, unable, even, to control my own actions." He was seized with horror by the thought. "Sister, when I have reverted to my state of madness, I am no longer master of myself. I could be a danger to Guendoloena. Or to you!" Wildly, he looked around. He tried to flee, but Taliesin had grasped him firmly by the arm. Merlin's eyes were darkening. He seemed to be engaged in a battle with himself, a battle which he was rapidly losing. "Please, Ganieda, you must let me go," he pleaded.

"Try to fight it, Merlin," she urged.

"Sister, can you believe that I am not at this very moment fighting to stave off the madness which is overwhelming me? It is taking all my power merely to continue speaking to you. Ganieda, please, my mind, what is left of it, is almost gone. You must allow me return to the woods. That is where I belong now."

She replied, "Merlin, dearest brother, we are going to take you back to Brocavum where you will be safe and cared for. Your condition will not matter when you are among family and friends."

He shook his head vigorously "No, Ganieda, no. I am warning you. I will be a danger. Please, you must…let me go. Don't…let me…hurt…those…I love. Please…sister…let me…"

He struggled to continue speaking but could mouth only incomprehensible babble. Then, with great effort, he managed to gasp a single word: "Beware!"

His eyes were dark brown again when he stopped struggling to speak. Quite placid now, Merlin looked at them quizzically and without recognition. Taking her brother's arm, Ganieda asked Taliesin to play again, but the music had no effect the second time. Disappointed, the bard put the lyre back in its case and slung the strap over his head. Then, each taking firm hold of one of Merlin's arms, Ganieda and Taliesin led him down through the wooded valley to where Hermogenes was waiting with the horses.

Hen and his wife were standing in front of the door of their dilapidated cottage as they waved goodbye to their departing guests. Before leaving, Queen Ganieda had given them a sizeable purse of gold coins, more than enough to buy a good farm south of the wall, a plow and a team of oxen, a cow or two, a large flock of sheep, a horse and cart to ride to market and with plenty to spare to pay for helping hands. Hen kissed his wife's cheek, the first kiss that he had bestowed upon her in many a year. She looked at her husband with surprise, a slight smile brightening her drawn and careworn face.

Chapter 3

The Prisoner

Merlin was riding docilely on the horse that had been brought for him as the four made their way south to Brocavum. Ganieda had discovered that as long as she supplied her brother regularly with bread and cheese and other food, he seemed content enough to follow them. Camping under the stars that night, she and the others took turns watching him, but he slept soundly and made no move to escape. The next day, however, as they approached Luguvalium and began passing other travelers on the road, Merlin became increasingly agitated. Taking no chance that he might attempt to ride off, they placed a halter on his horse and attached a short lead to the pummel of Taliesin's saddle, since, of all of them, the bard had been found to be the most effective in calming him.

When they reached the great wall just north of Luguvalium, the gates were opened for them, and soon they were crossing over the River Eden on the old Roman bridge. As they made their way through the city's busy streets, they were hard-pressed to keep Merlin under control. Panic-stricken by the crowds, the wild-looking man being led on a horse became increasingly frantic as his odd appearance and behavior attracted ever more attention. With great relief they finally cleared the town precincts and were once again riding on the open road.

Having witnessed Merlin's erratic behavior in the presence of other people, Ganieda decided it was best to enter Brocavum well after dark. It was nearly midnight as they rode along the city's empty streets. Passing through the deserted market square, they turned their mounts up the hill to the royal residence. At the queen's approach, the gates of the palisade were opened, and the four riders quietly made their way inside. After leaving the stables, they walked across the darkened courtyard to a fine, two-storied, timber-framed building. Merlin, who had been looking around curiously, but calmly, became visibly agitated when he was led inside, and the door was closed behind him. Leaving her brother in the care of Taliesin and Hermogenes, Ganieda hurried upstairs to tell her family the wonderful news that Merlin was back. A minute later, a jubilant Guendoloena, clad in her nightdress, came running down.

"Merlin, dear heart, dearest husband!" she said joyfully. Bounding across the room, she opened her arms to embrace him, but he jumped back, recoiling in terror from her touch. A moment later, a young woman entered the room. Crying, "Uncle Merlin!" Olwen ran to her beloved uncle. Reaching up on tiptoe, she wrapped her arms around him. When she lifted her head to give him a kiss, he roughly pushed her away. Not anticipating the rebuff, she lost her balance and fell backward, hitting her head against the stone floor. She lay quite still. Gwyn, who had come in just behind his sister, gave a horrified shout and ran to her side as Merlin bolted for the door. Hermogenes, anticipating his move, stepped in front of the door to block his way. Panic-stricken, Merlin turned and made for an interior door, but Taliesin, who had been standing nearby, reached it first. Darting frantically this way and that and finding no escape, the wild man finally retreated into a darkened corner, cowering in fear.

When Ganieda returned with her husband, anticipating a scene of joyful reunion, what she found instead horrified her. Guendoloena and Gwyn were both kneeling on the floor comforting Olwen, who was now sitting up and sobbing. Gwyn, looking concerned, was examining the bump already rising on his sister's head, while Guendoloena, with tears running down her pale cheeks, looked utterly stricken. Hermogenes and Taliesin, unhappy witnesses to the distressing scene, were guarding the doors. Meanwhile, Merlin, looking every part the wild man, was crouched in the corner with his back to the wall. He resembled nothing so much as a hunted animal brought to bay and turned to face its tormentors.

Rodarch was as appalled as his wife by what he saw. Both parents immediately rushed to their daughter's side as Gwyn explained what had happened. To their great relief, they learned from Olwen that she had suffered no more than a bump on her head. After being assured by their daughter that her tears were caused by sorrow rather than injury, Rodarch and Ganieda rose and turned to Merlin. He snarled in response. Speaking soothingly, Rodarch slowly approached, but the wild man's fear only heightened. Retreating again, Rodarch whispered to his wife that he had something that might please Merlin and left the room. Minutes later, he returned, carrying a circlet of gold. Showing it to the man crouched in the corner, he said, "Look Merlin, your crown was recovered from the battlefield. I thought you might be pleased to have it."

Merlin stopped snarling and looked at the glittering object with interest. Holding it out in his hand, Rodarch slowly approached again. Suddenly, the madman sprang to his feet. Snatching the crown from Rodarch's hand, he hurled it across the room. As the gold circlet crumpled against the wall, Merlin bolted for the outside door. Knocking Hermogenes flat on the floor, he wrenched the door open and raced outside.

Merlin sped to the gate, but finding the doors barred and the porter standing by, he veered away again. Meanwhile, the porter, catching sight of a figure running in the dark, shouted a warning to the guards standing on the walkway above. As shouts were taken up all around by the guards, the fugitive began scaling the ramparts. With amazing alacrity, he reached the walkway and began climbing the surrounding battlements. He was about to leap wildly from the top when two of the guards reached him. Grabbing him, they yanked him down again. When Rodarch, Ganieda and the others reached the scene, the two guards were wrestling with Merlin along the top of the embankment. Shouting up to the guards not to hurt King Merlinus, they watched aghast while the three men continued to struggle. Merlin was fighting savagely with teeth and nails when one of the men gave a sharp cry of pain. As the guard grabbed his bleeding finger, Merlin managed to twist from the other man's grasp. Running along the ramparts, he had not gone far when a young guard, hurrying to the scene from the opposite direction, tackled him hard. The impact sent them both flying. They were rolling along the brink of the precipitous embankment when the young man tumbled off the edge. Falling some twelve feet, he gave an agonized cry when he hit the ground. Merlin quickly sprang to his feet and began climbing the parapet again when some dozen soldiers reached him. Pulling him down, they finally subdued him. Directed by King Rodarch, the guards led their panting and disheveled captive to a large, upper-story room in the royal residence.

Once the door of the room had been secured, Rodarch ordered the guards to release their captive. Merlin immediately bolted for the window. He was halfway through before he was wrestled to the floor, and another scuffle ensued. Ganieda, who was standing next to her husband, frantically begged the guards not to injure her brother. When Merlin was eventually brought under control, Ganieda bade Taliesin to play his lyre for her brother. The bard's songs briefly calmed him, but only minutes after the music stopped, the wild man began struggling anew. When Taliesin played a second time, the music had no effect at all. Each time Merlin was released, he immediately ran to the window, though guards now stood by, poised and ready to catch him. When morning finally dawned, a distraught King Rodarch had the blacksmith summoned.

A short while later, the blacksmith entered the room. He was shocked by what he saw there. Slumped abjectly on a chair in the middle of the large chamber was a thin and unkempt prisoner, rather ludicrously surrounded by a dozen burly guards. The bearded man's head was bent listlessly towards the floor, so that his long, straggly gray hair obscured most of his face. Madoc, the smith, was an amiable man, and he knew that Rodarch was a good king who would never order a man to be deprived of his freedom without just cause. All the same, he felt sympathy for the poor man, whoever he might be. He was further surprised when two of the guards grabbed and held down the unresisting man with what seemed to be unnecessary force, even though the captive had made no move to escape. Approaching him, Madoc removed a short measuring cord from the bag at his belt and lifted one of the prisoner's limp hands. As he wrapped the cord around the man's wrist, he said, "I'm sorry, sir. Measuring a man for shackles is a smith's sorriest job, but I promise I'll use the lightest weight chain possible and make sure that it's long enough so your shoulders don't get pulled in. Don't worry, sir, it won't be too bad." The captive remained mute and unmoving. After measuring the man's wrists and ankles, Madoc walked to the door and nodded to the guard who opened it for him.

When the smith returned later that day, he found the prisoner still seated on the chair and in the same abject posture as before, appearing not to have moved the entire time. Walking to the middle of the wall opposite the window, Madoc put down his toolbox next to an oaken beam and removed from a leather sack a ten-foot length of chain. Attached to one end of the chain was a large iron ring to which was fastened a metal strap pierced with four holes. Holding the strap against the beam, he hammered four long spikes through the holes, angling them so they could not be pulled out. Affixed to the other end of the chain was a pair of shackles. As he was extending the clattering chain to where the captive was seated, he was discomfited to see the poor man's shoulders shaking with silent sobs. Kneeling, Madoc opened one of the iron bands and was about to slip it around the prisoner's ankle when the chair suddenly overturned. Agilely, the prisoner somehow managed to twist from the grip of the two guards holding him and made a dash for the window. The startled guards, positioned to either side of it, were able to seize hold of him but not before he had almost climbed through. With difficulty they dragged the struggling captive back into the middle of the room as he thrashed about violently, trying to break free from their grasp. Two more guards had to rush to the aid of their fellows before the snarling wild man was finally pinned to the floor.

The captain of the guards shouted to the blacksmith to hurry. Quickly slipping the iron cuff around the prisoner's ankle, he began pounding the rivet flat against the small anvil that he had placed next to the man's foot. With each blow, the prisoner let out an unnerving cry of anguish.

"Please hold still," begged the smith. "I'm trying not to hurt you, but the way you're moving around I could hit you with the hammer. It'll go easier on you, sir, if you'd just stay still."

The prisoner, unheeding of the advice, continued to resist, and it was with great difficulty that the smith managed to slip on the second cuff and hammer it closed. When he had finished, he hurried back to the bag and brought out a pair of manacles. Kneeling at the prisoner's side, he noticed that the struggling captive seemed to be having trouble breathing. When he reached down and cleared the hair from the man's face, he sat back on his heels in surprise.

"This is King Merlinus!" he exclaimed.

Nodding grimly, the captain of the guards replied. "It's him all right. Merlinus Ambrosius, King of Dyfed, brother of Queen Ganieda, Chief Advisor to the High King of Britain and crazy as a coot."

"But I thought King Merlinus had disappeared after the battle of Arfderydd."

"He had. One of the queen's agents found him out in the woods somewhere in Caledonia. They brought him in last night, and he's been nothing but trouble since. The man's gone moon mad. Almost bit off a guard's finger and broke another man's arm. He fights like a wild animal, but we're under strict orders not to hurt him. It's hard to restrain a man when you're not allowed to fight back. I can't tell you how many bites and scratches he's given us. King Rodarch ordered him shackled to stop him from escaping." The captain shook his head. "If you ask me, they should let him go. No good will come of keeping him here. Send him back to Caledonia and good riddance to him. Of course, you didn't hear that from me."

In a shaken voice, Madoc replied, "I knew King Merlinus when I lived in Derventio. He used to come in to have work done at my smithy. No one in town knew he was a king back then. It took everyone by surprise, me included, when we found out, I can tell you that. Fact is, it was King Merlinus himself who recommended me for this job when King Rodarch needed a new smith in his household." He shook his head sadly. "I'll tell you this – a kinder and wiser man than Merlin you could not hope to find. It just breaks my heart to see what's happened to him." As the blacksmith spoke, the captive had become quiet, lifting his eyes to scrutinize the smith's face and furrowing his brow. Since the prisoner was no longer struggling, the guards warily relaxed their hold. Merlin raised himself to a sitting position on the floor and extended his hands submissively to the smith. With an embarrassed cough, Madoc thanked him and slipped the iron cuffs around his wrists. When Merlin obediently placed the manacles on the anvil, the smith had to fight back his tears as he pounded the rivets flat. "I'm sorry I have to do this to you, King Merlinus. Someday I hope I can take off these shackles for good."

Wrapping his massive arms around the prisoner in an emotional embrace, the smith then quickly gathered his tools and hurried to the door before his tears could be seen by the guards.

Ganieda was in an adjacent room with Rodarch as she heard the hammer blows and her brother's anguished cries. Angrily, she rounded on her husband, "Couldn't bars be installed on the window instead?"

"And have your brother attack everyone who enters the room? You've seen his behavior, Ganieda; you know how violent he can become."

"But Rodarch…"

"Good God, wife, your brother nearly bit off a guard's finger and broke another man's arm," he replied with some heat. "And it was sheer luck that our daughter's injury wasn't far worse."

Seeing his wife's pained expression, he added more gently, "I'm sorry, my dear. I know this is hard on you, but it really is the only way to insure that Merlin will not pose a danger to himself or to others. Besides, having him restrained is only a temporary measure. As soon as your brother becomes used to his situation and is calm again, he will be freed. Meanwhile, I've instructed Gwasawg to have a bedstead brought in so that your brother will have a comfortable place to sleep. Once Merlin has had a little time to settle in, we'll go over to see him." Rodarch kissed his wife's brow. "I offered prayers every day that Merlin would be found, and – see? – were my prayers not answered? Now, I shall humbly pray to God that He, in His infinite mercy, might deliver Merlin from this terrible affliction." Ganieda smiled, trying to look hopeful, but felt far from assured or satisfied.

A few minutes later, Gwasawg entered with a bow to inform the king that the blacksmith had finished his work and that the bedstead had been moved into place. Thanking his steward, Rodarch offered his hand to Ganieda, and together they made their way to Merlin's room. When Ganieda entered, she was appalled to see her brother, chained to the wall and lying on the floor like a dog. "Merlin!" she cried as she hurried over to him. Kneeling next to her brother, she looked up at her husband reproachfully. Rodarch turned to the captain of the guards for an explanation.

Sheepishly, the captain said, "I'm sorry, Lord King. We've tried leading King Merlinus to the bed several times, but as soon as we move away, he goes back on the floor again. I'm sorry, Lord King, but nothing short of tying him will keep him there, Lord King."

Nodding curtly as reply, Rodarch joined his wife, and together they helped Merlin to his feet. Obediently, he shuffled between them and sat at the edge of the bed as they sat on either side of him. Rodarch patted Merlin's knee. "There, brother. The bed is much more comfortable than the floor, is it not? Merlinus, I realize that you may not understand why I have had you restrained in this way, but please believe me when I say that my sole intention is to help you. I was afraid that if you were allowed to escape again, you would simply run back into the forest, there to die of hunger and privation. Merlinus, you should know that your sister did not wish you to be chained. Having you restrained in this manner was my decision and mine alone, so if you feel you must blame someone, blame me. I promise you, however, that as soon as you demonstrate your willingness to abide with us peacefully, I shall have the chains removed."

While Rodarch spoke, Merlin's head had been slumped downward, his eyes fixed on a knot in one of the floorboards. Ganieda touched his arm, and he looked up at her. "Rodarch is concerned about you, brother, and only wishes to help. Is there anything we can do for you? Anything that you might want?" Receiving no response, she went on. "Your wife Guendoloena is so happy now that you have returned. She'll be coming up soon with your supper. She says it's something special that she knows you'll enjoy." Merlin cocked his head, listening to words he could no longer comprehend. Listlessly, he turned his eyes back to the knot on the floorboard.

Rodarch patted his brother-in-law's shoulder. "We'll visit you several times every day, Merlinus, to make sure that you are comfortable. Please let us know, if not by speech, then by sign if you need anything." Merlin remained mute and unmoving, his eyes still fixed upon the floor. Glancing toward his wife uncomfortably, Rodarch rose and gave her his hand. With promises of Guendoloena's imminent arrival, they made their farewells. At the door, when they turned to look back at Merlin, they saw that he had already slipped off the bed and had curled up on the floor again. Glancing at each other, Rodarch and Ganieda left the room. Once they were back in their own chambers and beyond earshot of the guards, Ganieda accosted her husband. "Rodarch, was it really necessary to have his hands manacled as well?"

Rodarch replied somewhat testily. "Ganieda, must I state again what you already know to be true? That your brother has become violent and unpredictable? Until Merlin has proven through his actions that he can be trusted again, I am afraid I must insist that his hands remain chained, if not for his own safety, then at least for the safety of others."

Ganieda was about to retort that the manacles would only serve to make him more dangerous rather than less, but seeing the expression on her husband's face, she stopped. Instead, sighing resignedly, she said, "I know, Rodarch, I know. It's just that Merlin looked so listless. I'm afraid this humiliation is breaking his spirit."

Rodarch put an arm around his wife and kissed her brow. "You must have faith, Ganieda, as I do. I know that my prayers will be answered. Just as I know that your devotion to your brother will be rewarded."

Guendoloena had been warned by Ganieda what to expect before she entered the room. Even so, she could not help but be distressed when she saw her husband lying on the floor in chains. At her request, one of the guards moved a small table within reach of the prisoner, and she placed on it the heavy tray that she had been carrying. Noticing that none of the guards were making any motions to leave, she said to their captain, "I was hoping to spend some time alone with my husband."

Looking doubtful, he considered her request. "I'm sorry, Queen Guendoloena, but the prisoner is dangerous and unpredictable. You could be hurt if he becomes violent again. It's best that we remain in the room while you are with him."

"Please, captain, I know my husband would never hurt me, and I want to be alone with him tonight. I will take full responsibility should anything happen."

"As you wish, Queen Guendoloena," he said, bowing. "Guards will remain posted outside in the hallway. Call them if you need help."

"Thank you, captain, but I'm sure I'll have no need of their assistance."

The guards bowed to her respectfully though she did catch sight of one of them winking surreptitiously to another as they left the room. When the door closed, she breathed a sigh of relief.

After bringing two chairs to the table, she walked to her husband, who was still curled up on the floor. Greeting him cheerfully, she said, "Merlin, dearest, it's me, Guendoloena." Receiving no response, she reached down and touched his shoulder. His skin twitched like that of a horse bothered by flies. She tried again. "Merlin, wake up, it's me, Guendoloena, your wife. Come look, dear heart, I've brought you your supper." Opening his eyes, he looked at her blankly, but the smell of food brought him to his feet, and he shuffled to the table. When Guendoloena encouraged him to sit, he complied, eyeing the food with interest.

Sitting in the chair opposite him, she poured wine from a flagon into a glass and offered it to him. Sniffing the wine suspiciously, he pushed the glass away, though he did accept from her hand a cup of cool well water. Smiling, Guendoloena removed the lid from a small tureen and ladled the soup it contained into two bowls. Grabbing one of the bowls, Merlin lifted it to his lips and began to drink noisily. Guendoloena picked up a spoon, thinking to re-instruct her husband in its use but, changing her mind, put it down again. Instead, she raised her own bowl and began to slurp as noisily as her husband. After Merlin finished his soup by licking the bowl clean, he seized a loaf of bread from the table and tore off a large chunk with his teeth. Guendoloena, mimicking her husband, did the same. When Merlin picked up one of the two plump roasted partridges from a platter, she grabbed the other, and both birds were devoured in the same wolfish manner. A cake dripping with honey, the final course, was unceremoniously torn in half and crammed into their mouths. Finishing his meal, Merlin sucked the honey from his sticky fingers and wiped his lips on his sleeve. Then, he looked at his wife expectantly.

Quietly, Guendoloena rose from her chair and walked around the table. Taking him by the hand, she led him to the bed. He sat at its edge, and she sat beside him. Gazing at her husband lovingly, she said, "Merlin, now that you are back again, I am so happy. All those long months without you were almost unbearable for me. And then, when everyone believed you were dead, and I thought myself a widow – I can't begin to describe the grief I felt, thinking that I had lost you forever. And now that I have you back again, I can't begin to express my joy. To have you here beside me, my dearest husband, my dearest love." While she had been speaking, Merlin's eyes had been fixed, not upon his wife, but upon the opposite wall. Turning to see what he was looking at, she saw the moon, just short of full, framed by the window. As she watched the moon with him, it seemed to grow ever brighter while the sky around it darkened to the deepest indigo. She exclaimed, "Isn't the moon beautiful!" Smiling, she added, "Do you remember, dear heart, how you used to compare me to Diana the huntress, goddess of the moon? Do you remember that, my love?" She moved closer to him and gently stroked his arm. He turned to her, looking intently into her face, as though trying to recall who she might be. Frowning, he gave up the effort and turned his eyes back to the small square of night sky.

Rising to her feet, Guendoloena moved in front of her husband, blocking his view of the window. Reaching up, she pulled the ribbon from her hair, allowing her honey-colored curls to spill in a lovely golden cascade down over her shoulders. Then, gracefully, she slipped off her tunic, letting it fall beside her onto the floor. Barefoot and clad only in a gossamer, white linen shift, her lissome form was limned by the moon's silvery light. Moving closer to her husband, still seated on the bed, she placed her hands on his chest and slowly slid them to the tie at the throat of his tunic. Delicately, she plucked it open. Slipping one of her hands inside, she stroked her fingertips lightly across his chest. She could feel him shiver. Suddenly and impulsively, she threw herself against him, and he fell backward onto the bed. Straddling him, she parted her lips and kissed him passionately. Merlin grabbed her by her shoulders. Pushing her off roughly to the side, he sat up again and wiped his mouth with the back of his hand. It was a simple, childish gesture, but it stabbed Guendoloena to the heart to see it. She chided herself that it meant nothing, that her husband was not yet in his right mind. Still, it hurt her pride. Then, reminding herself that rekindling her husband's love would take time and patience, she said to him gently, "Merlin, dearest, I know that you may not remember what we once meant to each other and how you used to love me, but I want you to know one thing: I love you. I have always loved you, and I shall always love you. It doesn't matter to me that you have changed. The only thing that matters to me is that you can return my love."

Both were sitting on the edge of the bed again. He had been inching away, and she now moved closer to him. Taking one of his hands, she kissed his palm and held it pressed against her cheek. As soon as she released his hand, he snatched it back again. Looking at her fearfully, he rose from the bed and shuffled as far away from her as the chain would allow. Then, after giving her another apprehensive look, he curled up on the floor, trembling. Sighing, Guendoloena took two blankets from the bed. Covering him with one, she wrapped herself in the other and lay down on the floor beside him, being careful not to let any part of her body touch his.

Weeks went by in dreary tedium. There was no improvement in Merlin's condition and never so much as a glint of recognition in his eyes for his wife. If anything, his condition had grown worse. Soon losing his appetite for food along with everything else, he became even more gaunt than on the day that he had been found. Guendoloena was near tears one day when she knocked on the door of her sister-in-law's study. Ganieda invited her in to sit and poured wine for them both. Thanking Ganieda, she took the proffered glass. Holding it between her hands, she stared into the cold hearth as she spoke. "I'd been trying to think of ways to divert Merlin when it suddenly occurred to me that even though he can no longer speak, he might still be able to read. So this morning, after I cleared away his breakfast, I found one of his favorite books. When I offered it to him, he grabbed the book from my hands and tore it to shreds before my eyes."

Ganieda said, "I'm sure that it wasn't an intentional act on his part, Guen. No more purposeful than when a puppy tears apart a shoe."

"I'm not so sure, Ganieda. He looked at me so angrily. And then…then he threw the pieces into my face."

"Oh, Guen, I am so sorry. I fear that my brother can no longer be trusted. Actually, Rodarch and I were just discussing how we think you should be more careful when you are around him. We both believe that you should never allow yourself to be alone with him."

"Are you suggesting that my husband might try to hurt me?"

"I don't know, Guen," Ganieda replied. "I would hope that there is enough of his old self somewhere inside to prevent him from harming you." Emotion suddenly choked her voice. "That the most brilliant scholar in all Britain has been turned into a dumb, mindless brute is a more heinous crime than his murder would have been! It would have been a mercy if the poison had simply killed him!"

Guendoloena was shocked by her words. "Ganieda, how can you say that about your own brother?"

"That miserable animal chained to the wall is not my brother."

"That poor, miserable man is my husband," Guendoloena replied indignantly. "I have no need of a 'scholar.' I have accepted what he has become for the sake of what he once was – a kind and gentle and loving man. It is my duty, no, it is my privilege to stay by his side no matter what. My love for Merlin will never die."

"Ah, my dear Guendoloena. How strong you are. Far stronger than I! You are right to rebuke me. But what is the solution? We cannot keep my brother locked in a room and chained to the wall forever, yet if we release him, he will simply run away and die of privation. Frankly, I can see no solution. For months now, I've been racking my brain, trying to come up with some plan. I sent out my agents to find Morwen and force her to reveal the antidote, should there even be an antidote, but she seems to have vanished from the face of the earth. I've consulted with the most respected doctors and herbalists in all of Britain, read every book I could find on the subject of poisons and their antidotes, but so far, as you know, none of the remedies have had the slightest effect."

"I'm sorry, Ganieda, I shouldn't have spoken to you like that. I know that you are doing your best to help Merlin. But if even you cannot find a solution, I'm afraid that there may not be one." Guendoloena, who had been fighting back her tears, now sought solace in Ganieda's arms.

Patting her friend's shoulder comfortingly, Ganieda said, "Rodarch believes that all is not lost as long as we have faith." Though, in truth, she felt but little hope as she said it.

That night, Guendoloena went to her room and sat at a small table by her bedside. Lifting the lid of a wooden box which lay next to her mirror and comb, she removed a beautiful amber necklace and fastened the honey-colored strand around her neck. As she gazed at her reflection in the polished surface of the bronze mirror, tears began to well in her eyes. The necklace, intended to be a gift to mark their first wedding anniversary, had instead been given to her by Merlin just before he had departed for the ill-fated battle. That was the last time she had seen her husband as the loving man whom she had married. Sorrowfully, she unfastened the necklace and put it back in its box, closing the lid and seemingly closing the life which she had shared with her once adoring husband.

The next morning, as Guendoloena and Ganieda and Rodarch were making some desultory remarks about the weather, no one said a word about what was really on their minds: Merlin's unchanging condition, which hung over them like a pall. After they exhausted the topic of the weather, the silence was finally broken when Rodarch put forth a proposal. "I have been considering Merlin's situation, trying to come up with ways to relieve the monotony of his confinement."

Both women looked at him, Guendoloena's expression one of hope, Ganieda's one of guarded concern. "What did you have in mind, husband?"

"Well, I thought we might take Merlin on an excursion. Being chained in a room for weeks on end would make any man grow dull and morose let alone…" Rodarch stopped, embarrassed.

"Let alone one already mad," finished Ganieda.

In a sudden burst of anguish, Rodarch exclaimed, "This is all my fault. Before Arfderydd, Merlin had wisely advised caution, but I arrogantly overruled King Arthur's own wise and trusted advisor and charged headlong into battle. Now, thanks to my overweening conceit, hundreds of men lay dead. And Merlin, my own brother-in-law, once the most brilliant man in Britain, has been reduced to madness, thanks to my foolishly inviting his poisoner into my own kitchens! This is my fault! Everything! All of it!"

Ganieda had never seen her husband so distraught. Trying to comfort him, she answered, "No, my dear, none of it is your fault. All the military men, including King Peredur himself, had unanimously agreed that immediate action needed to be taken against Gwenddolau. You were hardly alone in that decision. And when, out of charity and kindness, you thought to help a poor and destitute old woman, how were you to know that it was Morwen in disguise?"

Rodarch replied bitterly, "You would think that I should know by now that the world is full of treachery and deceit. How naive I was to trust a complete stranger, bringing her into our own household."

Ganieda said, "No one could have detected deceit arrayed in such innocent garb. You were simply doing what you do best: helping those in need. You must never hesitate to give aid and comfort to the poor and destitute because of a single instance of deceitfulness. Your inherent generosity and kindness are among your many virtues, my dear," she said, squeezing his hand. "They are why I love you so much." Rodarch, smiling gratefully at his wife's reassuring words, lifted her hand to his lips to kiss.

Guendoloena, witnessing the love and tender regard that Ganieda and Rodarch had for one another, turned her thoughts back to her own husband. "What sort of excursion did you have in mind, Rodarch?" she asked.

"Oh, nothing too ambitious to begin with, just a short walk through town. Since tomorrow is market day, there should be plenty of activity and things for him to see."

Guendoloena, brightening perceptibly, said, "I think that's a wonderful idea."

Looking worried, Ganieda asked, "Do you really think we should take my brother into town? And on market day? What would prevent him from escaping? You know how fast he is."

"Of course Merlin would need to be restrained," replied Rodarch. "But I'm sure that being in the fresh air and seeing some sights other than four blank walls can only prove helpful."

Ganieda was not so sure that an excursion through town on market day with her volatile brother was a good idea, but seeing Guendoloena's hopeful expression and not wishing to dampen the others' enthusiasm, she also voiced approval of the plan.

Early the next morning, the blacksmith entered the prisoner's room with a cheerful greeting. "Good news, King Merlinus," Madoc said. "I hear you're going to go on a little excursion today." Taking a pair of pliers and a stout iron bar from his toolbox, the smith pried open the link attaching the chain to the iron ring and handed the end to one of the guards. Bobbing a bow to Merlin before leaving the room, the smith said, "I hope you enjoy your walk, Lord King."

As soon as the door had closed, the guard holding the end of the chain asked one of his fellows, "What now?"

"Dunno," replied the second. "Wait for orders, I guess. But taking him out for a walk doesn't sound like a good idea to me," he said, jerking his head toward the prisoner cowering at the other end of the chain. "And he don't look too happy 'bout it neither."

A third said, "I still don't get why our king and queen are wasting their time botherin' with him. Let him go and have done with it, I say. And if the damned bugger starves to death in the woods, wha' of it?"

"Watch it," whispered the second, glancing at the prisoner. "Sometimes I think he can understand what we say."

The third shrugged. "So wha' if he does? He can't talk, can he? I don't know 'bout you two, but I've got one too many bite marks on me ta care 'bout him too much one way or t'other."

"Keep quiet," hissed the first. "The king or queen could be coming through that door any second now."

"All right, all right, I'll keep quiet. But if I was you, I'd keep a good grip on tha' chain."

Making her way down the hill to the market square with Guendoloena, Rodarch, and the four guards who were accompanying them, Ganieda was relieved that Merlin had made no move to escape. Since his feet were still shackled, his gait was somewhat shambling, but, in spite of that, he was easily managing to keep up with the rest of the group. She was also pleased that her brother was looking more alert and animated than he had in many weeks.

When they entered the bustling market, the people bowed respectfully to the royal party, though there were backward glances and murmured whispers at the strange sight of their king and queen accompanied by a man being led in chains. Most recognized the man as King Merlinus, and the crowd was soon buzzing with speculation. Merlin looked around nervously at the increased scrutiny, but Ganieda and Guendoloena, walking on either side of him, patted his arm and reassured him with soothing words.

After passing the stalls of the wool dealers, they were proceeding to the more colorful displays of the cloth sellers. At their approach, the cloth merchants, who had been chatting together near one of the booths, bowed low to the royal party. Knowing that it was King Rodarch's custom to speak with people informally on market day, the merchants took the opportunity to have a few words with their king. While Rodarch was thus engaged, Ganieda could see that her brother was becoming restless and suggested to Guendoloena that they should keep moving. Rodarch nodded to his wife when she signaled her intention to him, and the two women resumed their stroll through the market. They were passing a baker's booth when the enticing aromas caused them to pause. As they were looking over the tasty offerings, Merlin pointed to one of the nut cakes. Ganieda, delighted to see her brother taking an interest in food again, purchased two of the cakes, sharing one with Guendoloena. They were walking along, eating their cakes, when Merlin motioned to the center of the square where the animals were displayed. More than pleased to comply, the women redirected their steps to the farmers' tents. Reaching one of the pens, they stopped to look inside, and two friendly nanny goats immediately came over to them. Holding out his hand, Merlin fed the remnants of his cake to one of the goats, as Guendoloena, smiling happily, fed the remainder of her cake to the other. While Merlin and Guendoloena were petting the goats, Ganieda chatted with their owner, who was flattered to be speaking to his queen. When Merlin and Guendoloena turned to go to the next pen, Ganieda pressed a coin into the pleased man's hand.

Continuing their walk among the animals, the three admired beautifully groomed horses, enjoyed the antics of playful calves and lambs and piglets, and patted the noses of inquisitive colts and fillies. As they were leaving the animal pens, Ganieda looked back to find that Rodarch, who had almost caught up with them, was now being approached by a group of farmers. Judging that her earnest husband was about to be engaged in another lengthy conversation, Ganieda indicated to him with a gesture that they would be continuing their stroll through the market, and Rodarch, once again, nodded to her in reply. After viewing the offerings of a potter and then a basket maker, they were making their way to a tinsmith who was hawking his wares from the back of a cart. As they were passing by an alley, a group of children who had congregated there giggled at the sight of an odd man wearing chains. Conspiratorially, they whispered to each other. One of the boys, challenged by the rest on a dare, darted from the alley and came running up behind the chained man. Three of the guards caught sight of the boy just as he slapped the prisoner on the back before darting off again. The fourth guard, who had been distracted by the sight of a pretty girl selling flowers, gave a yelp when the chain he was holding was wrenched from his hand. Merlin, his eyes wide with terror, was running headlong through the market square as the guards set off in pursuit, pushing their way through the crowd. Soon, amid shouts and confusion, many of the market goers also began chasing after the fugitive. Merlin, surprisingly fast and nimble even with his legs hobbled, was managing to elude his pursuers as he ran around carts and barrels and darted between the stalls. Racing past the last booth, he was almost out of the square when a burly butcher, seeing the long chain trailing behind the fleeing man, thought to step on it. Brought up short, Merlin was pitched headfirst onto the ground. Soon surrounded by the mob, he crouched on the ground, panting like a cornered animal, his dirt-streaked face twisted into a snarl. Some of his tormentors grabbed the chain while others thought to take hold of the fugitive himself. Rushing forward, several of the men tried to seize him but hastily retreated back into the crowd when the wild man lashed out at them, growling threateningly.

Ganieda reached the excited crowd just behind the guards and ordered to be allowed through. Hearing their queen's commanding voice, the throng parted for her. Walking to her brother, she held out her hands to him. Obediently, he rose to his feet and stood close beside her, hanging his head to avert his eyes from those of the staring crowd. The queen addressed the people. "Thank you, good citizens of Brocavum, for your assistance in restraining my unfortunate brother. I apologize for the disruption. I promise that it will not happen again. Now please return to your businesses and shopping and enjoy the rest of your market day."

The people stood aside and bowed respectfully as their queen, with great dignity, led her brother through the square. Rodarch, holding the arm of a tearful Guendoloena, ordered one of the guards to take up the end of the trailing chain, and they remorsefully made their way back up the hill to the royal compound.

Chapter 4

Fulfillment

Later that spring, King Rodarch received word from Cathures in Caledonia that Morken, King of Alclud, had finally died after suffering an extended illness. Writing to Bishop Kentigern with the news, Rodarch urged his pastoral friend to return to his ministry in the north since the way was now clear for him. It was nearly midsummer, however, before the bishop's reply arrived. Opening the letter, Rodarch was pleased to read that Kentigern had decided to take up permanent residence in Cathures and would be stopping at Brocavum on his way north. In his letter the bishop confided that, upon receiving Rodarch's appeal, he had at first hesitated to leave the comfortable and thriving monastery which he had established in northern Cambria, the place where he had expected to be spending the rest of his days. After weeks of indecision, he had finally turned to God for help. As he knelt in prayer seeking God's guidance, he wrote that a heavenly messenger, bearing a rod, had appeared to him. Striking him sharply with the rod, the angel of the Lord had commanded him to rise and return to Cathures. There, the angel revealed, Kentigern would flourish among his chosen people, collecting a rich harvest of souls for salvation until he, at a goodly old age, should pass in glory to his Father in heaven. As the angelic vision faded, Kentigern, weeping freely, humbly gave thanks to the Lord, his heart now set on doing what would be most pleasing to Him. The bishop closed his letter with a blessing for Rodarch, a most generous and Christian king, who had supported and sheltered him when Morken, infected with the venom of the devil, had sought his death. Rodarch's account of the manner of Morken's death, the bishop concluded, was clear testimony of the just punishment which God metes out to the arrogant.

Twenty-five years earlier, Kentigern had set out on foot to bring the word of God to the people of Caledonia. Traveling widely and ministering to those whom he met along the way, the young bishop had soon discovered that many of the Britons living north of the wall were pagans who had yet to hear the good tidings of the Lord. Others, though calling themselves Christians, had been led astray by the teachings of Pelagius who had falsely asserted that people could attain salvation through their own good deeds, while still others were apostates who had sinfully renounced their faith. All of them, Kentigern could see, were sorely in need of a good shepherd to guide them to the true faith. Seeking a place where he could establish a church and monastery, Kentigern found himself led by divine inspiration to a particular hill near Cathures, a remote British outpost near the western end of the old Roman wall of turf and timber that crossed Caledonia some hundred miles north of the one built of stone by Hadrian. Climbing to the top of the hill, Kentigern and his followers lifted their eyes and hands to the Lord to thank Him for His guidance in choosing this place. Then, after fashioning a cross of wood and erecting it next to their tents, they immediately began felling trees, leveling the hilltop, and measuring and staking the outlines of the church and the monastic buildings. Following a fortnight of hard work, after the posts had been set in place and the buildings were being framed, Morken, the King of Alclud, arrived at the head of a large troop of soldiers. Outraged that Kentigern had begun construction of a monastery on crown land without first seeking the king's permission, Morken threatened to tear the structures down. The bishop, asserting that he had been granted approval by the highest authority of all, countered royal threats with the retribution of God. Following a vigorous and heated exchange, a compromise was eventually reached, Morken agreeing to grant his approval for the project upon receiving the bishop's formal request for the king's permission. The damage had been done, however, and the smoldering animosity between the two men was never extinguished.

Some time later, after a particularly bad harvest from the monastic fields, Kentigern went to Morken's court and petitioned the king for grain to feed his brethren. The king, though an apostate, was not unfamiliar with Holy Scripture. Mockingly he replied, "Is it not telling that I, who seek neither God nor his justice, am rewarded with an excellent harvest while you, who fear God and obey his commands, find yourself lacking in this most basic necessity? Since you admonish others that there is no want among those who pray to God, cast thy burden upon the Lord, and He shall sustain thee."

When Kentigern rebutted that just and holy men often experience poverty and want while sinful and arrogant men are sometimes elevated even so high as a kingship, Morken brusquely dismissed him. As the bishop turned to leave, Morken taunted that if God could manage to transfer the grain from the king's storehouses to the monastery without human intervention, then he and his holy brothers would be welcome to it. Kentigern left the king's hall with the jeering laughter of Morken and his followers still ringing in his ears.

That evening, as Kentigern poured out his prayers to the Lord with tears flowing freely from his eyes, rain, as if in answer, began pouring down from the heavens. After five days of unremitting rain, with the River Clud overflowing its banks, King Morken belatedly gave orders to move the grain from his storehouses near the river to buildings on higher ground. By the time carters arrived on the scene with horses and wagons, however, raging floodwaters were already encircling the royal granaries. The men could do nothing but watch as the rapidly rising water lifted the wooden granaries off their stone piers and dragged them into the channel. Swept downstream for several miles, the buildings were finally brought to a halt against a tangle of fallen trees and debris that had jammed together, not a hundred yards from the monastery door. As soon as the water began to recede, Kentigern sent some of the younger and more athletic monks to look inside the granaries. Climbing over the wreckage and prying open the doors, they found that bags of grain were still inside. Although some had been soaked through, a greater number were quite dry and the grain they held usable. Thanking God for this miracle, Kentigern directed the monks to carry the grain into the monastic storehouses.

News of this miraculous event soon reached the king's ear. He was hardly pleased, but his own declaration, publicly made, prevented him from taking any direct action against the bishop, however galling it was for him to watch Kentigern's popularity rise as the monks distributed grain to commoners who usually petitioned the king for help. Since Morken could not attack the bishop's person, the king instead attacked his character, charging that this so-called miracle was clear evidence that Kentigern was not a man of God, but a sorcerer and a worker of evil. Declaring that such a man would no longer be welcome at his court, the king threatened severe penalties should Kentigern ever again come into his sight. When the bishop responded by appearing before the king and admonishing him in the manner of a forgiving father patiently lecturing a wayward son, the festering ill will between the two men finally came to a head. Morken, in a fit of anger, rose from his chair. Approaching the bishop who had been standing at the bottom of the dais, the king stopped halfway down the flight of stairs. Lifting his foot to the level of Kentigern's stomach, he pushed the bishop over, knocking him flat on his back. When Kentigern regained his breath and rose to his feet, he raised his hands and rejoiced, praising God that he was deemed worthy to suffer shame and humiliation for Him. Then, leaving his vindication from the king's false accusations in the Hands of the Highest Judge, Kentigern summarily departed from the king's hall.

Still infuriated by the bishop's parting words some weeks later, Morken offhandedly mentioned to his henchman that any injuries or deaths caused by stray arrows during the following day's hunt near the monastery, while regrettable, would never be questioned as anything more than an unfortunate accident. Since the king had been fingering a fine gold torque at the time, the message was understood. The next day, when Kentigern was walking to the stream where he was wont to immerse himself every morning while reciting prayers, an arrow flew by his head and landed, quivering in a tree beside him. As Kentigern turned to run back to the sanctuary of the monastery, a second and third arrow missed him by inches. Choosing to follow the example of Paul who had hidden in a basket to avoid a fruitless death in Damascus in order to embrace one many times more profitable in Rome, Kentigern departed from Cathures that night under the cover of darkness.

Some weeks later, as Kentigern was passing through Brocavum on his way further south, he was received and warmly welcomed by King Rodarch. Invited by the Christian king to stay for as long as he should wish, Kentigern decided to remain in Cumbria for a time. Traveling west into the more remote mountains, the bishop found many Cumbrians who were erring in their faith and even some who were still practicing idolatry. After spending several months roaming the hills and valleys and sowing the seed of the divine word wherever he trod, he was satisfied that he had collected a rich harvest of souls for God. Then one day, having received divine instruction that he should direct his steps further south, Kentigern returned to Brocavum and cordially took leave of the king, blessing Rodarch for his charity and other good works. Since then, the two men had kept up a friendly correspondence. Not long after Kentigern had begun work on his new monastery in northern Cambria, he had received a letter from Rodarch, conveying the news that King Morken had developed a tumor in his left foot, the same foot which he had raised in anger against the bishop less than a year earlier. Crippling the king over the years with increasingly agonizing pain, the malignancy later spread to other parts of his body, and it was this illness which had eventually killed him. Kentigern, knowing that this clear example of divine retribution would instill, if not love or reverence, then at least fear and obedience among his former persecutors, decided to use this opportunity to the advantage of God. Gathering his monks together, Kentigern revealed to them how the Lord, through His holy messenger, had commanded him to return to Cathures. While acknowledging that his decision to leave them had been difficult, Kentigern explained how no one should dare conceal the words of God or go against Him in any way, but should always obey His will and commands in all things. The following week, after an able young monk named Asaph had been unanimously elected and elevated as his successor, Kentigern met with the brethren one final time. Bidding them all farewell, he exhorted them to stand firm in their faith. Then, after raising his hand in blessing, Kentigern took his leave through the north door of the church, turning his thoughts and his steps back to Cathures.

When Bishop Kentigern arrived at the gates of Brocavum a month later, he was graciously met and attended by Gwasawg, the king's steward, and shown to a fine room in the royal residence. Once he had refreshed himself from his journey, he was conducted by the steward to the great hall where the entire court had been assembled to greet him. Carrying his simple wooden crosier, he slowly made his way down the central aisle, his hand raised to all in a sign of blessing. As the holy man approached the dais, King Rodarch rose from the throne. Removing his crown as a token of respect, the king descended the flight of steps and knelt to receive the bishop's blessing. Following a formal ceremony of welcome, the bishop delivered the Mass to the congregation. Then, after dismissing the court, Rodarch escorted Kentigern to a chamber behind the dais where they could speak in private. As the two men conversed, each bringing the other up to date on recent news and developments, Rodarch, at one point, broached the subject of his brother-in-law's unfortunate condition. Briefly describing the events leading to Merlin's madness, Rodarch expressed his hope that a cure might be affected through divine intervention and asked the bishop if he might intercede on King Merlinus's behalf. Kentigern, already quite familiar with King Merlinus and his malady, acquiesced to King Rodarch's request, promising to recommend the course of action which would be most pleasing to God.

The next day, after morning Mass, Rodarch conducted Kentigern and the two monks who were his traveling companions to Merlin's room. Ganieda, insisting on being present during the bishop's meeting with her brother, also accompanied them. Inside, they found Merlin lying on the floor as usual. The shackled man looked up warily as they entered and trembled when the bishop stepped closer to better examine him. Upon completing his inspection, Kentigern turned and addressed the king and queen. "Those thinking themselves beyond the hand of God would do well to look at the example of this wretched man. Thus the impious, imagining themselves to be outside God's jurisdiction, learn otherwise and to their regret when they are laid so low as to be like unto the beasts of the woods. This," pronounced Kentigern, pointing to the man cowering on the floor, "is the wage of sin."

Ganieda protested immediately. "My brother, who is not sinful, has always done good works and has been kind and generous to both Christians and non-Christians alike. He is a friend to Archbishop Dubricius and prophet to all Britons."

"There is no man without sin, particularly a man known to be a demon's son," he declared, looking at Ganieda pointedly. She began a retort, but the bishop cut her off. "Take care, King Rodarch. A man not able to control his wife could easily be thought not able to control a kingdom. A husband must rule his family as absolutely as a king rules his realm. Particularly," he added, "when the wife, thinking herself clever and intelligent beyond her sex, exceeds her proper place. A firm hand is essential to curb such unseemly womanly ambition."

Ganieda, furious, took a step toward the bishop and opened her mouth to speak, but Rodarch grabbed her hand in a grip so hard that the words choked in her throat. Giving her a reproving look, Kentigern quoted, "There is no poison above the poison of a serpent, and there is no wrath above the wrath of a woman." He continued. "Dubricius, our beloved and worthy archbishop, who has withdrawn to the Island of Bardsey to spend the remaining years of his life in divine contemplation and prayer, verily suffered the presence of pagans in his midst. But the time for such tolerance is past! No man can now pretend that he has not heard the good news of God's word, and no man can achieve salvation through his own efforts without the grace of God. As to this person being a prophet," he added disparagingly, "when in any of his prophecies was Merlin ever heard to say 'Thus spake the Lord God.' Never once! It must be remembered that the spirit of prophecy was given not only to the holy but also to unbelievers and even to the wicked, such as Balaam and Caiaphas. Further," Kentigern declared, "wicked men often would not only prophesy but perform miracles as well. No man shall be exalted just because he is granted knowledge of the future. For prophecies fail, tongues are curbed and knowledge, as we can see, vanishes away," he said, gesturing to Merlin. "This miserable pagan, offensive to the sight of God, is being punished with this affliction for his wicked obstinacy. He will never be cured until he comes humbly into the church and confesses his sins to receive his chastisement. Only after he has repented and mortified his flesh will he be acceptable to plead unto God for forgiveness. Only after he has been shriven and comes into the true faith, can this sinner ever hope to receive the blessing of God's grace."

Merlin began laughing loudly, and the bishop looked at him in outrage. Rodarch quickly intervened. "Lord Bishop, please forgive my unfortunate brother-in-law's unseemly behavior. I am afraid that his present condition renders him incapable of self-control." Intrigued by Merlin's outburst, however, Rodarch added, "Frankly, I am curious to know why Merlin would break so many weeks of silence with such an untoward and unprovoked display. I would give anything to understand what might have caused his laughter and what it might possibly signify."

"Even my freedom?"

Ganieda's heart leapt with joy to hear her brother speak.

Taken aback, Rodarch did not answer immediately. After some deliberation, he replied, "Yes, Merlinus, even your freedom."

Upon hearing those words, Merlin rose to his feet and full height while direly surveying the assembled company. Ganieda looked to see if his brown eyes had become blue again but saw that they appeared to waver, giving him a terrifying aspect which was not lost on the three clerics who crossed themselves. Speaking with the force of strong emotion, Merlin said, "I laughed for joy because I foresaw that I would be released today, but my happiness is tinged with sorrow and my laughter is mixed with tears. For," he pronounced gravely, "someone in this room is fated to die by falling from a great height."

There were sharp intakes of breath and glances all around. Kentigern declared, "It is blasphemy for you to speak of fate. Knowledge of the future is the purview of God alone." Indignantly, he inquired, "And just when is this death supposed to occur?"

Merlin answered, "Within a month, he or she will die by being hanged from a tree."

Kentigern countered, "False prophet, you have just contradicted yourself! By which of those two deaths is this person supposed to die?"

Merlin replied, "A man in this room will die by drowning in four days' time."

Now realizing that these were merely the ravings of a lunatic, everyone breathed a sigh of relief. Merlin's eyes were brown again as he silently resumed his place on the floor. Once more, Rodarch begged forgiveness for Merlin who clearly did not know what he was saying.

Sternly, Kentigern declared, "Merlinus Ambrosius, it is to be your lot to roam the woods and wild places of the earth, communing only with animals, until your death, since your sinfulness renders you beyond hope of receiving salvation through the gift of God's grace."

Galfridus, the younger cleric, who had been looking with sympathy at Merlin, spoke up at the bishop's pronouncement. "Reverend Father, could we not at least pray on behalf of this poor man?"

Kentigern bestowed a look of disapproval upon Galfridus. Giraldus, the older cleric, mimicking the bishop's expression, inquired, "Brother Galfridus, have you so soon forgotten your vow of obedience? Or perhaps an acolyte believes that he knows more about religious matters than the bishop." Giraldus concluded with a deep bow to Kentigern who acknowledged him with an approving nod. Galfridus, blushing, lowered his eyes and quietly apologized for his presumption.

Clearing his throat, Kentigern said, "Although unrepentant pagans are beyond hope of redemption, it is possible that, through the intercession of prayer, this wretched man may be brought to see the error of his ways. We shall pray every day that, through God's mercy, this man will come into the true faith before his death so that his soul may yet be saved." Magnanimously, Kentigern raised his hand above the captive in a sign of blessing. Then, taking leave of the king, he departed from the room with the monks.

As soon as the door had shut, Ganieda angrily declared, "I cannot abide the pomposity of that man!"

"Be quiet, woman," said Rodarch sharply as he grabbed her hand.

Pulling her hand from his grasp, she said reproachfully, "I can see that you have heeded the bishop's advice on how a husband should rule a wife."

"That remark is not worthy of you." In a lower voice, he added, "Please, Ganieda, you know that I have always respected you and your wisdom, but you must be circumspect. Do you wish to see me shamed before the bishop?"

Ganieda could see that her husband was extremely distressed. Upon reflection, she said, "I'm sorry, Rodarch. I would never wish to see you shamed before anybody. You know that I have only the greatest respect for you."

"Then why won't you demonstrate your respect by embracing my faith?"

Ganieda sighed. "I made clear my position on this subject before our marriage and several times since. My position remains the same. I respect your faith, but I cannot embrace it."

"But why, Ganieda?"

"What I have said to you before continues to hold true. I refuse to be a hypocrite. Do you wish me to mouth words that I do not believe in my heart? Besides, did not the bishop himself, in his sermon to us last night, declare that the vice of hypocrisy is the repudiation of faith, the destruction of all virtues and the moth of religion? I am certainly in agreement with the bishop regarding hypocrisy."

"I am glad that you are able to find accord with the bishop in some things."

"In some things, yes. Though I must say that I find my husband to be a better exemplar of the Christian faith."

Rodarch chided, "Hush, Ganieda, you mustn't say such a thing. The bishop is the man who has been chosen to spread the word of God."

"I might wish that a different man had been chosen."

"It is not up to the sheep to choose their shepherd."

Ganieda was about to make a rejoinder to his analogy which compared people to an animal not highly regarded for its intelligence when she was interrupted by the rattle of chains. Merlin, who had risen to his knees, was stretching his hands towards Rodarch in an imploring gesture. Rodarch nodded. "You are right Merlin. It is time for me to fulfill my promise to you."

Anxiously, Ganieda asked, "Rodarch, what are you going to do?"

"I am going to have your brother's chains removed."

"But Rodarch, if Merlin is released, he will simply run away again."

"Then that is what will happen," he replied brusquely. "Ganieda, was it not you yourself who most vehemently expressed your disapproval to me when I had your brother shackled?"

"Yes, but to release him now, so suddenly, without notice or preparation…"

"I'm sorry, Ganieda, but I shall not rescind the promise that I made to him. Your brother may stay if he wishes, but I shall inform the guards that they are not to stop him if he chooses to leave."

"At least allow me to have some time alone with him once he is released. Please give me a chance to convince him to stay with us."

"You are free to do as you like Ganieda, however, I believe it only right that Guendoloena should be here as well."

"Of course."

"Then I'll see that Guendoloena is informed of my decision," he said briskly as he exited through the door.

Within minutes of Rodarch's departure, the blacksmith entered, carrying his toolbox. Putting a small anvil on the floor in front of a chair, he politely motioned to the prisoner to sit. Needing no additional encouragement, Merlin eagerly sat on the chair and placed one of his feet against the anvil so that the shackle could be struck off. Once freed from all of his bonds, the unfettered man gratefully rubbed his ankles and chafed his wrists. Then, rising to his feet, he swung his arms in wide circles and stretched them high over his head. Meanwhile, the smith removed the chain from the wall and dropped it, clanking, into a leather bag. Smiling, Madoc said to the obviously jubilant man, "Lord King, I told you on that sorry day, when I first put these chains on you, that I was looking forward to the time when I could strike them off again for good. Well, that day's finally come, Lord King, and now I can be a happy man again." He tried to say more, but found himself choking on his words. After wiping his eyes with a sleeve, he wrapped his arms around Merlin in a heartfelt embrace. Then, bobbing a respectful bow to the queen, he heaved the heavy bag across his broad shoulders and departed.

Merlin was about to follow him. Alarmed, Ganieda put a restraining hand on her brother's arm and begged him to stay. Heedless to his sister's entreaties, he shook off her hand. Despairingly, she said, "If Rodarch had given me more time, I could have summoned a bard to restore your mind with music. I'm sorry, brother, but I'll have to try another way."

He was almost at the door when Ganieda grabbed him forcefully by his shoulders. Spinning him around, she slapped him hard across the face. Wincing in pain, he shut his eyes. When he opened them again, they were clear and blue. Touching his face gingerly, Merlin said, "Ow! Was that really necessary, sister? I think I would have preferred the music."

Ganieda, overjoyed to hear him sounding like his former self, said, "Now that I am able to speak with you, brother, I hope that I can convince you to stay with us in Brocavum."

He shook his head adamantly. "Stay here and become a permanent embarrassment to my family? 'Please pay no attention to the lunatic snarling in the corner of the feasting hall, that's only my brother, Merlin the madman.'" He laughed grimly. "Besides, I'd scare away too many dinner guests. No, Ganieda, I shall not even consider staying to become an object of scorn or pity. I must return to the woods, far from the eyes of men."

"But what is Guendoloena supposed to do? Surely you will not abandon your devoted and loving wife who now lives for you alone?"

"Guendoloena!" he cried, in sudden remembrance.

Just at that moment, the door opened, and Guendoloena herself appeared on the threshold. She hesitated, looking at Merlin apprehensively. Then, when she saw him joyfully throw open his arms to her, she flew across the room. Merlin, clutching her in a tight embrace, lifted her off her feet and covered her face with kisses. Holding him just as tightly, she returned his kisses with equal ardor. After the two had finally broken off a particularly long and passionate kiss, a radiantly happy Guendoloena said, "My husband is back! Now we will be as we were!"

Jolted back to reality by her words, Merlin gently lowered her to her feet. When she tried to embrace him again, he held her by her shoulders at arm's length. Looking at her sadly, he said, "Alas, dearest wife, we can never again be as we were. Soon, I shall revert to that state of madness which is now my lot in life. I knew when I asked you for your hand in marriage that I would cause you sorrow, but my selfish love and desire overwhelmed what should have been my greater concern for your welfare."

Shaking her head vehemently, she declared, "But I know no sorrow, dearest husband. When I am with you, I know only complete happiness. And that is where I wish to be! With you, at your side, now and forever!"

Merlin said sadly, "Ah, dearest Guen, but that is where you may not be. Soon, I must return to the woods, alone, where I can no longer hurt you or anyone else."

Steadfastly, she replied, "Merlin, I am willing to take any risk to be with you. I will live in the forest and sleep under the stars with you. I will endure snow and rain and hunger and privation. I will face wind and storm, wild beasts and anything else just to be with you. I will be your helpmate and your comfort. I will be your kindred spirit. All I ask for in return is your love."

Merlin had been looking at her intently while she spoke. Now, turning his eyes from her, he said, "I am sorry, but I no longer have any love to give to you. Nor do I wish to receive your love. My only wish is to be left alone."

Guendoloena stood speechless, devastated by his words. Angrily, Ganieda demanded, "And what is your wife supposed to do? Is she to re-marry? Or do you expect her to live like a widow? Merlin, you have a beautiful, caring, intelligent, loving woman who is willing to make any sacrifice just to be with you, and you think to reject her so lightly?"

Sorrowfully, he bowed his head. "You are right to rebuke me, sister." Merlin turned to his wife. "Guendoloena, please find a deserving husband who is able to return your love and affection. I am sorry, Guendoloena, but I am beyond love. You must forget me."

Abruptly, he turned his back to them. Then, he walked to the door and departed without a backward glance.

Four days later, Bishop Kentigern and his two companions were nearing the village where they were intending to spend the night. Shortly after setting out that morning, Kentigern had chosen the shorter of the two routes which they could have taken. Although the shorter route was also the rougher, they were not overly concerned since their mounts were sure-footed mules. The track, still muddy from the heavy rain that had fallen the previous night, closely followed the course of a river for much of the way. At one point, as it climbed to traverse a height of land, the already narrow track became an even narrower defile, hugging the very brink of the riverbank. Galfridus, who had been riding in the forefront, reined in his mount and stopped to survey the way ahead. With thickly wooded land rising steeply to the right and a precipitous drop to the turbulent river hidden somewhere below the trees to the left, their only options were to continue along the path or turn back. When Galfridus questioned the safety of proceeding along such a dangerous-looking track, Kentigern answered that they would lose two days of travel if they went back to the junction where they had turned off early that morning. Observing that it would soon be nightfall, he added that while there were no likely looking places to camp nearby, the town ahead was now only minutes away. Reminding the young monk that he was in God's hands, Kentigern told him to proceed. Galfridus urged his mount forward, but the mule jibbed, refusing to budge. When he heard the bishop make an impatient sound, Giraldus wondered aloud if Brother Galfridus had forgotten that man had been given dominion over the beasts, advising him that a stubborn mule was best controlled with a firm hand. Flustered, Galfridus gave his mount a gentle kick and crossed the most precipitous section of the track, halting where the path broadened again. Kentigern, kicking his own mount forward, followed Galfridus without incident. When Giraldus kicked his mount, his mule also balked. Even after he had given it several sharp jabs to its flanks, the animal stubbornly refused to take a single step forward. Irritably, Giraldus loosed his whip and gave the beast a stinging lash across its croup. When the mule jumped forward under the stroke, the ground suddenly gave way under its hooves as the path collapsed into the gorge. Scrabbling frantically, the mule managed to regain a foothold, but its hapless rider was pitched headfirst into the gorge. Kentigern and Galfridus watched in horror as Giraldus disappeared into the trees below. Leaping from his mount, Galfridus hurriedly tied the reins of the two mules to a protruding tree root and half-ran, half-slid down the steep side of the gorge. When he returned several minutes later, panting from exertion, his face was flushed and his eyes were wide with shock. Badly shaken, he informed the bishop in a trembling voice that their companion was dead, and that he would need help to recover the body. Stunned, Kentigern followed Galfridus with difficulty down the steep slope to the river's edge and gasped when he saw Giraldus. The cleric was hanging upside down from a tree. With his right foot wedged in the fork of a branch which extended over the river, his head was submerged beneath the surface of the water. Unnerved, the bishop fell to his knees, his hands clasped together in prayer.

Chapter 5

The Gift

Over the past weeks King Arthur had received letters from Rodarch and Ganieda, keeping him apprised of Merlin's unfortunate and unchanging condition. On more than one occasion during that time, Arthur had intended to visit his ailing mentor when something had intervened, preventing him from doing what he most wanted to do. Now all those concerns, which had seemed so crucial at the time, were barely remembered trivialities, while what really mattered – seeing his dearest friend in all the world – would most likely remain forever unrealized. Ganieda's latest letter detailing the episode with Bishop Kentigern, her brother's release and subsequent disappearance, and the tragic fulfillment of Merlin's prophecy made Arthur realize with deepest regret and sorrow that he might never again see the man who had been like a father to him. With the heaviest of hearts, Arthur picked up his pen to write a reply to Ganieda's letter.

In early autumn, rumblings began to be heard of political upheavals inside the Saxon treaty lands, and anxious British farmers living along the border hurried to bring their harvests to the nearest hillfort for safekeeping. Ever since King Arthur's decisive victory over the Saxons at Badon Hill ten years earlier, the Britons had been enjoying peace with their neighbors and erstwhile enemies in the south and east of Britain. Now that precious and precarious peace could very well be in jeopardy.

As soon as he learned that a new leader had risen to power among the Saxons, Arthur, concerned about the potential consequences of the power shift, dispatched his shrewd and trusted chamberlain, Lord Ulfin, on a diplomatic mission to parley with this new king. Ulfin, a gray-haired but spry man in his early-sixties, had been chamberlain to the previous High King of Britain, Arthur's father, Uther Pendragon. Merlin himself had recommended the worldly-wise Ulfin to the post when the then fifteen-year-old Arthur had been named High King.

Ulfin returned a fortnight later with a cautiously optimistic report. His first impressions of Cerdic, the West Saxons' new king, had been favorable, and the preliminary discussions had gone well. Learning from his chamberlain that Cerdic wished to speak to the British High King face-to-face during future negotiations, Arthur decided to oblige by moving his court from his capital city at Isca to Camalat, which was closer to the treaty land borders. Camalat was the old British fortress that Merlin had rebuilt shortly after Arthur had become High King. Through pure hard work, Arthur's chief advisor had transformed the long-abandoned hillfort into an easily defendable, yet comfortable, stronghold. With its lofty and imposing ramparts crowning a high, flat-topped hill, the fortress, ringed by a series of deep ditches and sheer-sided walls faced with ochre-colored stone, shone like gold in a low-angled sun. As Ulfin cannily noted, the mighty and glittering citadel made a suitably impressive and awe-inspiring setting at which to both welcome and intimidate Cerdic and the members of the Saxon delegation.

A week later the Lord Chamberlain, accompanied by a large British honor guard, rode out to meet King Cerdic and his entourage at the border. With pomp and pageantry, the Britons escorted their Saxon guests to Camalat, where they were received with appropriate ceremony and fanfare. As Ulfin had earlier observed to King Arthur, Saxons always seemed to enjoy a bit of a show, and it would not be impolitic to provide it. The meeting between Kings Arthur and Cerdic was cordial, and during the days that followed, their rapport grew warmer. The early negotiations went well, and some small disputes regarding boundary lines were soon settled. When the subject turned to coastal fishing rights, the discussions that followed led to an equally amicable conclusion. Upon the successful resolution of those two items, Cerdic brought up for discussion the pithier and potentially more divisive topic regarding trade.

After the Battle of Badon, the borders between the Saxons and the Britons had been officially closed to all trade and commerce under the terms of surrender to which the Saxons had agreed. This ruling had, of course, led to a thriving and lucrative business of smuggling goods across the border. Conducted by Saxons and Britons alike, this illicit activity led to an inordinate amount of time and effort being spent by their respective leaders trying, mostly in vain, to prevent the clandestine practice. Cerdic argued persuasively that if an agreement on trade could be reached and put into effect, the kings on both sides of the border would no longer have to waste time and resources attempting to enforce an unenforceable law, while lawful trade could be regulated and tariffed.

Cerdic, who clearly had a witty side, made a joke when he had first brought up the issue regarding trade. Relating that his mother had been a Briton, he humorously noted that commodities were not the only things that managed to cross the border. Adding that his British name had been the source of endless gibes when he was growing up, Cerdic laughed that his parents might have actually done him a favor since he had secured his reputation as a fighter at an early age by cracking the heads of more than a few who had dared to taunt him.

Arthur, somewhat surprised to find himself in agreement with the practicality of what Cerdic had advocated, accepted the idea of a new trade policy in principle, and over the next few days the details of that and several other proposed policies were hammered out and finally approved by both sides. To ratify the new treaty, the document was read aloud by the herald before the full court in the great hall at Camalat, and the two kings put their names to parchment. Then, after vowing to honor the contract as a binding trust, they solemnly pledged to maintain into perpetuity the peace which had been achieved between their two peoples. As the two kings raised silver goblets to confirm their pledge to peace, everyone in the hall did likewise, raising whatever vessel was in his or her hand. This toast was only the first of many that followed as five days of drinking, toasting, feasting, boasting, music-making, story-telling, gift-giving, gaming, dancing and general carousing ensued.

At the end of the week, with banners flying and a musical fanfare playing, King Cerdic departed from Camalat at the head of his train, riding the fine bay stallion that the British High king had bestowed upon him as a gift. As Cerdic passed through the gates, King Arthur and Queen Gwenhwyfar, standing together on the ramparts above, smiled happily and waved farewell to their Saxon guests. When the last member of the Saxon delegation finally disappeared down the cobbled road, Arthur and Gwenhwyfar each let out a long, unconscious and simultaneous sigh of relief. Laughing together over the little incident, Arthur wrapped his arms around his wife's waist and kissed her. Holding hands, they walked to their private chambers where they could at last relax, each vowing to the other that he or she would not be able to eat or drink another thing for a month.

Arthur and Gwenhwyfar, content in each other's company, had long become resigned that their marriage would most likely remain childless.

Earlier, there had been murmurings for a time among the Britons that their king should put aside his barren wife and take a new queen, but Arthur, who deeply loved Gwenhwyfar, had rejected such a notion out of hand. Sternly, he had silenced the discontent by reminding the Britons that shortly after becoming High King, he had named King Cador of Dumnonia, his mother's brother, heir to the throne. Since Cador's grown son Constantine already had two healthy and thriving young sons of his own, a long and peaceful line of succession to the throne had been insured. Although Arthur, in truth, was disappointed that he did not have a son to become High King after him, he was, at least, untroubled by any fears that his country might be thrown into turmoil upon his death. Now that a new treaty with the Saxons had been forged, the future appeared especially bright with the promise of many peaceful years ahead. Arthur decided to remain at Camalat until winter, ostensibly as a pleasant change of scenery for himself and Gwenhwyfar, while also keeping a watchful eye on the border now that it had been opened to regulated trade. Thankfully, all appeared to be going well in that quarter.

A fortnight after the treaty had been signed, one of the regular messengers from the north, bearing three letters from Anna, Queen of Lothian, arrived at Camalat. One of the letters, delivered to her half-brother, King Arthur, offered her felicitations on his achievement of a new accord with the Saxons. The second, given to her eldest son Gawain, was pleasant but mundane, advising him that all was well in their realm and sending him her love. The third letter was delivered to her other son Mordred who, along with Gawain, was one of King Arthur's companions. Although there was nothing in the letter that could not comfortably be shown to others, Mordred, as a matter of course, tossed it onto the fire of a brazier as soon as he finished reading it. Making his way into the great hall at Camalat, he asked the herald if he might have a few words with the king. When it came his turn to speak, Mordred bowed politely to his king and begged permission to take leave of court for a few weeks to visit his mother, who was hoping to see him before winter weather made traveling to Lothian too difficult. Arthur readily granted Mordred's request and asked his nephew to kindly convey his warmest regards and best wishes to his sister, Queen Anna. Promising to do so, Mordred thanked the High King and, after another courtly bow, left the hall. He was walking down the cobbled road to the small, but thriving village, which had sprung up in the shadow of Camalat, when his brother Gawain came hurrying after him. A big and blustery but good-natured man, Gawain had been in the hall when Mordred made his request and had followed his younger brother through the gates. With a broad smile, Gawain called out, "Hey, Mordred. I hear our Mummy wants to see her little boy again before it gets too cold for him to travel."

Mordred stopped and turned to face his brother. He said icily, "Gawain, I am so glad that you are my brother since I am wearing my good clothes today. The last time a fool made some such remark to a similar effect, I found my garment quite spoiled by the man's blood."

Gawain could see that his brother was in deadly earnest. Flustered, he tried to make a face-saving remark. "Listen, Mordred, I was only joking. You know I didn't mean anything by it."

Coldly, Mordred continued to glare at his brother. Then his face broke into a wide grin. Gawain, very relieved, said, "Damn you, Mordred! You had me going there for a while. I thought you were really angry at me."

"Me? Angry at my dearest brother? Perish the thought!" said Mordred, laughing. "And you are my dearest brother since you're the only one I've got!" he added, still grinning. "Here. I was just going into town for a drink before I leave. Why don't you join me? Drinks are on me." He wrapped his arm around his brother's shoulders as they walked to the inn. After spending an hour or so enjoying a couple of pints, the brothers got to their feet, and Mordred casually flipped a coin to the innkeeper. A short while later, with his horse saddled and standing in the courtyard outside the stables, Mordred embraced his brother. Promising to deliver Gawain's dutiful message of love to their mother, he vaulted into the saddle.

Mordred made good speed and arrived at Queen Anna's stronghold at Din Eidyn a week later. He met his mother privately in a tower room. Bidding him to sit beside her, the lovely, raven-haired woman kissed her handsome son and stroked his hair, as dark and glossy as her own.

While the hot-headed and high-colored Gawain favored his father, the late King Lot, in both appearance and personality, Lot's other son Mordred had the fine features and the dark eyes of his mother. Anna, in turn, had also favored her mother, Queen Igraine, the parent whom she shared with Arthur, though her sharp and piercing eyes were those of her father Gorlois. In temperament, too, she was unmistakably her father's daughter. Gorlois, the fierce and proud king of Dumnonia, had rebelled when a lesser man, Uther Pendragon, had been named High King of Britain. After fighting several costly battles, just as peace was being patched up between the two men, Uther had first set eyes upon Gorlois's beautiful wife Igraine. What was on his mind was clear to all to see, and war broke out anew, but this time over the woman. To protect his wife and his honor, Gorlois put Igraine in his fortress at Tintagel on Dumnonia's wild and rocky northern coast. Linked to land only by a knife-edged isthmus and surrounded on all sides by a restless sea pounding incessantly against its high, sheer cliffs, the fortress was considered impregnable. Meanwhile, Gorlois placed himself and most of his army in the nearby fortress Dimilioc, where he was soon besieged by Uther's forces. The sturdy fortress could have been held almost indefinitely, but one evening, after seeing Uther ride from the field with two other men, Gorlois made the unwise decision to attack the High King's forces and was killed during the action. Some hours later, under the cover of darkness and pouring rain, Uther, who had been made to resemble Gorlois, was admitted into the fortress Tintagel. His two companions, who were also disguised, then led their High King to Igraine's chamber. One of the men was Ulfin, Uther's chamberlain. The other, younger man was Uther's advisor Merlin. Having foreseen in a vision a future king who could be conceived only on that one wild and stormy night, Merlin had, against his own scruples, resorted to guile to bring Uther and Igraine together. But the tryst had been no rape. Earlier, Merlin had revealed to Igraine that the son she would conceive that night with the High King would be nothing less than the savior of Britannia. And truth be told, Igraine had felt herself more than a little attracted to the impetuous and handsome Uther. Later, when it became known that Gorlois had died prior to his supposed arrival at Tintagel, Merlin had willingly taken the blame for having deceived Igraine to protect her reputation, and the queen had gone to her grave with her honor intact. Although Anna never found out that Igraine had known who was in her bed that night, she despised her mother, nonetheless, for marrying King Uther just thirteen days after Gorlois's death. Luckily for Igraine, her daughter had never learned the full truth.

Anna now questioned Mordred about affairs at court, especially the meeting between Arthur and Cerdic, and he freely revealed more than he had deemed prudent to write in his earlier letter to her. When her son brought up the subject of Merlin and told her how saddened Arthur had been upon learning that his dear old mentor had, once again, disappeared into the woods, Queen Anna beamed with pleasure.

"Of course, my agents at Brocavum have been keeping me informed about Merlin, but it is especially satisfying to hear how pained my dear brother has been about it," she said. "I must confess that I was at first very disappointed when I learned that Morwen's poison hadn't killed Merlin outright, but after learning of his public humiliation being paraded in chains through the market square, I have found his madness to be a far sweeter revenge than his mere death would have been." She smiled maliciously. "How utterly delicious! To think that the great Merlin will be spending the rest of his days living miserably in the woods with only dumb animals for company, and he just as dumb."

Mordred snickered. "That reminds me, mother. I've been thinking about going to the Caledonian Forest on a hunting trip. I hear the game's good over there, and I was hoping to catch a stag, a boar and a merlin. A mixed bag is always nice and should provide some good sport."

His mother declared, "My dear boy, what a charming idea! But, unfortunately, not a prudent one, at least for the moment. You must remember that Merlin's clever sister is always watching, and we cannot afford to have our intentions revealed until you are sitting comfortably on the throne. After that you can serve him up for dinner as far as I'm concerned. Believe me, Mordred, I shall celebrate on the day that Merlin dies. And who better to deal the blow than you, the grandson of the man he betrayed!"

Mordred smiled inwardly at her increasingly passionate words. His mother's public demeanor was invariably cool and collected. Only in front of him did she ever allow her true feelings to be shown. "And I shall celebrate with you! Actually, mother, speaking of having our intentions revealed, I was wondering if we should be worried that Morwen might give us away or try to blackmail us some day."

Anna laughed. "I'm afraid that you are a little behind the news since discretion prevented me from writing to you about the terrible tragedy. It seems that the ship Morwen had boarded must have hit some heavy weather before it reached Isca. The poor old dear, who wasn't too good on her feet, was pitched overboard and tragically lost at sea." She added slyly, "One of my agents who happened to be on board saw the accident happen. It is such a loss."

Mordred smirked. "Then it's fortunate that I had that package from her."

Queen Anna said, "Fortunate indeed, and I believe the time is now right to use what is inside. Actually, that's why I sent for you. I'd like you to go on a little mission for your mother."

"Oh, before you tell me about it, Mother, I almost forgot. Arthur sends you his warmest regards and best wishes."

"How kind of my darling brother!"

Some weeks later, King Arthur was holding court in the great hall at Camalat when he was informed by his herald of the arrival of an emissary sent by King Cerdic. Bidding the herald to admit him immediately, Arthur was amazed when a flaxen-haired woman stepped into the hall. She was young and beautiful, and Arthur smiled when he heard Gwenhwyfar, who was sitting by his side, give a little exclamation of surprise. The emissary approached the throne and placed a handsome wooden chest which she had been carrying on the floor beside her. Then she dipped in a deep and respectful curtsy to the king and queen, who responded with courteous greetings. Arthur signaled to Ulfin to step forward and act as translator, but the emissary, thanking the king politely in the British tongue, said there was no need. She spoke fluently, though with a strong Saxon accent. "Hail King Arthur, High King of the Britons," she declaimed. "Cerdic, King of the Saxons, sends you his greetings. King Cerdic gives to you this gift, King Arthur, as a token of his great esteem and to further strengthen the bonds of friendship and goodwill between our two peoples." Stooping, she opened the lid and lifted from the chest a magnificent, ermine-trimmed robe, embroidered with gold thread and encrusted with precious gems. Excepting King Arthur's great sword Caliburn itself, a more magnificent object of craft and beauty had never been seen. As the emissary lifted the garment, it brought gasps of wonder from everyone in the hall and an exclamation of delight from Gwenhwyfar. The Queen, leaning closer, whispered to her husband, "Arthur, we must give King Cerdic something in return, but what in all the kingdom could match such a splendid gift!" She mused. "Perhaps an enameled bronze hanging bowl or a gold torque? Or perhaps several of them since any one of those objects would pale by comparison with this magnificent gift!"

The emissary held the garment out to Arthur, and Gwenhwyfar encouraged her husband to don the robe. Smiling, Arthur rose to his feet. He was descending from the dais when everyone in the hall was shocked to hear a woman's voice loudly command the king to stop. The court was thrown into chaos, and the herald, vigorously thumping his staff upon the floor, called for order. Striding forward with her arms dramatically raised, Nimue, Arthur's chief advisor, stepped between the king and the emissary. Gwenhwyfar expressed her outrage over the presumptuousness of Nimue whose presence, in fact, she had never more than barely tolerated.

Nimue, a beautiful young woman who had been Merlin's student, had once saved Arthur's life. When Accolon, a nobleman from Lothian, had somehow managed to steal Arthur's sword, he had then publicly insulted the king to instigate a duel. Having disguised Caliburn by wrapping its hilt with leather, Accolon had wielded Arthur's own sword during their combat, shattering the blunted and brittle copy that had been substituted in Arthur's scabbard. Nimue, who had detected the fraud in a vision, had intervened and revealed Accolon's deception. Although badly wounded, Arthur was able to recover Caliburn when it slipped from Accolon's grasp and kill his adversary. Knowing that Merlin had wished his former student to be his successor, Arthur, in gratitude, asked Nimue to fill the vacant post of chief advisor. She had readily accepted. Although no one could ever take the place of Merlin, Arthur had always found Nimue's advice good and her judgment sound. Until this moment.

As the Lord Chamberlain hurried forward, making his apologies to the Saxon emissary, Arthur whispered under his breath, "Nimue, what are you doing? This is a terrible insult to King Cerdic and could very well shatter the treaty that he and I have just ratified."

Ignoring the king's words, Nimue demanded that the emissary don the robe first. The Saxon protested. "It would be unseemly for a woman to wear a man's garment." Quickly sidestepping around Nimue, she took several steps toward Arthur. As she held the robe open for the king, Nimue wrenched the garment from her grasp and threw it over the emissary's shoulders instead. Everyone gaped in disbelief at the actions of Nimue. Even Arthur could only stare in shock as he fumbled for the words of an apology. The Saxon woman's face twisted and became livid as in anger. Suddenly, she shrieked. Frantically, she tried to tear the robe away, but Nimue, overpowering her efforts, continued to hold it firmly over her shoulders. Giving an agonized moan, the Saxon collapsed onto the floor, writhing in pain. Arthur took an instinctive step toward the woman, but Nimue put her arm across his path to prevent him from going any closer. Moments later, the woman's movements stopped.

"The inside of the robe," said Nimue, "has been poisoned."

The hall was in an uproar as everyone shouted to avenge this latest example of Saxon deceit. "There must be a swift reprisal against Cerdic's treachery!" "These Saxon dogs poisoned King Aurelius and King Uther, and now they are trying to poison King Arthur as well!" "Death to Cerdic!" "This time no mercy, no surrender until the Saxons have been wiped from the face of the earth!" was heard among the many angry shouts.

It was Nimue's commanding voice that finally silenced the court. "The Saxon woman lied. King Cerdic had no hand in this plot against our High King's life."

Arthur asked, "Do you know who is responsible?"

Nimue, with much frustration, shook her head. "I saw in a vision the man who had instigated this plot and had given the poisoned robe to this woman, but his face was not clearly revealed to me. I am sorry Lord King, but I only saw enough to know that the man was not Cerdic."

Arthur said, "Lady Nimue, once again I am in your debt. Thank you, Chief Advisor, for saving my life."

Signaling to his steward, the king spoke a few words with him, and minutes later several servants entered with blankets. Nimue cautioned them not to touch the inside of the lethal garment as they carefully wrapped the body in several layers of the heavy woolen fabric before carrying it away.

Gwenhwyfar, although still badly shaken by the ghastly scene which had played out before her, rose to her feet and descended from the dais. Nimue tried to curtsy to the queen, but Gwenhwyfar stopped her and bade her to rise. Thanking Nimue for saving her husband's life once again, Gwenhwyfar embraced the young woman with heartfelt goodwill and kissed her.

Some time later, through his informants, Ulfin found out that the Saxon woman was the fanatical sister of an equally fanatical Saxon leader unable to tolerate the idea of bending the knee to a "half-breed king," his disrespectful moniker for Cerdic. No doubt had his sister's attempt on King Arthur's life been successful, fighting between the Britons and Saxons would have resumed, and in the ensuing turmoil he would have tried to seize power from Cerdic. Cerdic, upon learning of the assassination plot, was more than happy to use the incident to permanently rid himself of his hostile and outspoken rival. The Britons and Nimue herself, believing that Cerdic's rival was the man whom she had seen in her vision, were content that those who had been responsible for the assassination attempt had paid the ultimate penalty, and peace was maintained.

When word of the plot against Arthur's life reached Brocavum, Ganieda, once again forced to acknowledge Nimue's usefulness to the High King, was now better able to understand Merlin's motivation for not having revealed his student's treachery towards him. For although everyone knew the story of how a rockfall had left Merlin trapped inside a cavern, few knew that the ambitious Nimue had caused the rocks to fall. Before he had met Guendoloena, Merlin had become infatuated with the beautiful Nimue. Blinded by love, Merlin had angrily rejected Ganieda's warnings and traveled with his clever but guileful student across the British Sea to Armorica. Later, Nimue had returned alone to Arthur's court, claiming that Merlin had chosen to remain in Armorica to pursue his studies there. Ganieda, suspicious of the woman who had assumed her brother's mantle, was determined to find him. After a journal belonging to Merlin had been discovered by a hunter near the blocked entrance to a cave, Ganieda forced Nimue to accompany her there. After Nimue's efforts had failed, Ganieda invoked powers she never believed she possessed to shatter the huge boulder sealing the cave's entrance. Terrified of Ganieda's apparent powers, Nimue had fled. Searching the labyrinthine cavern alone, Ganieda had found Merlin inside, very weak but alive, sustained by his protecting spirit and a supply of food kept in what had always been one of his favorite retreats. Although Merlin had allowed Ganieda to reveal Nimue's treachery to Rodarch, he had been adamant that no one else should know the full story. Now that Nimue had once again saved King Arthur's life, Ganieda was finally able to understand why her brother had shielded his duplicitous student and why, incongruously, she now found herself hoping for Nimue's continued success.

Chapter 6

The Bridegroom

Almost four years had passed since Merlin's release, and during all that time no one had caught so much as a glimpse of him. While nearly everyone had assumed that King Arthur's old chief advisor had long since died of privation in some lonely woods, Ganieda had staunchly continued to believe that her brother yet lived. Merlin's wife, however, had been less certain.

Not long after Merlin had left her, Guendoloena had returned to the house of her father, Lord Rhiwallon, a well-respected landholder whose modest estate lay about a half-day's ride from Brocavum. For the first two years or so following her husband's disappearance, Guendoloena had often returned to visit Ganieda, who had always been her dearest friend. On several occasions during that time, the two women had traveled together as they had done in their younger days, walking the high fells, hunting and foraging for their food, and camping under the stars. As time had passed, however, though neither had consciously made any decision to do so, the two women had slowly drifted apart. Having had no word from Guendoloena in more than six months, Ganieda was pleased to receive a note from her, inquiring if she might come to Brocavum for a visit. Happily, Ganieda penned a reply that her dearest friend was always most welcome.

Two days later, when a guard informed the king and queen that Guendoloena had arrived, they went out into the courtyard to greet her. Both were surprised to find three men with her. Two of the rather brawny men were strangers to them. The third man, however, Ganieda recognized immediately though she had not seen him in many years. Although some twenty years older than Guendoloena, he was tall, broad-shouldered and not unhandsome. As Guendoloena introduced him, Ganieda was dismayed even before she heard her friend speak his name – Dinabutius – Merlin's childhood nemesis. Ganieda's dismay turned to shock when Guendoloena presented him as her fiancé.

No one had failed to notice Ganieda's expression of unhappy surprise when Dinabutius was introduced to her. Quickly falling to his knees before Cumbria's queen, he bowed his head contritely. "My Queen, I know the memories you have of me from our childhood days in Moridunum are not the most pleasant, but a person may change. A stupid and thoughtless boy may grow to become a wiser man. Please believe that I deeply regret my childish deeds and have long since repented them. Let me prove to you, My Queen, how I have changed."

Coldly, Ganieda bade him to rise. Guendoloena, who had been very anxious about this first meeting, was visibly upset by Ganieda's reaction. As an awkward silence was becoming prolonged, King Rodarch stepped forward and, with decorum, welcomed them all to enter their home as honored guests.

Once she had been shown to her room, Guendoloena sought her friend. Learning from the steward that Ganieda had retired to her study, Guendoloena gently knocked on the door of that room. When she heard Ganieda's voice bid her to come in, she entered and closed the door softly behind her. She immediately took the plunge. "Ganieda, I was afraid that you might be disappointed in me for wishing to remarry."

"Please sit down, Guendoloena," Ganieda replied, pointing her to a chair. "You have misunderstood my reaction. I am not troubled that you plan to remarry. After all, Merlin himself had made it clear that he wished for you to do so. It is whom you have chosen that I find so troubling. I know Dinabutius. He is a cunning and manipulative liar who cannot be trusted. I simply do not wish to see my dearest friend fall under the power of a devious and brutal man."

"But Ganieda, he really has changed," Guendoloena protested. "I met Dinabutius quite by accident while I was taking a walk in the woods near my home. He's never been anything but a perfect gentleman to me and to everybody else. He had no idea who I was when we first met, but once he found out, he never tried to conceal who he was and what he had been to Merlin. He speaks only with remorse for his past behavior which he now so regrets. Ganieda, you know how devastated I was when your brother abandoned me. Dinabutius has been my comfort and support just when I needed a shoulder to lean on."

"I'm sure he has," replied Ganieda acidly. "Please, Guen. You mustn't allow yourself to be misled by this man. A stoat may change his coat to white in the winter and be called an ermine, but underneath he's still just a stoat. Dinabutius is an artful deceiver who cannot be trusted."

"Dinabutius is no deceiver, Ganieda. I've been with him long enough to know that. Please, Ganieda, just give him a chance. You'll see for yourself how different he is from the boy you once knew."

"Guen, you are my dearest friend in all the world. It's not too late. Please reconsider your decision to marry this man."

"Believe me, I gave Dinabutius's proposal of marriage long and careful consideration before I accepted it. During all that time, he was very patient and very understanding. He never pressured me for an answer and was nothing but joyous when I finally gave it to him. I know in my heart that I have made the right choice. Please, Ganieda, at least say that you'll give him a chance to prove himself before you judge him."

"I will only say that I hope Dinabutius will indeed prove himself before you have irrevocably bound yourself to him."

"I'm sorry you feel that way, My Queen," said Guendoloena. Rising from her chair, she curtsied formally before departing.

As the days passed, Dinabutius became increasingly well liked by everyone, both at court and around town. He showed himself to be thoughtful to the elderly, generous to the poor, amusing to children, and the epitome of propriety and politeness to women of all stations. He was particularly popular among the soldiers, regaling them with funny stories and buying them drinks in town when they were off duty. Even his two companions, Tomos and Cadog, who at first glance appeared to be rather rough fellows, were exemplars of polite behavior. Rodarch thought Ganieda wrong for continuing to be suspicious, but she remained skeptical of Dinabutius, in spite of that man's efforts to ingratiate himself with her. Regardless of Ganieda's misgivings about her intended, Guendoloena proceeded with making arrangements for the wedding which was planned to take place the following month.

On a cold evening in early spring, a man was lying on his back on the top of a high and remote mountain. Alone, he was staring up into the arching vault of the heavens, watching while the stars slowly became visible in the growing darkness. He was gazing at Venus, shining more brightly than the brightest star when a ray from her cut across the ether. While he watched, the ray split so that twin beams now streaked across the sky. In alarm, the man sprang to his feet and began racing down the steep mountainside in the dark with surprising speed and ease.

In the first light of dawn, a group of guards manning the ramparts at Brocavum gave shouts of amazement as a bizarre sight came into view. From a small copse around the side of the palisade, a large herd of deer came trotting placidly toward the gates. They were drawn up neatly into two ranks, hinds on one side, harts on the other. Most of the harts had already shed their antlers, but the lead animal, an immense and thick-necked stag, was still sporting a full rack. Amazingly, a man was sitting astride the great beast's back as easily as if he were sitting a horse though he was using neither saddle nor bridle. Barefooted, he was tanned, tall and wiry with long grey hair and beard. His dress was an eccentric garment made of animal skins, stitched together with sinew, and a girdle of lime bast was knotted around his waist. When he reached the gate, he lifted his hand, and the deer halted. Dinabutius, who had been out all night with a group of soldiers, was still with them when they had returned to duty on the ramparts. He called over to the guards standing above the gates to find out what they were looking at. One of them shook his head and replied, "You've got to see this to believe it, Dinas."

Joining them, Dinabutius leaned over the parapet. After a moment of surprise, he roared with laughter. "That, unless I'm very much mistaken, is none other than King Merlinus Ambrosius himself at the gate."

The soldier standing next to him nodded. "It looks like King Merlinus, all right, though he hasn't been around here in years."

"And by the way he looks, I'd wager that he hasn't had a shave or a haircut in all that time. Or a bath," he added merrily. "Once Merlin's subjects were the proud people of Dyfed, but now they are the furry creatures of the woods, and he looks just as hairy as one of his subjects," said Dinabutius, grinning. The soldiers all laughed at his joke.

"Still," he said, "I bear him no ill will. Actually, I had always hoped that my old childhood friend might still be alive." He paused for a moment. "I'm thinking. Could one of you gentlemen show King Merlinus and his… ah…steed to the stables and give me a little time to talk to him before he's announced to the king and queen? I'd like to try to convince him to stay in Brocavum with his family since nothing would please Queen Ganieda more. As you know, the queen still holds a bit of a grudge against me. If I could convince her brother to remain here with his family where he can be properly cared for, I think she'd finally realize that I'm not such a bad fellow after all. And nothing would make me happier than to help this poor man. Besides," Dinabutius added, "we Britons owe King Merlinus so much." The soldiers nodded in agreement at his generous sentiments.

When the porter opened the gates, Merlin rode through into the courtyard. The other deer would have followed, but Merlin turned and raised his hand, and they quickly melted back into the woods. The soldier who had come down from the ramparts to show Merlin to the stable might have thought that his eyes had deceived him, but the stag in front of him was real enough. It sidled nervously, and Merlin patted its neck and put a hand on one of its antlers to steady the animal. Saluting, the guard cordially invited King Merlinus to come with him to the stable where his mount could be safely housed and where an old friend was hoping to have a few words with him. Silently, Merlin inclined his head and followed the soldier. The building was deserted, and the soldier pointed out several empty stalls at the far end where he could stable his mount and await his friend. With another salute the soldier left to return to his post.

Merlin dismounted and led the stag into the farthest stall. He was murmuring soothingly into the animal's ear when the ear suddenly swiveled to a sound at the stable's entrance. When Merlin turned, he saw three men silhouetted in the light of the open door. Stepping into the aisle, he was squinting toward the men when one of them shut and barred the door, plunging the stable into semidarkness. The stag was stamping nervously as the three approached. When they stopped in front of Merlin, the tallest of them said, "Hello, Ambrosius. Do you remember me?"

Silently, Merlin scrutinized the man's face. "No?" asked Dinabutius as he looked Merlin up and down. "Actually, letting you continue to live like a mindless madman would be the best revenge, but somehow two bridegrooms seem to be one too many."

He nodded, and Tomos and Cadog rushed forward, each grabbing one of Merlin's arms. He struggled to break free but was held fast in their iron grip. Noticing a knife at Merlin's belt, Dinabutius reached over and removed it. Made of bone, it was sharpened to a keen edge. After feeling it with his thumb, he tossed the knife from hand to hand as though weighing it. "What a quaint little tool," he said, "and how distinctive. You always were good at making things, weren't you?" Dinabutius slipped the knife under his own belt. "Still don't remember me, Ambrosius? Here, maybe this will help," he snarled, punching Merlin in the jaw with his fist.

Grimacing in pain, Merlin closed his eyes. When he opened them again, they were clear and blue. A trickle of blood was running from the corner of his lips into his beard. He spat the blood from his mouth. "Let me see," replied Merlin. "A coward, a bully, and a liar. No, Dinabutius, you haven't changed a bit in all these years. And still good at getting others to help you do your dirty work," he added, glancing at his captors.

Dinabutius's hand clamped into a fist again. Merlin turned his head to try to deflect the blow, but Dinabutius stopped himself. "No, much as I would like to, I can't afford to have too many bruises showing up on your face." Dinabutius smiled. "By the way, Ambros, I have to tell you how much I've been enjoying the company of your wife. When I heard that you had run off into the woods again, I knew that she must have been devastated. When a little job brought me up to Cumbria a few months ago, I decided to seek her out. It's amazing what consoling words and a few gifts can do. Your stupid wife's been completely charmed by me. Of course, I've been a perfect gentleman throughout and a comforting shoulder for her to lean on. I can't wait to introduce her to the real Dinabutius on our wedding night."

"Please, you mustn't do this to her. If it's revenge you want, kill me. Only promise that you will leave Guendoloena alone."

"Keep begging, Ambrosius, I'm enjoying it, but you are hardly in a position to bargain. I'm simply going to take it all – your wife, your life, and that nice piece of venison you were thoughtful enough to bring along. And once I'm married to the Queen of Dyfed, I'll be taking your crown as well." Dinabutius laughed. "No, Merlinus, I'm afraid I must decline your feeble offer since I much prefer to have everything. And just think, next week I'll be sleeping with your lovely wife. I'm going to enjoy that best of all."

Merlin struggled in vain to break free as Dinabutius pulled the bone knife from his belt. Dinabutius winced as he gashed himself in the side and tossed the knife a few feet behind him. He laughed at Merlin's look of surprise. "I can see the great prophet is confused. Obviously your death can't look like a murder, now can it? Here, Ambros, let me explain. I came to the stables to try to convince you to return to your family, but when I happened to mention Guendoloena's name, you suddenly attacked me, stabbing me with your knife. In desperation, I drew my sword to try to hold you off, but in a madman's frenzy you lunged at me with the knife again. Unfortunately, you ran yourself onto my blade. These two gentlemen here were witness to the whole unhappy accident. The knife, of course, will be placed in your hand after you're dead."

Genuinely interested, Merlin asked, "Why have you always hated me, Dinabutius? I know no reason for it."

With sudden passion Dinabutius cried, "Because I was the King of Dyfed's son but never got anything just because my mother was a servant while Merlin the bastard, sired by a demon on the king's whoring daughter, lived like a prince in the king's palace and was made king! It wasn't fair. Now I'm finally going to get what I always deserved!" He said to the two men, "Let him go. It has to look like there's been a scuffle before I run him through."

When he was released, Merlin tried to dodge past them to the door, but Tomos and Cadog barred his way. Dinabutius grabbed him and hurled him backwards onto the floor. Jumping to his feet, Merlin tried to push his way through, but was again blocked and thrown to the floor. The big man grinned. "This reminds me of our happy childhood days when I used to enjoy beating you in our fights. Unfortunately, all good things must come to an end," he said, drawing his sword.

The stag, crazed with fear, was leaping wildly, its antlers clattering against the sides of the stall. Merlin rose to his feet, crouching slightly, poised to try to avoid the blow. As Dinabutius was about to lunge with his sword, the stag suddenly thrust its head over the stall door. Merlin saw that one of its antlers was hanging loose. Snatching the antler from the stag's head, he whipped it in front of him, holding it at arm's length to fend off the attack. Dinabutius, unable to stop the momentum of his lunge, ran himself onto the antler, a sharp tine piercing his throat. He stood there in shock, gasping for breath as blood bubbled from his mouth. When Merlin pulled out the antler, Dinabutius fell forward, dead, onto the stable floor.

Tomos and Cadog hesitated. Looking at Merlin, who was still holding the bloody antler, they turned and hurried to the door of the stable. Flinging it open, they ran into the courtyard crying, "Murder!" Merlin dropped the antler and opened the door of the stall. Swinging himself onto the stag's back, he galloped his mount out of the stable and across the courtyard toward the gates. The porter, who had just admitted a horse and wagon into the palisade, had heard the men's cries. He was hurriedly pushing the massive oaken doors closed as Merlin hurtled past him on the back of the stag. A few minutes later, mounted soldiers were pounding through the gates in pursuit of the fugitive.

Merlin was galloping his mount away from town across the fields to the east. Looking over his shoulder, he saw the soldiers leave the palisade. While his mount could put on faster bursts of speed, he knew that across open terrain over longer distances the horses would soon overtake the stag, especially since it bore his added weight. Thinking to elude his pursuers, he turned his mount to the north and galloped the stag into dense woodland. Doggedly, the soldiers followed after him. Inside the forest, Merlin's mount had the advantage, as it agilely bounded around saplings and over the trunks of fallen trees. But as the trees began to thin, the horses once again began gaining on the stag. When Merlin finally broke from the cover of the forest to cross a meadow bordering the River Eden, the horses were galloping only minutes behind him. Reaching the river, he plunged his mount into the water without hesitation. The exhausted animal began swimming across the river, but soon started to struggle in the swift current. Giving the stag an affectionate pat, Merlin slipped from its back and watched as it swam across. He was relieved to see it climb out onto the opposite bank and, after shaking itself, disappear into the trees. With a sigh of resignation, Merlin did not attempt to swim but allowed himself to be carried by the river's current.

Meanwhile, the soldiers had reached the river. Galloping their horses downstream along the bank ahead of the man floating in the river, they quickly dismounted. Holding onto one of the ropes that they had brought with them, they waded out into the river and intercepted the fugitive as he was swept into their midst. Seizing him, they dragged him up the slippery bank and threw him onto the ground at the river's edge. When they tried to pin him down, he began to struggle violently. One of the soldiers gave a yelp of pain. "The filthy bugger just bit my arm," he cried, kicking the prone man in the ribs.

"Stop!" shouted another. "He's the queen's brother, you know."

"More the queen's embarrassment, I'd say," the soldier replied, examining his arm. "I say we finish the murderin' bastard."

"He's right," said another. "The man's a murderer. Let's save our king the trouble of executing 'im. Someone bring over that rope."

While four of the soldiers restrained him, the others tightly bound the prisoner's wrists and ankles. When they finished, the seven soldiers glared down menacingly at the shivering captive.

"Should we hang 'im?" asked one.

"Naw," replied another. "Why bother carrying 'im all the way back to the woods? I say we tie a rock to the murderin' bastard and drown 'im in the river like the animal he is."

One of the soldiers, looking doubtful, said, "I don't know 'bout this; shouldn't we wait for orders?"

"Wait for orders? Tomos and Cadog saw 'im murder Dinas. We know fer a fact he did it. Why wait? The king'll just have to execute 'im anyway. But jus' so there's no trouble later on with the queen, we'll take the ropes off 'im once he's dead and tell 'em he drowned when he was trying to swim across the river." After the others had all agreed to the plan, he said, "Here, one o' you get me another rope while I look fer a rock big enough to sink the bastard. The rest o' you stay here and make sure he don't escape."

When he found a suitably large boulder from the riverbed, the soldier who had become the ringleader carried it over and dropped it with a thud next to the captive's head. While the others watched, he took the rope and wrapped it around the stone several times. Then, after knotting it securely, he looped the other end around Merlin's neck. Hearing the sound of hoofbeats, he turned and swore under his breath when saw his commanding officer approaching.

Riding up, the captain shouted, "What do you think you're doing, soldier?"

"Executing a murderer, sir," the soldier replied with a hint of defiance in his voice.

"It's not your place to execute this man, soldier. That's the prerogative of our king alone." At his words, the soldiers began muttering among themselves. The captain could see they were angry. He understood their feelings because he shared them.

"Listen men," he said. "We're all upset about Dinabutius's murder, none of you more than me. Dinas was a good friend to us all, as generous and open-handed a man as you could hope to meet. Believe me, I want to see this murderer punished for his crime as much as you do. But like I said, it's not our place to execute him. Don't worry men, King Rodarch will see that justice is done. But for now, our job is to see that the prisoner is brought back to our king for judgment. Keep his hands and feet bound and sling him over one of the horses."

Looking obstinate, none of the soldiers moved. One of them said, "With permission sir, we've all seen how he has command over beasts. Even tied, he might still be able to get away."

After a moment's consideration, the captain nodded. "All right then. Tie that rope to his wrists and hand me the other end. The bugger can bloody well run all the way back to Brocavum. We may not have the right to execute him, but we can make him regret what he did."

Eagerly, the soldiers did as they were ordered. Once the captain had secured the rope to his saddle, he said, "Now cut his legs free. Right! Mount up, men! Let's see just how fast the murderer can run." Smiling grimly, he jerked his horse's head around and jabbed his spurs into its flank.

Ganieda was anxiously pacing up and down the ramparts when she spotted the returning soldiers. She gasped in dismay when she saw her brother among them, tied to the end of a rope and stumbling behind one of their horses. Although the soldiers were riding at a walk, she observed that her brother was panting, his garment torn and filthy, and he, cut and bruised. As they were making their way up the hill to the palisade, she caught her brother's eyes. He quickly cast them upon the ground and bowed his head, looking completely broken in spirit.

"Why did you allow yourself to be captured, brother?" she whispered to herself. "Why didn't you stay in the safety of your woods forever. Was it to prevent your wife from making a terrible mistake? Or was it simply to end your own unhappy life?" Rushing down the steps, she hurried to the gates.

Rodarch, striding briskly across the courtyard, arrived there first. When the soldiers rode through and saw their king, they saluted. After dismounting, the captain, looking slightly uncomfortable, said, "Lord King, I'm afraid the prisoner cut himself a little when he tried to avoid capture by running through a thorn brake."

Keeping any emotion which he might have felt from his voice, Rodarch replied, "No doubt it could not be helped. Escort the prisoner to the empty granary. He is to be held there by my personal guard until the trial. See that he is given a blanket and a pail, and some bread and water."

Ganieda looked to her husband appealingly, but Rodarch, ignoring his wife, said neutrally, "That is all, captain." As soon as he had given the order, Rodarch turned on his heel and walked back across the courtyard to the royal residence. Ganieda, hurrying after him, was about to follow her husband inside when she heard angry shouts and paused at the door. As her brother was being led away, the soldiers on the ramparts were hurling abusive shouts and taunts at him. One of the soldiers even threw a stone, which only narrowly missed its mark. While she watched, she saw two soldiers bring over the blanket and pail, and the bread and water. To the amusement of his fellows, the soldier holding the jug of water spat into it before placing it with the other items just inside the granary door. Then, the soldiers roughly pushed the prisoner into the stone building. The captain of the king's guard padlocked the door. Retaining the key, he directed eight men under his command to take positions around the building and on either side of the door.

Feeling nothing but powerless despair, Ganieda hurried inside to speak to Rodarch about her brother's harsh treatment. When she found him sitting in his study, she challenged, "Was it really necessary to have my brother locked inside a windowless building?"

Rodarch had expected his wife's protest. "And just how long, do you imagine, would your brother live if not locked in a windowless building surrounded by my own loyal guard? You have heard the soldiers' angry cries for justice. Your brother committed a capital offense, the most heinous crime imaginable against an honored guest in my own home. The criminal will receive no special treatment."

"The criminal?" she said. "So you have already found my brother guilty even before he is granted a trial?"

"Two people witnessed his crime, Ganieda."

"Two thugs of dubious character, just as deceitful as Dinabutius himself."

"That is what you believe, Ganieda, but I never agreed with your assessment of Dinabutius's character. Nor did any of my men. The soldiers all thought very highly of Dinabutius."

"Why?" she retorted. "Because he bought them drinks and amused them with ribald stories?"

"Ganieda, you keep telling me how terrible Dinabutius was, yet no one else seems to have shared your opinion. Good God, woman! Your own best friend was about to marry the man!"

"So you think I am lying?"

"No, I think you are mistaken. I believe the man had reformed. As does everyone else."

She was about to reply, but he cut her off.

"No, Ganieda, justice must be served. It is necessary for the people to see that the law is upheld and applied equally to all. And justice must be swift. In their current mood the soldiers will tolerate nothing less."

"When do you plan on holding the trial?"

"Tomorrow."

"Tomorrow! Tomorrow is too soon! Justice must also be fair! The facts must be learned before there is a trial."

Rodarch shook his head. "The facts are already known. Although Merlin himself had given Guendoloena permission to re-marry, he returned of his own free will with the sole intention of murdering his rival."

Ganieda protested, "He only returned because he knew Dinabutius's true character and was willing to sacrifice himself to save Guendoloena from making a terrible mistake."

"And sacrifice himself is what he has done," replied Rodarch gravely.

Alarmed, she said, "Rodarch, please. Postpone the trial, at least for a few days. I must have time to think."

After reluctantly considering his wife's request, he said sternly, "I shall grant one additional day, but only if you first pledge to me that you will use no devious means to try to help your brother escape justice. The security of our kingdom depends upon the loyalty of our soldiers, and they will be quick to detect any fraud. Ours is a kingdom run by law," Rodarch pronounced, "and the law must be applied equally to all. Otherwise our entire realm will be put into jeopardy. If for no reason other than the sake of our children, Ganieda, you should wish to see that justice is done."

She replied, "Since you feel it necessary to evoke our children's welfare to ensure my compliance, and since you imagine that I might stoop to devious means to accomplish my ends, I shall give you what you desire. I, Ganieda, vow to you, King Rodarchus, that I shall use no devious means to help my brother, King Merlinus Ambrosius, escape justice. Will that pledge suffice, Lord King?" After a deep curtsy, she walked across the room to the door. Pausing, she turned to her husband. "Lord King, I know that this trial will be even more difficult for you than for myself since it is you, and you alone, who will pass judgment on the man whom you once called your brother and your friend." Before leaving she added, "King Rodarchus, how, do you imagine, will the people of Dyfed respond when they learn that their beloved king has been put to death by your order? Will a war with the chieftains of Dyfed not also put our realm into jeopardy, Lord King?"

Chapter 7

Trial

On the day of the trial, the great hall at Brocavum was filled to overflowing. Those who could not find a place inside the cavernous chamber were pushing and jostling outside the doors, craning to catch a glimpse of what was happening inside. The people were all buzzing with speculation. When the herald thumped his staff of office on the floor and called for silence, a hush fell over the crowd. Everyone bowed respectfully as King Rodarch entered the hall from his private rooms behind the dais and took his place upon the throne. At a signal from the king, the herald called for the prisoner to be brought forward. A low murmur, punctuated by angrier sounds, ran through the court as Merlin was led into the hall. The prisoner's hair and beard had been roughly hacked short, and a plain, dun-colored tunic had been put on him, along with leather shoes. With his feet hobbled and fastened by a cord to his bound hands, he was able to shuffle only slowly down the center aisle. To prevent any possibility of escape, six guards surrounded him, and cords tied to his arms were also secured to the arms of the men walking on either side of him. When he reached the foot of the dais, he stood before the king with bowed head and downcast eyes. King Rodarch stared at him in silence. Everyone had become completely still, straining to hear what the king would say. The silence was shattered when Rodarch angrily struck the arms of the throne.

He declared, "You have put me in an untenable position, King Merlinus, and even now I am uncertain how to resolve this dilemma! How can I sit in judgment over another king? And yet how can I ignore this most serious crime, the murder of an honored guest in my own home? The prisoner is a madman and so is not fully responsible for his own actions. Yet there can be no excuse and no justification for this most heinous of all crimes."

At Rodarch's command, the herald stepped forward and read the charge of murder that had been brought against the prisoner. When the king asked the accused man if he would plead guilty or not guilty to the charge, he remained mute and unmoving. King Rodarch acknowledged to the court that, because of his condition, the accused man was usually incapable of speech. Taking another tack, Rodarch asked the prisoner if he would accept the king's judgment, even if the verdict were to go against him. Merlin, looking infinitely sad and weary, inclined his head. His gesture was accepted as his formal acquiescence, and the trial proceeded.

The first witness called to testify before the court was the guard who had led Merlin to the stable. Stepping forward, the soldier saluted the king and then climbed the steps to the top of the dais. After the witness was cautioned to speak nothing but the truth and had sworn his oath before God, he was asked to recount everything that he had seen and heard on the morning of the murder. Accurately, the soldier related the events as they had unfolded. His testimony seemed particularly damning when he repeated Dinabutius's words of kind intentions toward King Merlinus. Once he had finished his account, the king questioned him. "Why was King Merlinus's arrival not immediately announced to me?"

"Because Dinabutius wanted to try to persuade King Merlinus to leave the woods and return to his family so he could be properly cared for, Lord King," replied the soldier. "Dinabutius thought it would please Queen Ganieda."

"I see. And the reason for meeting in the stable?"

"Since King Merlinus came riding in on a stag, Dinabutius's suggestion of showing him to the stable made sense, being the best place to put his… his mount."

"Was anyone else in the stable when you entered with King Merlinus?"

"No, Lord King," the soldier replied. "The stable was deserted. When I left to return to my post, Dinabutius had not yet arrived."

"What happened after you returned to your post?"

"Nothing at first, Lord King. Then, a little while later, Tomos and Cadog came running out of the stable, yelling 'murder.' Just after that, I saw King Merlinus gallop his stag across the courtyard and out through the palisade gates."

"Why were the gates open?"

"The porter had just opened them to let in a horse and wagon. King Merlinus got through the gates before the porter could close them again."

"What did you do next?"

"Our captain ordered some of us to saddle our horses and apprehend the fugitive. He told the rest of us to stay at our posts. I was told to stay at my post, Lord King."

"I see. Thank you, soldier, for your testimony. You may step down."

The herald next called Tomos to the stand. The large, fair-haired man walked up the steps to the top of the dais and bowed deferentially to the king before taking his oath.

"Your name is Tomos?"

"Yes, Lord King."

"You were present in the stables when the murder took place?"

"I was, Lord King."

"Please relate to the court everything that you saw and heard in the stables on the morning of the murder."

Tomos bobbed another bow. "Thank you, Lord King. Er, yes, well, we went into the stable and saw him at the other end of the building, so we walked over, Lord King."

"Who is 'we'?"

"That would be me and Dinabutius and Cadog, Lord King."

"And when you say 'him,' are you referring to King Merlinus?"

"That would be him, yes, Lord King."

"Go on."

"Well, Dinas said hello to his old friend. He tried to get Ambros… that is, King Merlinus…to remember him by calling to mind some happy memories from when they were children together. Then Dinas told him how he should leave the woods and return to his family, saying how much they all must miss him. When Dinas happened to mention Guendoloena's name… Queen Guendoloena's name, that is…Merlin got mad. He pulled out a knife and stabbed Dinabutius with it just like that. Dinas knocked the knife out of his hand, but that only made him even madder. He reached over and yanked an antler right off the deer's head and stabbed Dinas in the throat with it. Dinas fell down dead, so we…that is, Cadog and me…raised the alarm."

Rodarch said, "When I went into the stables shortly after the crime had been committed, I saw that Dinabutius had a sword in his hand. At what point had he drawn his sword?"

Tomos swallowed. "Er, that point would be right after Merlin stabbed him with the knife. Dinas was just trying to keep Ambros…King Merlinus… from attacking him again."

"And a man with an antler was able to kill a man armed with a sword?"

"It's the truth, Lord King. He whipped that antler off the deer's head so fast that Dinas couldn't do anything about it, Lord King."

"And what were you and Cadog doing while all these events were taking place?"

"Yes, Lord King. Well, telling what happened like this makes it sound long, but the whole thing went by in seconds. When Dinas knocked the knife away, we were all surprised that King Merlinus could find another weapon. After Ambros…King Merlinus…killed Dinas, me and Cadog tried to grab hold of him, but he fought like an animal and stabbed at us with the antler. He's a lot stronger than he looks. That's when we figured we'd better go get some help, Lord King."

"Thank you, Tomos. You may step down for now. Herald, please call the next witness."

When Dinabutius's other companion Cadog took the stand, he essentially repeated the same story and, under questioning, confirmed everything that Tomos had said. After being thanked and dismissed by the king, he stepped down from the dais. The herald was about to call for the next witness when a woman's voice rang out from the back of the hall.

"They lie," she shouted. The court was in turmoil as a tall, dark-haired woman strode down the center aisle. Reaching the foot of the dais, she stopped and curtsied to the king. Rodarch did not look happy to see his wife standing before him.

Gesturing to her brother, she said, "Lord King, I ask for your permission to speak on behalf of a man who is unable to answer in his own defense."

Sternly, Rodarch replied, "Queen Ganieda, must I publicly remind you of your pledge?"

Turning, she addressed the people in the hall. "I should inform the court of a pledge which I made to King Rodarchus. Two days ago, I solemnly vowed to our king that I would use no devious means to help King Merlinus evade justice. I stand by my pledge. My only interest is in revealing the truth, wherever it may lead."

Turning back to her husband, she asked, "Do I have your permission to speak for the accused, Lord King?" Rodarch was silent as he considered this turn of events. He finally gave his nod of assent, but looked far from pleased.

"Thank you, Lord King." Looking at her brother, she asked, "King Merlinus, will you allow me to speak in your defense?"

All eyes were on the prisoner. When he inclined his head in assent, Cadog and Tomos glanced at each other nervously.

"Thank you, King Merlinus," she said. Curtsying again to King Rodarch, Ganieda climbed the steps to the top of the dais. When she asked to question the witness who had first testified, Rodarch nodded his assent, and the soldier was recalled to the stand.

After thanking the witness, Ganieda asked, "I understand that you were with Dinabutius on the ramparts on the morning of King Merlinus's arrival?"

"I was, My Queen."

"Did Dinabutius have a sword in his scabbard when he was with you on the ramparts?"

"I don't recall that he was wearing a sword belt at all, My Queen."

"In fact what is the regulation regarding civilians carrying weapons on the ramparts?"

"Civilians are not allowed to carry a weapon on the ramparts, My Queen."

"So it is indubitable that Dinabutius did not have a sword in his possession when he was with you on the ramparts."

"That is true, My Queen."

"Were Cadog and Tomos with Dinabutius that morning on the ramparts?"

"No, My Queen."

"Thank you, soldier. That is all. You may step down. If you please, Lord King, I would now like to question Tomos." Rodarch signaled his assent, and the herald called for the witness to return to the stand.

Tomos climbed the steps and regarded Ganieda apprehensively. She had a small bag hanging from her girdle. Silently, she opened the bag and removed a distinctive knife made from bone. Handing it to Tomos to examine, she asked, "Is this the knife which you assert was used by King Merlinus to stab Dinabutius?" she asked.

Tomos replied with emphasis, "This *is* the knife that King Merlinus used when he stabbed Dinabutius."

"Could you explain the circumstances which led up to the alleged attack upon Dinabutius by King Merlinus."

"I already have…My Queen"

"Then if you could kindly repeat the circumstances which led up to the alleged attack. I simply wish to recall the chain of events so that they are quite clear in my mind."

With considerable exasperation, Tomos said, "Dinabutius said Guendoloena's name, Merlin got mad, drew his knife and stabbed Dinabutius in the side."

"Thank you. Now if you could demonstrate to the court how King

Merlinus stabbed Dinabutius. I would like you to play the part of King Merlinus and your friend Cadog to take the part of Dinabutius."

Tomos appealed to the king. "Is this really necessary, Lord King? I think my words made it clear enough for anyone to understand."

Rodarch frowned. "I agree that this does seem to go a bit beyond reason."

Ganieda countered, "Lord King, a capital charge has been brought against the accused. I wish to leave no doubt in anyone's mind as to exactly what took place that morning in the stables by having Tomos show the court how Merlin used this knife to inflict the wound."

"Proceed," said Rodarch, though he was still frowning.

When Cadog returned to the dais, Ganieda said, "Thank you, Cadog. Just over there, please, where everyone can see you. Yes, thank you. Now Tomos, if you would mimic the actions of King Merlinus when he attacked Dinabutius."

Shrugging as if to humor her, he tucked the knife under his belt. Walking up to Cadog, he pulled the knife from his belt and made a thrusting motion with it, showing where Dinabutius had been stabbed. Thanking him, she took back the knife. She said, "I saw Dinabutius in the stable shortly after his death and can verify that there was indeed a slight wound on his left side."

Tomos replied defensively, "I never said it was a deep wound."

Ganieda suddenly held the knife aloft and in a ringing voice audible to all said, "And I say that it was impossible for King Merlinus to have inflicted the wound in the manner that Tomos has just demonstrated."

At her words, the court was thrown into an uproar, and King Rodarch himself angrily called for silence. Addressing her sternly, Rodarch said, "You must have proof to make such a statement. On what basis do you make your claim?"

"On the basis that a left-handed man would not draw a knife with his right hand to stab someone. King Merlinus is left-handed!"

The commotion in the hall went on for several minutes before Rodarch silenced the crowd. "Queen Ganieda is correct," affirmed the king. "I can attest to that fact myself. Whenever King Merlinus wrote or held a knife or any other tool, it was always with his left hand." Rodarch flashed an admiring glance at his wife. "Do you have an explanation for this, Tomos?" he demanded.

Tomos, visibly nervous, replied, "Maybe he did draw with his left hand and was standing a little more to the side. It all happened so fast it's hard for me to remember. But he did stab Dinabutius with the antler!"

Ganieda nodded. "I agree. I believe that King Merlinus did indeed stab Dinabutius with the antler. But in defense of his own life!" she declared. "Let me now recount to the court what happened in the stable according to the evidence. Two days ago, Dinabutius happened to be on the ramparts when King Merlinus arrived at the gate. Realizing that with King Merlinus's return, his plan to marry Queen Guendoloena would be shattered, Dinabutius quickly hatched a plot to eliminate his rival. He stopped the soldiers from announcing King Merlinus's arrival, which would have been normal protocol, with a flimsy story of hoping to first convince him to return to his family. Then, instead of going directly to the stable, Dinabutius went out of his way not only to arm himself with a sword but also to enlist the aid of two…" Here Ganieda paused and raised her eyebrows as she looked significantly at the two burly men, "…companions. Surely not the actions of a man with nothing but kind intentions in his heart. As to happy childhood memories, I myself can attest that they do not exist; the Dinabutius whom I remember well was a bully and a liar who always enjoyed tormenting my brother. What words Dinabutius spoke in the stable I cannot say, only they were not the words of tender concern as related by Tomos and Cadog. Dinabutius then used the distinctive knife to make it look as though King Merlinus had attacked first, the slight wound actually being either self-inflicted or made by one of his accomplices. Dinabutius planned to cover his crime by pleading self-defense, using his two partners to back his story with their false testimony. When Dinabutius drew his sword to murder his rival, King Merlinus, in desperation, grabbed the only thing at hand with which to defend himself. Tomos's saying that they were all surprised when King Merlinus found something with which to defend himself is undoubtedly the only part of his story that is true."

Tomos, having recovered his composure, said with defiance, "These are only words, Lord King. She wasn't there, so she can't know what happened!"

In the hush that followed, as everyone was waiting to hear the queen's response, a small voice from somewhere in the back of the hall said, "I was there, and that is what happened."

When King Rodarch ordered the speaker to come forward, a young man stepped from the crowd and walked up the aisle. He looked nervous as he bowed to the king, holding his cap in his hands.

Addressing Tomos and Cadog, the king said, "Both of you may leave the stand and return to the front with the other witnesses. Young man, please step up onto the dais. Thank you. Tell us your name."

"My name is Dafydd, Lord King."

"Dafydd, do you swear before God to speak nothing but the truth?"

"I do, Lord King."

"Now tell us, Dafydd, what you were doing in the stables."

"Yes, Lord King," he replied, bowing. "I'm one of the stable hands. I used to be the smith's apprentice when I lived in Derventio, but ever since my master came to Brocavum, I've worked in the stables. I was never very good at smithing, Lord King, and was happy when my master found me a job with the horses. My master told me I just didn't have the knack for blacksmithing. Or the body," explained the small, thin lad somewhat sheepishly. His last remark brought a few laughs from the crowd, and he looked around awkwardly.

"And how is it, Dafydd," the king asked, "that you say you know what happened in the stable when everyone else has testified that the stable was deserted?"

"Because I was up in the loft, Lord King," the young man replied. "No one could have seen me from below. I'd been up all night dosing a sick mare. When the head groom came in before dawn to see how the mare was doing and saw how good she looked, he told me to get some sleep. The loft is where I sleep, Lord King. I woke up a while later when I heard someone talking. He was saying some bad things to someone, so I crept to the edge on my stomach to see who they were. When I looked down, I saw it was Dinabutius talking to King Merlinus."

"You said that Dinabutius was saying 'some bad things.' Exactly what did he say to King Merlinus?"

"He…he said letting a mindless madman live was the best revenge but… but two bridegrooms were one too many."

"What did King Merlinus do after Dinabutius said this to him?"

"Nothing. He couldn't. Dinabutius had those two men grab his arms."

"Which two men?"

"Them," he replied, pointing to Tomos and Cadog.

"What happened after that?"

"Dinabutius took a knife from Merlin's belt and stuck it under his own belt. Then he punched Merlin in the face. When he said some things about Queen Guendoloena, Merlin begged him not to hurt her."

"What 'things'?"

The young man looked embarrassed. "Well, he…he called her stupid, Lord King. And he said…" The boy stopped.

"You must not hold anything back. You must tell the court exactly what you heard and saw."

"Yes, Lord King. He said…how he couldn't wait to introduce her to the real Dinabutius on their wedding night and…" The boy reddened.

"And?"

"And how much he was going to enjoy sleeping with Merlin's wife. I'm sorry, Lord King."

"Go on."

"Yes, Lord King. Well, King Merlinus told Dinabutius to kill him if he wanted, only not to hurt his wife. Dinabutius just laughed and said that he would take everything – Merlin's life, his wife and his crown. Then Dinabutius stabbed himself with the knife. That surprised Merlin and me, too, but he said how he couldn't have Merlin's death look like a murder. He was going to tell everyone that Merlin stabbed him first and that he had drawn his sword in self-defense. He was going to say that Merlin accidentally ran himself on the sword when he tried to stab him again. After King Merlinus was dead, Dinabutius was going to put the knife in his hand. Then Dinabutius told Tomos and Cadog to let Merlin go so it would look like there had been a fight. King Merlinus tried to get away, but they kept grabbing him and throwing him on the ground. When Dinabutius drew his sword to kill him, the stag stuck its head out of the stall. King Merlinus grabbed an antler from the stag's head – just to hold him off – but he ran himself right into the tines. When Dinabutius fell down dead, Cadog and Tomos ran out of the stable shouting 'murder,' and King Merlinus jumped on the stag and galloped it out through the door."

The king said, "How is it, Dafydd, that you could have watched all these events taking place without helping or at least summoning help?"

The young man was silent as he searched for words. "I…I'm not a brave person, Lord King. I was afraid if I climbed down and tried to open the barred door, I would get caught before I could get out. I was trying to think what to do, but it was all over before I did anything. I'm sorry for being such a coward, Lord King."

Ganieda, who had been standing to one side on the dais, looked at him kindly. "On the contrary, Dafydd. Coming forward as you have has taken great courage. Not the kind of courage that comes from physical strength, but courage of a far nobler kind that comes from strength of character." The young man brightened considerably at her words.

The king said, "Thank you for your testimony, Dafydd. You may step down. Herald, summon the head groom to the stand."

At the herald's call, the groom made his way through the crowd and walked up the center aisle. After bowing to the king, he took the stand. In answer to the king's question, he replied, "It's as the lad says, Lord King. A mare had been doing a little poorly, and the lad offered to stay up with her. Since he's a good hand with horses, Lord King, I agreed to let him tend her with the strict understanding that he should call me if the mare took a turn for the worse during the night. I checked on them well before dawn and, with the mare looking as sound as ever, I sent the lad off to get some well-earned sleep. As the lad says, he sleeps in the loft. I saw him climb up there just before I left, Lord King."

"Thank you. You may step down."

Once the witness had left the stand, the king addressed the court, "I have now heard enough evidence to render a verdict. Captain, take Tomos and Cadog into your custody."

As guards approached the two men, Tomos suddenly pushed Cadog into them, knocking over the captain and several others behind him. As the guards were scrambling to their feet, Tomos darted up the steps toward the throne. The people in the hall cried out in horror when it appeared that Tomos was about to attack their king, but he merely ran past the throne. Rushing to the door behind the dais, Tomos flung it open and disappeared into the king's private chambers as the captain and a dozen guards pelted after him. Meanwhile, Cadog had been seized and was being restrained by some dozen more. Within minutes the guards reappeared, dragging Tomos in their midst. Surrounded by their captors, the two men were pushed to their knees before the king. Tomos remained mutely defiant, but Cadog, without being asked, freely confessed their part in the attempt on King Merlinus's life.

"For your confession, Cadog," King Rodarch pronounced, "I shall be merciful. Tomorrow morning you will both be granted the swift death of the axe. The prescribed penalty for treason against a king is usually not so kind. Captain, keep these criminals on their knees a while longer for it is imperative that I immediately make amends to two people whom I have grievously wronged."

The king addressed his wife. "Thank you, Queen Ganieda, for preventing me from committing a gross miscarriage of justice. Once again, Queen Ganieda, you have exhibited wisdom and prudence when I was all too quick to rush to judgment."

"Thank you, Lord King," she replied, curtsying deeply.

The king then turned to Merlin who had been standing all this time, unmoving. "Now to rectify a great injustice," said Rodarch, rising from his throne. Stepping down from the dais, he stood before the prisoner. "Never again shall I doubt your inherent goodness, King Merlinus. And never again shall I suffer you to be fettered or restrained in any way," he declared. Requesting a knife from one of the guards, the king himself carefully cut Merlin free from his bonds. Then, with profound humility, King Rodarch fell to both his knees and bowed his head. Following the example of their king, the people in the hall did likewise, kneeling in respectful obeisance to King Merlinus. With his head still bowed, Rodarch said, "King Merlinus, I most humbly beg you for your pardon. Can you find it in your heart to forgive me?"

With great emotion, Merlin lifted Rodarch to his feet and embraced him. His eyes now clear and blue, Merlin replied, "King Rodarchus, it is rather I who should seek forgiveness of you for all the trouble which I have brought to you. I forgive you, dear brother, with all my heart. But I must also beg a favor, King Rodarchus."

"Anything which you desire will be willingly granted," declared the king.

"Then do not execute these two men," said Merlin.

Rodarch protested. "But King Merlinus, these two criminals showed you no mercy when they abetted an attempt to murder you and later when they falsely accused you of a capital crime."

"It is true," Merlin replied. "Nevertheless, I do not wish to have their deaths on my conscience."

"Then for your sake, and for your sake alone, I shall grant your request." The king pronounced, "Tomos and Cadog, you are to be forever exiled from the fair land of Cumbria. If either of you so much as set foot in this kingdom again, you will be put to death and not by the swift mercy of the axe. Captain, see that these criminals are put in chains and escorted to the border under close guard. Now take these wretches from my sight!"

The guards jerked Tomos and Cadog to their feet. As Cadog was walking past Merlin, he suddenly fell to his knees again. With tears in his eyes, he took one of Merlin's hands and kissed it. Tomos, though, remained standing, merely staring at Merlin in wide-eyed wonder. Merlin said nothing to either but nodded to Cadog before that man was pulled back to his feet by the guards. Once the convicted men had been led from the hall, King Rodarch pronounced that justice had been served and dismissed the court. After respectfully bowing to their king, the people began chattering excitedly about the amazing turn of events as they slowly filed from the hall. Merlin, scanning eagerly for one particular face in the crowd, looked disappointed when the last of the spectators had finally exited through the door. After embracing Rodarch again, Merlin said, "Please excuse me, brother, but if I might have a word with Ganieda while I am still able to speak?"

"Of course, brother," replied Rodarch. "I shall leave you two to talk then." Kissing the hand of his wife, he then bowed to them both before departing from the hall.

When they were alone, Merlin said, "Ganieda, how can I ever repay you? I can never thank you enough! Yet here I am, ready to ask another favor of you."

Joyously, she replied, "Dear brother, ask me anything! You know that I am only too happy to give you whatever you wish."

"Then, dear sister, could you please, on my behalf, entreat Guendoloena for the favor of coming to see me?"

"With pleasure, brother! I know that Guendoloena will be overjoyed to see you."

"Will she? I hope so. I fear that my wife has much to reproach me for."

"Nonsense, Merlin," replied Ganieda. "Of course, she'll be overjoyed to see you."

"Do you really think so, Gani? Four years ago, I rejected her heartfelt pleas to come with me because I was afraid that I might hurt her. I now realize that I would never hurt my dear wife, not even when…when I am in my usual state. Also, Gani, over the years there has been some small improvement in my condition. Although I am still unable to speak, I have found that I can often understand much of what people are saying. So there can be at least some small communication between Guendoloena and me. If she'll have me back, that is."

Ganieda felt her spirits soar. "Of course she'll have you back, Merlin! This is wonderful news!" She kissed her brother. "I can't wait to see the look on Guen's face! Especially when she sees your haircut," she added mischievously.

"I can see that my sister has not lost her keen sense of humor over the years," he said, ruefully running his fingers through his closely and badly shorn hair. "I'll have you know that this haircut was not exactly by my request, sister dear."

"Don't worry, brother dear. Given time, I'm sure your hair will grow back. And still be just as gray," she added, grinning broadly. "Merlin, why don't you wait here. I'll be back with Guen in a thrice! Just as soon as I find her, that is!"

Ganieda's spirits were buoyant when she entered her sister-in-law's room and found Guendoloena staring out the window. Joyfully, she announced, "Guen! Merlin can speak again, and he is asking to see you!"

Without turning, Guendoloena replied darkly, "And what is that to me?"

Ganieda was startled by her response. Then she realized that Guendoloena had probably not yet heard the good news. Quickly, Ganieda recounted the events in the court, telling her how her husband had been cleared of the crime and how Dinabutius had been a scoundrel who had plotted Merlin's murder. She was about to go on but saw that Guendoloena was starting to cry. She apologized. "I'm sorry, Guen, I should have realized that this would be hard for you to absorb all at once."

Turning to Ganieda, Guendoloena shook her head. Through her tears she said, "At least four other people have already happily brought me the news, and everyone is in high spirits over it. And how is this supposed to make me feel?" she asked. "Until a few minutes ago, I believed that Merlin was a crazed murderer who had killed the man whom I thought I loved enough to marry. Now I am told that Dinabutius was a scoundrel who thought I was a stupid fool for believing in his sincerity. No doubt I am since I was so easily deceived by him. Obviously, Dinabutius had only been interested in me as the means for achieving the crown of Dyfed. And this man, to whom I was going to give myself in marriage, coldly plotted the murder of my husband who stood in the way of his ambition. My husband who, having rejected my entreaties of love and devotion four years ago, now suddenly wants to see me again and somehow this is supposed to make everything all right?" She covered her face with her hands and turned away, weeping.

Silently, Ganieda reproached herself for not considering the conflicting emotions of her friend. When she tried to embrace her, Guendoloena pulled away. "I don't want you or your sympathy, Ganieda, and I don't want your brother!"

Ganieda said, "I'm so sorry, Guen, I've been unforgivably thoughtless. Thank you, dear sister, for opening my eyes. But for your own sake as well as for the sake of Merlin…"

Guendoloena interrupted. "I thought I could start a new life, but that dream is gone. I suppose I should be grateful; my new life would have been a misery, I can see that now. But I do not feel grateful – I just feel numb. I'm going home."

"Please, Guen, you are my dearest friend. Please reconsider before you make any hasty decisions which you will later regret. At least say a few words to Merlin. Even if only to say goodbye."

Guendoloena shook her head. "No," she said through her tears. "Because if I see him again, I will never be able to leave him."

Ganieda returned to the hall and walked to where Merlin was standing. He was eagerly looking past her towards the doorway, but Guendoloena was not there. Sorrowfully, Ganieda said, "Guendoloena is not coming, Merlin. She is very conflicted and emotional just now and said she is going to return to her father's house. But she also said that if she were to see you again, she would never be able to leave you. Perhaps if you were to go to her…"

"No, Ganieda," he interrupted, "I shall not impose myself upon her if she has chosen not to come to me." He shook his head sadly. "No, I'll not have Guendoloena return to me simply because she feels pity or, worse, because she feels obligated to do so."

"Then I have lost my best friend, and you have lost your wife. I am very sorry, Merlin."

"As am I. Goodbye, Ganieda. I must go now so that you will always remember me as I was while still in my right mind." He embraced her and kissed her cheek. Then, with resignation, he turned and walked from the hall.

Merlin slipped out of town unnoticed. When he reached the hut of a poor man he had known from years past, he removed his shoes and left them at the door. Then he hesitated, first looking to the north, then to the west. Making his choice, he turned towards the mountains to the west.

Trotting quickly, he soon reached the ancient woodland that blanketed the lower slopes of the high fells of Cumbria. Walking in the midst of enormous fern and moss-covered trees and crossing clear mountain streams tumbling in deep shady glens, he climbed steadily and ever higher up the mountain's flank. Finally, leaving the last meager and stunted trees far behind, he reached the rocky and windswept summit. Pausing only briefly to survey the forlorn and formidable landscape around him, he continued along the knife-edged crest of the ridge toward an even higher peak. As he was skirting around a ravine that deeply gouged the mountain's side, movement caught his eye. Below him, at the edge of the ravine, an emaciated she-wolf painfully lifted herself to her feet. She was trying to drag herself from his sight, but with her left hind leg hanging uselessly, she soon collapsed from the effort. Merlin slowly made his way down to her while holding out his hand. When he touched the wolf's head, she became calm and allowed him to examine the injury. An arrow shaft was deeply embedded in her leg, and the wound had festered. Gently, he pushed the broken end of the shaft and felt the point of the arrow near the surface of the skin on the other side. Giving the wolf a reassuring pat and murmuring soothing sounds, he held her leg firmly. With a sudden skillful movement, he pushed the arrow through and pulled it out the other side. The wolf yelped in pain but made no attempt to bite him. After giving her another reassuring pat, he climbed down into the ravine to a small rivulet. Tearing a strip of fabric from his sleeve, he dipped it into the water and wrung it out. Then, after plucking a large handful of sphagnum growing at the stream's edge, he returned to the wolf's side. Once he had cleaned the wound, he squeezed the excess water from the clump of moss and bound it neatly in place over the injury with a dry strip of fabric torn from his other sleeve. Gently lifting the wolf, he carried her into the ravine and placed her at the stream's edge. Eagerly, she began lapping the water, her tail beating feebly against the ground. Then, cradling her in his arms, he walked down the steep slope to look for a sheltered place to care for her.

Once again, Merlin melted into the forests and lakesides and mountains without a trace, far from the eyes of men.

Part II

Chapter 8

Homecoming

In the twentieth year of King Arthur's reign, Britannia and her people continued to prosper. With border raids, smuggling and highway robbery now almost entirely things of the past, the Britons' feelings of well-being and confidence had never been greater. Much of the credit for these improvements was thanks to King Arthur's use of his military during times of peace to help keep the country safe and secure. Every year, as before, recruits from each of the kingdoms of Britain were sent to Isca for military training. Also as before, the young men competed fiercely to be among those selected for entry into the more elite of the military units. Competition was particularly stiff to gain entry into the King's Eagles, a mobile cavalry force led by the dashing and charismatic Lord Pelleas, husband of Lady Nimue. When Nimue had first arrived in the capital, she had been captivated by the handsome young commander, considered at the time to be the most eligible bachelor at court. The attraction had been mutual, and the two had wed three years later. Their marriage, though childless, had been a happy one.

Since not all talented young men were able to join the King's Eagles, another unit called the King's Harriers, had been created to accommodate those who had not quite made the cut. Headed by Prince Mordred of Lothian, this light cavalry force had, in fact, been so gaining in prestige over the years that many of the new recruits now sought entry into the Harriers as their first choice of assignment, no doubt due to the popularity of its leader. The rivalry between the two cavalry units and their respective leaders, though keen, was mostly good-natured. Meanwhile, on the high seas, another development had been the creation of a coastal patrol dubbed the King's Sea Hawks, commanded by King Arthur's longtime friend, Lord Drustan of Dumnonia, nephew of the late military leader, Lord Marcus. Since the establishment of the Sea Hawks, piracy and coastal raiding, too, had become virtually things of the past.

While most Britons were lauding this new and golden age of peace and prosperity, Arthur's uncle, King Cador, took continued pleasure in grumbling at almost every meeting of the High King's Council about how peace was making the soldiers soft. In reality though, Cador's facetious grumblings were those of a happy and well-contented man. Besides, the old warrior had managed to find solace in these "trying" times of peace by showing his two grandsons, now aged eleven and thirteen, how to throw a spear, wield a sword, control a warhorse and plan a military campaign. Cador proudly and often proclaimed that both boys already had the makings of great leaders, no doubt thinking of the day when one of his grandsons would sit upon the throne as High King of Britain.

Although King Arthur and Queen Gwenhwyfar had never had any children of their own, they found continued contentment by happily doting on the children of their friends and family. And there were many of these to dote upon. The families of Cei, Arthur's foster brother and seneschal, and Bedwyr, Arthur's closest friend and cupbearer, for instance, were growing almost as bountifully as the crops in the fields. Bedwyr's wife Annwr had just given birth to their fourth daughter, keeping pace with Cei and his wife Alys's tally of four sons. Good planning for the future, laughed Arthur and Gwenhwyfar and both sets of parents, thinking of potential marriage pairings.

One fine spring day, after dismissing his court, Arthur had remained in the hall while awaiting the arrival of Cei and Bedwyr to discuss the festivities and events planned for the annual midsummer games. He had begun to look over a list of vendors and the schedule of events when the two men entered with Cei's four-year-old son between them. Crying "Uncle Arthur," the boy immediately ran across the room and climbed onto the king's lap. Happily setting aside those pieces of parchment with the rest, Arthur began bouncing the boy on his knee as Cei and Bedwyr pulled up chairs to begin work.

After going over the list of vendors and determining the best placement for the various stalls and booths, the three men were discussing the merits of some of the new sporting events that had been proposed for the games when the little boy started tugging on the king's beard in a bid to gain some attention. Cei was chiding his son when the door opened, and one of the king's couriers was admitted. Looking solemn, the man walked across the hall and fell to one knee before delivering news of the death of Lord Ector, Cei's father and King Arthur's foster father. The old warrior had gone easily, the messenger assured them all, dying peacefully in his bed, surrounded by friends. Cei's son, not fully understanding but sensing that something bad had happened, began to cry, prompting Arthur to lift the little boy from his lap and place him into his father's arms. After thanking the messenger, the three men immediately left to inform their wives of the sad news. They found the three women together, as they often were on a fine day, just outside in the courtyard of the old Roman bathhouse. Alys and Annwr were sitting on a shaded bench in the colonnade, nursing their newborns, while Gwenhwyfar was nearby, minding her friends' five older children, who were splashing in the rectangular pool at the center of the large quadrangle. Upon learning of Lord Ector's death, the women concurred with their husbands that it would be best if they remained at Isca rather than attempt such a long journey with nursing infants.

Within the hour, after bidding their wives farewell, Arthur, Cei, and Bedwyr were cantering their horses through the fortress gates and across the bridge, heading for Glevum and the main road which would take them north to Cumbria. By riding hard and changing horses at every posting station, they reached Derventio three days later.

After crossing the river on the old Roman bridge and riding past the blacksmith shop, they reached a junction just after the market square and turned right onto the narrow lane that would take them to Lord Ector's seat, some five miles beyond the village. As they were walking their tired mounts on the final leg of the journey, Arthur's thoughts carried him back to a fifteen-year-old boy riding in the opposite direction along that very lane, setting off for Isca with Cei and Bedwyr and his foster father, Lord Ector. Never in his wildest dreams could that boy have imagined that his first adventure away from home was about to lead him to the High Kingship of Britannia. Even now, over twenty years later, Arthur was still struck with amazement at how an obscure country lad of then unknown parentage had become High King. Of course, it never would have happened without Merlin, the man who had been more like a father to him than any other. While Lord Ector had treated him as well as his own son Cei, Arthur had always felt that something was missing in his life. That void had been filled one stormy night when a tall, black-haired stranger had appeared at their kitchen door, carrying a little bundle which appeared to be all that he owned. At the time, Arthur was surprised when Lord Ector had given the stranger permission to move into an abandoned cottage about a quarter-hour walk beyond the house. Watching the drenched and apparently destitute man step back outside into the rain and darkness to make his way to the ramshackle cottage, Arthur had felt more than a little sorry for him.

When Arthur went there the next day to see if he might lend a hand with the repairs, he soon discovered that the stranger, whose name was Merlin, was not only a skilled craftsman, but a learned scholar as well. After a while their casual question-and-answer sessions had taken the form of more formal and structured lessons in reading, writing, history, mathematics, philosophy, and literature. Eager to learn and equally eager to try to emulate his master, Arthur had been a diligent student, though with Merlin as his teacher, there had also been time for fun. Merlin, who could give the impression of a solemn academic, hoary with age and wisdom, more often acted like a mischievous younger brother, always ready for games or a prank. Arthur smiled as he remembered some of their practical jokes, both given and received. Then one day, after three idyllic years, Merlin had revealed his identity as King of Dyfed and departed almost as suddenly as he had arrived. At the time Arthur had been devastated, imagining that he would never see his beloved mentor again. Only after becoming High King of Britain, did Arthur finally learn the full truth: how Merlin, foreseeing the danger, had brought him as a baby to be raised in obscurity in a remote corner of Cumbria, far from the eyes of those who would not have hesitated to eliminate High King Uther's six-year-old son and successor who stood between them and their ambitions. Later, during the early and contested years of Arthur's reign, Merlin had always been at his side to advise him. Even now Arthur somehow felt bolstered, simply knowing that Merlin was alive and somewhere in Britain. For although his old chief advisor had once again disappeared without a trace, Queen Ganieda had assured him that her brother still lived.

As Arthur looked around at the familiar fields and mountains, a strong feeling of regret came flooding into his mind. Too late, he realized that he should have taken the time to visit his foster parents more often. He owed them both so much. Since becoming High King of Britain, he had returned home only four times. The last occasion had been three years ago to attend his foster mother Drusilla's funeral. Now he was back for another funeral.

Arthur was drawn from his reproachful thoughts as he and his two companions turned their mounts up the hill toward the house, and a dog, which had been dozing next to the kitchen door, suddenly flew to the end of its chain and began to bark excitedly. A moment later a man whom Arthur recognized as Bedwyr's younger brother Llew stepped through the door. When Llew saw who they were, he looked flustered and called to someone inside, and a woman came out, wiping her flour-covered hands on a towel. Seeing the High King of Britain riding up the lane, Llew's wife became equally frantic. Obviously, neither had expected the royal party to be arriving so soon. As two grooms came hurrying over from the stable to take their horses, Llew and his wife tried to direct the king to the rarely used front entrance, but with a few kind words, Arthur soon put both at ease. Commiserating with them over their mutual loss, the High King of Britain entered his childhood home through the kitchen door, as he had always done.

The next morning, following a simple ceremony, Lord Ector was laid to rest, buried next to his wife Drusilla on a hillside not far from the graves of his parents. During the week that followed, Cei took time to travel to every farm on his landholding so that he, as the new lord, might speak with each of his tenants. Since Llew, who had been Lord Ector's steward, would be staying on to manage the estate in his absence, Cei was able to reassure his tenants that nothing would be changing. Once he had spoken to all the farmers, Cei had similar conversations with the residents of Derventio. Upon hearing their concerns over the safety of the old Roman bridge, damaged after another recent flood, Cei hired a local work crew to undertake its repair and made arrangements for a mason from Luguvalium to oversee the project. Once Cei had settled these and other sundry affairs on his estate, the three friends took a ride for pleasure prior to their departure the following day. Knowing that Llew's wife was preparing a special meal for them that evening, they returned from their outing well before supper. They were walking to the house from the stable when Llew's dog, tail wagging, came trotting over to Arthur. While he was petting the dog, Arthur looked toward the track that led to Merlin's old home. Not once during his stay had he taken the short walk to visit the little cottage. In fact, Arthur had not been back to the place since leaving his childhood home over twenty years ago. Now, as before, he was torn between wanting to see it again and wishing to keep his memories of the place intact. Coming to a decision, Arthur gave the dog a final pat and began walking up the track. Cei started to follow, but Bedwyr put a restraining hand on his friend's arm. At first surprised, Cei then gave a nod of understanding, and he and Bedwyr turned to go into the kitchen.

Even from a distance, Arthur could see that the old cottage had become derelict. The door was missing, along with much of the thatching, and some stones, which had tumbled when the lintel above a window had collapsed, lay scattered about in the tall grass. Stepping gingerly through the rickety doorframe into the cottage's single room, Arthur was happily surprised to see that the table was still there – the same sturdy old kitchen table which had also served as his student's desk and Merlin's carpentry bench. Even now, though its surface was much encrusted with lichen, Arthur could make out a few chisel marks made by the usually precise Merlin. Arthur smiled as he remembered the mild oaths which had accompanied some of the missed strokes, given in any one of six languages. Looking around, Arthur found that the two chairs, which had been the only other major furnishings in the modest home, were gone, along with the precious books which had long ago been retrieved and returned to Merlin's library at Moridunum. But the shelves were not entirely empty. Lying on the uppermost shelf, a single waxed tablet had been left behind. With some trepidation Arthur reached up and took it down. It was almost with relief when he saw that the wax coating had melted, obliterating whatever words had been last inscribed on it. After placing the tablet back on the shelf, he continued his tour – the grand tour as Merlin had jokingly called it. Walking to the other side of the room, he found that the once cheery hearth was now a circular smudge of charcoal on the ground; the pantry was a few shards of pottery and broken glass half-buried in the dirt floor below; and the pile of straw in the corner which had served as Merlin's bed was now a mound of compost, covered by rank weeds thriving in the light streaming through a gaping hole in the wall.

Arthur emerged through the doorway abruptly, wishing that he had never returned. His eyes were tearing as he looked toward the dazzling sun and the hazy purple mountains rising distantly to the south. As he moved his gaze closer, to the nearer foothills where he and Merlin had taken so many of their pleasurable outings together, he gasped. On top of the highest hill, a tall, thin man stood facing him. At the man's side was what appeared to be a wolf. Wiping his eyes, Arthur looked again, this time shielding his face from the sun with his hand. The man was gone. For a moment, Arthur wildly thought of chasing after him. Then he realized who he must have been. A shepherd, of course, with his dog. Shepherds often moved their flocks to the higher slopes during the warm months. Disappointed, Arthur was reaching behind him to close the door when he remembered that there was no longer a door to close. With a sigh, he began walking down the track back to the house. Before reaching the curve in the lane which would hide the cottage from view, he allowed himself a last look. Wistfully, he gazed at the cottage, as if sensing that he would never see it again. Then he turned and continued down the path.

By the reckless way that the royal messenger was galloping his horse on the rough and pitted road, Arthur suspected that the man coming toward him from the south was bearing bad news. Some days earlier, he had left Derventio with Cei and Bedwyr. Since no pressing matters were at hand, he and his two friends had been taking the journey back to Isca at their ease, often stopping along the way to talk to people. Over the years the Britons had grown comfortable speaking with their High King, knowing that they could freely express any concerns, suggestions or even criticisms which they might have. The king always listened to everyone patiently and, if he could, would try to rectify any problems brought to his attention. Even if he were in disagreement with the person, he would always explain his reasoning with never a negative repercussion to the petitioner. Arthur had taken this idea from Merlin, who had found that the best way for a king to know what his people were really thinking was by being open and approachable. Based upon everything that Arthur had so far seen and heard, all appeared to be well in the realm. Until this moment. Now, as the rider drew near, his demeanor confirmed Arthur's fears. It was a look that he had not seen in many a year and had fervently hoped never to see again. As the royal messenger reined in his horse and saluted, King Arthur braced himself for the worst.

Chapter 9

Departures

When Arthur learned from the messenger that an envoy from Armorica had arrived, bearing urgent and troubling news from King Hoel, Arthur and his two friends rode hard back to Isca, stopping only to change mounts at the posting stations. Upon reaching the city late the following afternoon and with the grime of travel still on his clothes, Arthur spoke with his cousin Hoel's envoy and immediately called together his full council.

The news reported by the envoy was grave. Germanic warriors known as Franks were advancing into Armorican territory from the east, making brutal raids on farms and villages in their bid to seize control of land through fear and intimidation. King Hoel was being hard-pressed to repel the invaders, whose attacks were as unpredictable as they were savage.

"The Franks have been committing the most heinous outrages upon our innocent civilians," the envoy continued. "One of the atrocities has even touched our royal family," he said solemnly. "King Hoel's niece, our gentle Princess Helena, has been seized by one of the Frankish war bands. The princess had been traveling back to the capital from the house of her aunt and uncle when she and her escort were ambushed in the woods. The men in her escort were viciously slaughtered, and the princess and her old nurse taken hostage. Our king and her mother and father are frantic to find her. Since there have been no demands for ransom, there are grave concerns for her safety." The envoy, who had been keeping his emotions in check, choked on his final words and fell silent for a few moments. "I apologize, Lord King; Princess Helena is beloved by all who are privileged to know her," he said. "King Hoel had been reluctant to call upon you, Lord King, but the situation in Armorica has grown so desperate that he has sent me to request from you as many troops as you might be able to spare to help us in our fight against these barbarians who mean to take not only our country, but our very lives as well."

With passion in his voice King Arthur replied, "Good sir, please tell your king, my dear cousin Hoel, that he has my full support and backing, and let him know that British troops are on their way. I pledge to you, before my full council, that I shall not rest until Princess Helena has been restored to her family, and the Franks have paid dearly for her abduction and all their other outrages. Also, kindly tell King Hoel that the people of Greater Britain have not forgotten how he and the people of Little Britain came to our aid in our own time of need. Saxons, Picts and Hiberians have all learned to their regret what happens to plunderers who try to invade British lands. Now it is time to teach these Franks the same lesson as the peoples of Greater and Little Britain unite once again in common cause to defend all Britons, whether they live to the north or to the south of the British Sea!"

There were loud shouts of approval all around, and King Cador's fist came down on the table with a crash. "It's long past time that I put my battleaxe to good use again! By cleaving Frankish skulls! We'll make these curs pay for their crimes, and the coin will be their blood! Now, let's go and whip these barbarian dogs all the way back to the kennel that they came from!" At Cador's words, there were further shouts of approval and the pounding of fists all around.

"Thank you, good King Cador. I know I can count on you. As I know I can count on all of you." Turning to the envoy Arthur said, "Kindly inform King Hoel that I will be bringing fifteen hundred troops, half of them mounted, as soon as the ships can be gathered to carry them. I would gage that we will be arriving at my cousin's capital within a fortnight. Sooner, if we are able."

"Thank you, Lord King. King Hoel will be most thankful to know that he has your full support and that British troops are on their way. With your permission, Lord King, I shall sail with the tide to bring this good news back to my king and countrymen." Bowing deeply, the envoy took his leave.

King Arthur immediately sent out representatives of the crown to press into service all nearby vessels and to inform Lord Drustan to bring up the fleet from the southern coast. Then, after quickly discussing the preparations needed to be made and assigning tasks to all, Arthur dismissed his council. As the others were leaving the chamber, Nimue, who had remained silent during the meeting, quietly asked the king if she might speak with him. When they were alone she said, "Lord King, as your advisor, I must tell you that I have deep forebodings about your leaving Britain, even briefly."

Frowning, Arthur replied, "I'm afraid I cannot change my plans on something that vague, Chief Advisor. Can you be more specific?"

"I have had troubling visions of the future, Lord King. I say visions because there may yet be several outcomes, depending upon which paths you and others may choose to take. But all possible outcomes of one particular decision remained consistent: if you leave Britain and go to Armorica, the path that you will be on inexorably leads to one invariable and unchanging vision – the crown of Britain resting on another man's head, and the red dragon banner lying trampled on the ground."

"The man wearing the crown – could you tell who he was?"

"No, Lord King, only that the man was not you. His face was turned away from me, but his hair was black."

"Black hair? That could be Prince Constantine, or either of Constantine's two sons. Perhaps your vision is of something that will happen years from now, and the man could be one of my heirs. I shan't live forever, you know," he said, smiling. "Besides, a vision such as this could be interpreted in many ways, could it not? The red dragon banner lying on the ground? Perhaps it simply slipped from my bannerman's grip."

"The spirit of prophecy does not deal in trivialities, King Arthur. You know this as well as I."

"Yes, I do know. I apologize, Nimue. I didn't mean to offend or make light of your vision. I only thought to suggest that it might not be as dire as it seems."

"No vision is given without reason, Lord King. This vision has been sent as a warning to you. It is imperative that you choose the right path, and the right path for you, King Arthur, lies in Britain."

"I'm sorry, Nimue, but my decision is beyond choice. I must go. As you are aware, my cousin Hoel came to my aid without hesitation when I was a young, unknown and untried king. My reign had hung in the balance until the scales were tipped in my favor by the arrival of the Armorican troops. How can I possibly ignore my cousin's appeal for aid after what he did for me? Moreover, we have each sworn an oath to support the other for as long as we both shall live."

"Lord King, I am not suggesting that you should not support King Hoel. By all means send King Hoel your troops. Only do not lead them yourself. Send someone in your stead to lead them. King Cador, perhaps."

Arthur shook his head. "Impossible, Nimue. Not after Hoel himself came to my aid at the head of his forces."

"But Lord King," said Nimue, "if you go, I fear you will risk everything that you have fought so hard to achieve."

"If it is my fate to die, then so be it," Arthur declared. "At least I shall die with honor. For honor itself is at stake. And now, with the abduction of Princess Helena, this has become a family affair. I'm sorry, Nimue, but my decision in this matter is final."

Nimue was looking at him so tragically that Arthur thought to reassure her. "Besides, my dear advisor, now that I've had your warning, I shall be more on my guard than before. I promise that I'll have news brought to me on a regular basis to keep me informed of what is happening in Britain while I am away. Also, since King Cador is my heir, I'm considering naming him co-regent while I am away. I know that my good uncle will be vigilant in keeping Britain safe during my absence. And should anything happen to me, my heir will be in place in Britain and ready to rule. Will that content you, Chief Advisor?" he asked.

When she did not answer, Arthur looked and saw that her eyes had taken the same glazed and faraway look that his previous chief advisor's often had. In a voice not her own, Nimue solemnly intoned, "Arthur, High King of the Britons, listen to my words: never set aside Caliburn, the mighty sword forged on the Isle of Avalon."

"My dear Chief Advisor, it would never occur to me to do so."

"Listen, King Arthur, listen well! Heed the spirit of prophecy. For your own sake, for the sake of those who love you and for the sake of your beloved country, *never* set aside Caliburn, the sacred Sword of Avalon, forged of metal sent from the heavens themselves to protect the people of Britannia."

Drawing Caliburn from its scabbard and holding the gleaming sword by the hilt, King Arthur replied gravely. "Spirit of Prophecy, I have heard your voice and I shall heed your words: I, Arthur Pendragon, High King of Britannia, solemnly swear, on the sacred Sword of Avalon itself, that I shall never set Caliburn aside, neither in peace nor in war."

Nimue, still possessed of the spirit, did not speak but dipped her head. As Arthur had often done with Merlin, he waited for her eyes to become normal again before speaking to her. Then, after sheathing his sword, he said, "My dear Nimue, are you back? You may set your mind at rest; I assure you that I will never set Caliburn aside. Don't worry, Lady Nimue, I have heard the warning and shall heed the voice of the prophecy. But for now, my dear Chief Advisor, I must leave you to help with the preparations. And I know that you have much to do yourself, helping to organize the needed drugs and other medical supplies. I shall see you again before I leave." Nimue curtsied respectfully. Since her head was bowed, Arthur could not see the tears that were welling in her eyes.

When Arthur broached to Cador his idea of naming him co-regent, his warrior uncle's soldierly pride seemed so deflated that Arthur felt compelled to reconsider his choice. While he loved them both, Arthur knew that neither Cei nor Bedwyr was truly suited to the office, equally so his loyal and brave, but hotheaded, nephew Gawain. And Cador's son Constantine would be loath to leave the side of his valiant, but aging, father. Arthur considered his other nephew, Gawain's younger brother Mordred. Arthur knew Mordred to be a bold warrior, popular with citizens and soldiers alike. Mordred was also shrewd, and he possessed diplomatic skills should the need arise. The only thing which made Arthur hesitate was that he felt he really did not know his nephew well, for all the years that Mordred had been at court. Yet his younger nephew seemed to be the logical choice. Besides, Arthur did not expect any trouble in Britain while he was away since there had never been a more peaceful time in all his reign. Moreover, his wife Gwenhwyfar, who would be co-regent, knew his mind in all matters.

When Arthur asked Mordred to remain in Britain to be co-regent with Queen Gwenhwyfar, Mordred demurred at first, declaring his wish to be at Arthur's side, fighting the enemies of the Armoricans. Arthur was pleased when his nephew, after being given a little time to consider, finally agreed to accept the office.

Preparations proceeded smoothly, and five days later the army had assembled to board the ships that crowded the quay along the river Usk. On Prince Mordred's suggestion, the force left behind to garrison the fortress was comprised primarily of the King's Harriers, soldiers whose capabilities he was most familiar with, while a smaller cavalry unit headed by Lord Pelleas was detached from the King's Eagles to deal with any unexpected emergencies outside the capital.

King Arthur and Queen Gwenhwyfar were standing together on the quay, watching as the troops boarded the ships to the sound of a jaunty military march. As the last of the soldiers were boarding, King Arthur took leave of his wife with an emotional kiss and embrace. Then, as the martial music continued to play, the High King of Britain boarded the flagship to the cheers of townsfolk and soldiers alike. At a signal from Lord Drustan, the commander of the fleet, a drum roll sounded, and sailors simultaneously unfurled red dragon banners on all the ships of the fleet. The men on board the ships gave three rousing "hurrahs," answered heartily by the soldiers standing nearby along the ramparts of the fortress. As the flagship slowly pulled away from the quay, Arthur walked to the stern to wave farewell to his wife. Tears were flowing from Queen Gwenhwyfar's eyes as she waved back to her husband. The queen's co-regent Mordred, standing near her on the quay, was better able to control his emotions as he, too, waved farewell to the departing High King of Britannia.

Chapter 10

Mount Tombe

King Arthur was still looking toward the city when the helmsman steered the ship around a sweeping bend in the river, and the highest roofs and towers of Isca finally slipped from view. After traveling several more miles down the meandering river, the ship sailed out into the Sabrina estuary where a stiff westerly breeze was kicking up choppy waves against the outgoing tide. Upon receiving orders from Lord Drustan, who was standing with King Arthur in the stern, the helmsman set a course to the southwest, keeping the ship close to the wind as the long line of vessels fell in behind the flagship.

Arthur's hair, now tinged with a bit of gray at the temples, was whipping wildly in the wind as he and his old friend Drustan made their way to the bow, greeting soldiers and sailors alike. Although Arthur traveled only rarely by ship, he found that he enjoyed the pungent smell of the sea, the cries of gulls wheeling overhead, and the spray of salt water on his face as the bow rose and plunged against the waves. As the hours passed and the ship continued to beat its way down the ever-broadening estuary, Arthur spent most of his time amidship, helping to calm the restless horses that were stamping and shifting nervously on the pitching deck.

As evening approached, the fleet berthed in the protection of a wide bay along Dumnonia's northern coast. There the soldiers disembarked to cook their meals and stretch out on the sandy beach for the night. Everyone boarded again before dawn, and the ships set sail at first light. Several hours later, as they continued along the coast, they could see the fortress Tintagel, perched high on a cliff that dropped precipitously down to the ever-roiling sea crashing at its base. Soldiers and the civilian residents of the fortress, who had gathered on the cliff top to watch them, cheered boisterously as the fleet approached, while the men on board the ships replied with equal exuberance.

King Arthur smiled when he heard the voice of his Uncle Cador from several ships behind, booming clearly above the rest.

Anchoring that night in a sheltered cove further down the coast, the ships got under way again at dawn and rounded the horn at the end of the peninsula before noon. As they entered the channel, Drustan ordered the steersman to set a southeasterly course directly for Aleth on Armorica's northern shore. Having cast a weather eye to the sky, Drustan was able to reassure the king with the voice of experience that the conditions appeared most favorable for the crossing. That night, with stars shining brightly in a clear sky to guide them and a brisk wind holding steadily out of the west, the conditions were indeed optimal, although more than a few soldiers thought otherwise as they hung heaving over the gunwales.

The weather held as a new day dawned, and they could see the distant coastline of Armorica. As they neared land, the helmsman steered the flagship toward an imposing citadel, perched high on a rocky crag to the east of the river it overlooked. First built by the native Armoricans and later enlarged and strengthened by the Romans, the fortress Aleth guarded the port and the entrance to the river. Pilots, rowing out from the river's mouth at their approach, hailed the Britons and guided their vessels into the harbor at the foot of the fortress. As the ships were being secured to the quay, an honor guard of soldiers descended from the citadel and greeted King Arthur with respectful salutes. Their leader, identifying himself as the commander of the fortress, courteously explained that a messenger had been dispatched to let King Hoel know of their safe arrival. Meanwhile, he hoped that King Arthur, his retinue and troops might accept such hospitality as the fortress could afford for the night. Arthur accepted the offer with thanks for his men, knowing that solid ground, a good meal, and a full night's sleep would benefit both man and beast alike. For himself, however, he chose to proceed to the Armorican capital as soon as possible, so that he might meet with King Hoel without delay.

As the Britons and a small army of Armorican dockers began unloading the ships, Arthur himself assisted with the unloading of the horses. Of the seven hundred-fifty horses which had been brought, it was considered fortunate that only two had suffered injuries severe enough to have to be put down. His own fiery bay mare Llamrei, Arthur was relieved to see, had suffered no injuries and appeared as feisty and ready to be off as ever. After placing the British troops under King Cador's temporary command, Arthur set off with Cei and Bedwyr and their Armorican escort for the capital city, some forty miles to the southeast.

The sun was just dipping below the horizon when Arthur, riding in the forefront with the captain of the guard, first caught sight of Condate Riedonum. Placed strategically at the confluence of two rivers, the Armorican capital shone with a rosy and almost incandescent glow in the low-angled light. When Arthur commented on this breath-taking sight, the captain explained that the effect came from the color of the brick that the Romans had used to construct the city walls, accounting for the capital's other name, the "Red City."

As they approached an imposing gateway, the captain hailed the guards, standing above on the ramparts, who called down to the porters, and the massive oaken doors slowly swung open. Soldiers, standing at attention inside, saluted as King Arthur and the captain passed through. Proceeding with the escort down a broad thoroughfare lined with prosperous shops and houses that ran the length of the city, Arthur could see, even in the dwindling light, that the Armorican capital was many times larger than Isca and, arguably, more grand. Near the center of the city, they halted before an imposing and stately Roman townhouse identified by the captain as the royal residence. As several grooms stepped forward to take their horses, King Hoel and his retinue came out through the front entrance to greet them. Arthur tried hard to keep the look of shock from his face when he first saw Hoel. Although his cousin was only two years older than he, Hoel had taken on the shrunken and hollow-eyed look of a much older man, or a man suffering from a grave illness. Embracing Arthur, Cei and Bedwyr in turn, Hoel invited them inside, leading the way across the atrium and down a long colonnade lit by lamps hanging from graceful bronze stands. After placing Cei and Bedwyr into the care of his steward, Hoel escorted Arthur into a spacious suite of rooms next to his own. Only after the Armorican king had dismissed his attendants and the door had been shut could the cracks in his composure be seen. Fighting back his emotions, it took several moments before Hoel was able to speak.

"Please pardon me, Arthur, for showing such weakness," said Hoel, "but more terrible news has been brought to me. Four days ago, after we received word that the war band holding my niece Helena had been sighted, her father, Lord Gerin, left with a troop of soldiers to rescue her. You remember Lord Gerin?"

"I do indeed. It was Lord Gerin and the Armoricans under his command who bore the brunt of our first assault during the battle at Badon. Without Lord Gerin and your Armorican troops, I could never have taken the hillfort."

Hoel nodded. "Yes, yes. Then you will understand my current state of mind when I tell you that I learned yesterday that my beloved brother Gerin had been killed in an ambush by this same war band. Two badly wounded troopers, who had survived the attack, brought me the terrible news. Then this morning, just as I was about to send out an overwhelmingly large troop of men to hunt down and finally destroy these brutes, my scouts reported that a massive Frankish force is marching toward Condate Riedonum from the east. They estimate that the Franks could be here in three days' time. We have already made preparations for a siege, of course; we had been expecting such an attack upon the city for weeks. But how can I pull men away now, just when they are needed to defend the city? Such an action would be unconscionable. Yet my dear sister, already mad with grief over the abduction of her beloved daughter and now with the death of her husband Gerin…" He fell silent again, fighting back his tears. "I am sorry, dear cousin. This all seems like some horrible nightmare. I can hardy believe it is happening. To think that such a sweet and fragile child as my niece Helena, thin and graceful as a willow…her health has never been good, you know…in the hands of brutes…and now my dear brother Gerin dead…" Hoel began sobbing.

Arthur embraced him comfortingly. "Ah, my dear, dear cousin, I am so sorry for all your tribulations. Please know that you have my deepest sympathy for your losses. But please also take heart, dear cousin. You now have fifteen hundred fellow Britons at Aleth, ready and eager to help you rid your beloved country of this pestilence. During the wars with the Saxons, I cannot tell you how many times I was thrown into the deepest despair, thinking that all was lost. And then you arrived, dear friend, bringing me renewed hope and succor. I pray I may now do the same for you, dearest cousin."

"Thank you, Arthur. Thank you for your support and comfort, for both are sorely needed by me in these terrible times. As you have no doubt seen from my appearance…" He smiled thinly. "Yes, yes, I could see from the look on your face that you were startled by my appearance. It's that same reoccurring fever which strikes me from time to time, though I had been clear of it for years…until these horrific attacks by the Franks…that was when it struck again…I'm sorry, Arthur, if we might sit."

"Of course."

Wearily, Hoel sat on a chair next to the dying hearth. Although it was a warm night, he had started to shiver. "I am sorry cousin…I'm not entirely well yet…as you can see. Gerin has been helping me with decisions and the day to day running of the kingdom…I can't believe he is gone…this is a nightmare, a horrible nightmare."

Arthur gently patted Hoel's shoulder. Then he went to the hearth and placed several logs from a stack over the smoldering embers. After stoking the fire back to life, he walked into the adjoining bedroom and returned with a thick woolen blanket which he wrapped around his cousin. Looking at Hoel with concern, Arthur asked, "Should I call for a doctor?"

"No, no, Arthur, thank you, but it's not necessary. The fever always grows worse in the evening. There is really nothing to be done but let it run its course. Luckily, it is not the sort of illness that can be given to others. My doctors believe the malady comes from marsh vapors. Once contracted, it stays with you for life." He shook his head. "Just when my people need a strong leader, what they have is this," he said, holding out his hands despairingly.

Pulling up a chair, Arthur sat next to Hoel. "May I make a suggestion, cousin? A suggestion which, of course, you may freely reject. I would propose that you place my infantrymen inside the city to bolster your defenses while keeping my cavalry mobile and outside the city walls. I've put my uncle, King Cador, whom you know, in temporary command of my forces. While Cador is bold, he is also prudent, and you may rely on him for good counsel. He'll be here tomorrow morning with the cavalry. Meanwhile, I plan on seeking out this war band myself. Do you know how many men they have?"

"About thirty, I've been told. But Arthur, you mustn't underestimate them. One of them is a notorious Iberian mercenary of enormous strength, literally a giant of a man, whose sole task is to terrorize and intimidate through wanton acts of cruelty. His brutal atrocities to captives have been witnessed," added Hoel with a shudder. "Please, Arthur, you must not put yourself in personal jeopardy."

"Yet when I was a young and untried king, you put yourself in personal jeopardy when you came to my aid, good Hoel. Now it is time for me to return the favor. I mean to restore Princess Helena into the arms of her family."

"I thank you, Arthur. I thank you with all my heart. I beg God that He grants you success. How many men will you take with you?"

"Only two, but two of my best – Cei and Bedwyr. Also, I would ask you for one of your scouts, a man familiar with the area where this war band has been operating. It is my intention to use stealth to free your niece."

"You shall have Winoc, a good and reliable man. He grew up near Mount Tombe, not far from where Lord Gerin was ambushed. May God go with you Arthur Pendragon! I shall pray my every waking hour that God grants you success so that I may look upon Helena's sweet face again."

At first light the next morning, Arthur, Cei, Bedwyr and Winoc galloped their horses through the north gate and along the road that ran northeast from the capital. After several hours of hard riding, they were still some distance from the coast when they turned off onto a narrow lane and soon reached a modest farmstead, set back across a field. Earlier, Winoc, an amiable, ginger-haired man in his late-thirties, had explained that they would be stopping at the house of his aunt and uncle, who might be able to provide them with the latest information about the Franks. As they rode up, a man holding an axe emerged from the stables, poised to fight. He looked tremendously relieved when he recognized his nephew among the strangers. The four men dismounted, and after brief introductions, Winoc asked his uncle for any recent news about the war band. Judoc nodded. "I have some, nephew, and none of it good. You know old farmer Yanig who lives up by the crossroads?"

"I do. The old widower. My son used to do some work for him around his farm."

"Well, old Yanig was here just this morning on his way to his son-in-law's house. He was pretty badly shaken. Yesterday, a band of Franks came through and ransacked his farm. Lucky for him he heard them coming and hid in the woods before they saw him. Poor old Yanig couldn't do a thing but watch while they looted his house, slaughtered his livestock, and then set fire to the house and barn.

"Was the giant with them?" Winoc asked.

Judoc nodded grimly. "He was there all right, and as big as everyone says. Yanig said he was eight feet tall if he was an inch. After they set fire to his cottage, it looked like they were going to go on their way when a rider – one of their own – came up from the south. Yanig could make out through the man's gestures that they were supposed to return with him, but the giant and a couple others held back. Then the three of them started arguing with the leader of the war band, and Yanig said it was pretty obvious the argument was over their two women prisoners."

"These two women, did he say if they were Princess Helena and her nurse?" asked Winoc.

"Must'a been. One of them was young, maybe sixteen-years-old or so and the other somewhere in her sixties. He said neither of them looked too good." Judoc shook his head. "Poor Princess Helena; they've been dragging her around for weeks. I'm surprised she's still alive."

"What happened then?" interrupted Winoc.

"Well, the giant shoved aside the man who was holding the princess and made to grab her. When the man drew his sword, the giant swung his club and stove in the man's head as easy as if it had been a rotten turnip. Then a fight broke out – a falling out among thieves as you might say. After a minute or so, the leader of the war band, the messenger, and two more Franks were lying dead on the ground. When the giant dared any of the others to fight him, they all backed down. Then he grabbed Princess Helena, threw her over his shoulder and went on his way. His two companions took hold of the old woman and followed him. After milling around for a little while, the rest of the band headed east. Old Yanig was so scared that he stayed hid in the woods for the night. He's over at his daughter and son-in-law's place now. It's just down the lane if you want to talk to him."

"Did Yanig say which way the giant and the other two men went?" Arthur asked.

Judoc nodded. "He said they were heading north on the main road, toward the coast, Lord King."

"Do you wish to speak to Yanig, Lord King?" asked Winoc.

Arthur shook his head. "No. Now that the situation has changed, it's more vital than ever that we find the women as soon as possible. A delay of seconds could mean the difference between life and death. Thank you, Judoc, for your help."

" 'Twas no trouble all, Lord King. I just hope it's not too late."

With hasty farewells, the four men vaulted back onto their saddles. As they spurred their mounts to a gallop, Judoc shouted "Godspeed!" after them.

Riding hard, they returned to the main road and continued north, soon reaching the crossroads where the ruins of Yanig's cottage and barn were still smoldering. Sprawled amidst broken furniture and smashed household items, the bodies of the five Franks were lying where they had fallen. The four men galloped their horses past without a pause.

Not long after, they halted at the edge of a vast salt marsh, which stretched out to the east and west for as far as the eye could see. Ahead, to the north, the British Sea glimmered distantly on an ebb tide, while to the west, a dun-colored river meandered lazily through the marsh before discharging its silt-laden water into the bay. Beyond the river's mouth, a high, wooded island rose like a mirage above glistening sand flats that reflected its image like a mirror. Winoc identified the island as Mount Tombe. To the north, shimmering in the far distance, a second, unnamed island of almost equal size rose above the rippled sand of the bay.

Scanning the green expanse of the marsh, they could see no signs of life at all other than the sheep grazing placidly in the salt grass and a few sandpipers probing busily in the mud at the edge of a tidal creek that ran into the river. Next to the creek, about halfway between them and Mount Tombe, stood a small, forlorn-looking hut built on high pilings. A rickety ladder leaning against the sill of the door provided the only means of entrance. When Arthur suggested they ride to the hut for the better vantage that it would afford, Winoc advised that they had best proceed on foot since their horses could become hopelessly trapped in the treacherous mires of the marsh. Taking their guide's advice, they rode back a short way to a small ford that they had crossed earlier and led the horses far enough into the woods so they could not be seen from the road. Unsaddling them, they tethered them next to the stream in a grassy clearing where they could graze. Then, quickly returning, the men set off across the marsh on foot.

They were approaching the hut when Bedwyr spotted four sets of footprints off to the side in the mud. The feet that had made one set of tracks were gigantic. Bedwyr was pointing out the tracks to the others when the door of the hut flew open with a crash. A man, who had been inside, leapt wildly to the ground. Foundering in knee-deep mud, he was struggling to reach the creek. Only after Winoc had called over to him in his own language and identified himself as a fellow Armorican, did the man cease his frantic efforts to escape. He was still panting heavily as Winoc and Bedwyr grabbed him by the arms and pulled him from the thick, sucking mud. In answer to Winoc's questions, he said, still breathlessly, "I'm just a shepherd. I tend my sheep on the marsh and fatten a couple of pigs on acorns and beech mast up there on the mount every year. I keep a quiet life, or I used to, before these Franks arrived like the plague. Just yesterday, when I'd come back here for my midday meal, I heard some rough-sounding men coming this way. When I peeked through the window, I saw three men, and one of them was that giant."

"Were two women captives with them?" asked Winoc.

He nodded grimly. "Yes, a young woman – she must'a been Princess Helena – and an old one. Both of them were trussed up with ropes though the old woman was forced to do her own walking. The giant had the young woman thrown over his shoulder, carrying her as easy as I carry a new-born lamb."

"What did you do?"

"What could I do? Me being here all alone against three armed men and one of them a giant? I was going to make a run for the river. I figured drowning was better than getting caught by them in here. Luckily the giant shook his head and pointed to the island, not Mount Tombe, but the other island, the one further out in the bay. I ducked down and held my breath until they went by. I was afraid they might change their minds and come back, but they kept going all the way out to the island. The only thing I've been able to think of since is what must have happened to those poor women. But what could I do all alone on my own with nothing but a shepherd's crook against two men with swords and a giant carrying a club?"

"You are not at fault," Arthur replied briskly. "Can we reach the island on foot?"

The shepherd glanced at the creek. "You could; the tide's not coming in for hours yet. But what's the point of throwing away your lives? Trust me, no man without an army at his back could stand up against that giant. Besides, it'll be too late to help those two women by now."

"Nevertheless, we are going to try," Arthur replied. "We have come to free Princess Helena and her nurse and to bring justice to those criminals."

Looking at Arthur and shaking his head, the shepherd said, "I can see for myself that nothing I can say is going to change your mind. Well, just make sure you don't get caught out there on the flats when the tide turns. There's a spring tide, and the sea comes in as fast as a horse can gallop – faster than you or any other man can run, no offense meant."

"None taken," replied Arthur. "Thank you for your help."

"Help? What help? You're welcome to it, though I did naught. Good luck to you, sir, and to you too, sirs; I hope I'm wrong, but I don't imagine I'll be seeing any of you again."

Cei answered irritably, "Listen you, do you realize that it's King Arthur himself that you've been talking to? I'm Lord Cei and this is Lord Bedwyr. We're the king's companions," he said, motioning to himself and Bedwyr. "It's not our intention to get ourselves killed."

"No, Lord, I'm sorry, I didn't realize who you were – how could I? I can see for myself that you're fighting men and, no doubt, good ones. No offense meant, Lord, but getting killed is never anyone's intention, is it? Still it happens all the time, doesn't it, even to lords and kings."

Cei had opened his mouth to reply, but Arthur intervened. "My good man, could you kindly do us a great favor? We've left our horses tethered in the woods not far down the road. They're about a hundred yards east of the first ford that you come to, next to the stream. Do you know where I mean?"

"That I do, Lord."

"Should we not return by tomorrow, please take them to farmer Judoc who lives on the first lane to the right below the crossroads. I would consider it a great kindness if you and he would see that they are well-cared for until they can be taken to Condate Riedonum and given to my cousin, King Hoel." Removing some coins from the bag at his belt, Arthur placed them into the shepherd's hand.

Startled, the shepherd said, "Here, Lord King, take your coins. I'll do what you want without them. It'd be a sin to take money from a man – even a king – for doing his last wishes." Pausing, he stared down at the eight silver coins lying in his palm. "Of course, then again, it might be the greater sin to let these coins fall into the hands of our enemies. All right then, Lord King, thank you, I'll keep these coins safe." Dropping them into the bag at his belt, he added, "I know farmer Judoc – I get my two shoats from him every year in exchange for three of my lambs. Now wait just a minute," he said, while looking at the scout. "You're Judoc's nephew Winoc, aren't you? Yes, yes, I knew it," he replied, looking satisfied after Winoc answered in the affirmative. "I never forget a face, even though I haven't seen yours around here for some time now. Nice to see you again, Winoc." Turning back to Arthur, he said, "Don't worry, Lord King, I'll see that your horses are well cared for until Judoc and I can get them over to King Hoel."

"Thank you," said Arthur. "But you must take care; the city may soon be under siege. Before you go, you must first find out if it's safe."

"Don't you worry, Lord King. You can rely on me to be careful."

After thanking the shepherd and saying their farewells, the four men began making their way as quickly as possible to the island. Meanwhile, the shepherd climbed up the ladder into his hut and opened a shutter to watch them as they trudged across the marsh. He continued watching until they had become four small specks, moving resolutely across the sand flats toward the distant island. Shaking his head, he muttered, "I warned 'em, but they wouldn't listen to me. Those men must think they can't die just because they're royal."

Rummaging around a cluttered corner of the hut, he found a scrap of linen, laid the coins on top and secured the parcel with a bit of string. Then, climbing back down the ladder, he walked to the road to bury his little hoard in the woods to keep it safe and to look for those horses that he, no doubt, would be taking to farmer Judoc's the next day.

The trek across the marsh was made more difficult by the tidal streams that the four men had to skirt around or, more often, wade through. When they finally reached the sand flats, covered to mid-thigh with black, sticky mud, they all breathed a sigh of relief. After washing off the mud in a little rivulet winding across the sand, they continued on to the island. Even though walking on the wet, rippled sand was easy, Winoc urged them to remain cautious; seemingly firm-looking surfaces could sometimes give way, trapping the unwary in deep, hidden pockets of quicksand lying below. With Winoc as their guide to point out potentially dangerous patches, they managed to cross the flats without incident.

Scanning the island before them, now lit by the late afternoon sun, they saw nothing but raucous gulls, squabbling contentiously as they swooped down to feast on creatures left stranded by the tide among the rocks ringing the island. At a silent signal from Arthur, the four men clambered over the slippery, seaweed-covered boulders and began climbing up the island's wooded flank.

As they were making their way through the trees, they began hearing an intermittent but distinct clanking noise coming from above. Crouching low, they advanced stealthily toward the sound. At the edge of a clearing near the island's summit, they halted within the cover of the trees so they could observe what was making the sound. While they were watching, an elderly, gray-haired woman, wearing torn and soiled clothing, came limping into view. With one blackened eye, a bruised face and a cut, swollen lip, she was weeping silently as she laboriously carried a heavy stone to a low cairn in the middle of the clearing. After adding the stone to the pile, she turned and began walking back the way that she had come. She appeared to be alone. So that she would not be startled by their sudden emergence from the woods, Arthur called out softly that friends of King Hoel had arrived. Wiping hair from her face, she turned as the men approached.

With lowered voice, Arthur said, "Dear lady, I am King Hoel's cousin, King Arthur of Britain. We are here to free you and Princess Helena from your captors. Do you know where Princess Helena is?"

At his words the woman burst into tears. "Lord King, your help has come too late for sweet Helena," she said, gesturing to the cairn. "There lies my treasure and all my happiness. My little dear one, as kind and thoughtful a child as ever lived, who deserved a life filled only with joy, died when that cruel beast of a man threw her to the ground and tried to force himself upon her. She was always a frail child, and her poor, dear heart must have simply stopped beating from fright. Unable to satisfy his bestial lust, the foul monster then turned on me. A woman of my age…one would have thought…" She choked back her tears.

Arthur was devastated, but asked gently, "Do you know where he is now?"

She nodded and pointed to Mount Tombe. "The giant and the two brutes with him went to the other island as soon as the tide let them. I wanted to do nothing but flee from this place in case they might come back but could not bring myself to leave until my sweet nursling had some sort of burial. The birds, you see…" She stopped, sobbing, unable to go on.

"Dear lady, I vow to you that after today this monster will not harm you or anyone else ever again. My companions and I have come to put a stop to his outrages."

Shaking her head vigorously, she said, "No, Lord King, please, you and your companions must flee from this place. You must not underestimate the strength and brutality of that pitiless animal. I have seen what he does to captives. Lord Gerin, Princess Helena's noble father, tried to free us. The monster forced Helena to watch while he brutally butchered her beloved father. I say animal, but in truth this man is more cruel and vile than the most loathsome of beasts," she said, pulling her tattered clothing more tightly around her.

Removing his cloak, Arthur placed it around the old woman's shoulders and offered her the leather flask of water that he had with him. Drinking deeply, she thanked him gratefully. When she tried to return the flask, he insisted that she keep it.

Turning to the scout, Arthur said, "Winoc, could you please escort the lady to the shepherd's hut where she may rest and have some refreshment? Cei, Bedwyr and I will finish building the tumulus."

"Yes, Lord King."

Taking the scout aside, Arthur added quietly, "Should we not return by tomorrow, please see that she gets back to Condate Riedonum safely. Since the capital may soon be under siege, perhaps she might stay with your aunt and uncle until the way is clear. I know I can rely on you to inform King Hoel of what has transpired here. Please convey to my cousin my deepest condolences and my most profound regret that I was unable to save his beloved niece."

"You may rest assured that I will, Lord King, though I have no doubt that I shall see you soon."

"Thank you, Winoc. Until we meet again."

The sun was setting when Arthur, Cei and Bedwyr, their faces grimly determined, began walking across the sand flats to Mount Tombe. To the north, the sea was still a distant, but ominous, line of steely gray. Ahead, looking more than ever like some gigantic burial mound, Mount Tombe was silhouetted darkly against a blazing crimson sky. As darkness grew, the island's summit began to pulse eerily with the orange glow of an enormous bonfire. They had no doubt who had lit that fire.

They were about halfway across to the island when Bedwyr detected, even in the gloom of the moonless night, that the line of darkness to the north was rapidly widening. The tide had turned. Just minutes after, with the rush of oncoming water loud in their ears, the three men quickened their already rapid pace to a flat out sprint. Soon, the foaming water that had been lapping at their feet was swirling around their knees. By the time they were nearing the island, they were in waist-deep water, struggling to stay upright as they waded across the strong onshore current rushing into the river. Then, perversely, when they were less than a hundred feet from the island, an even stronger eddy current threatened to sweep them off their feet and carry them out to sea. Holding onto each other's wrists, they fought their way across the final yards of the rapidly deepening flow. Staggering out of the water, they threw themselves on the ground, panting for breath.

After resting, they began cautiously making their way up the wooded slope. Ahead, through the trees, they could see the glow of the fire still burning above. Advancing stealthily, they stopped just short of the grassy clearing at the summit of the island. There, by the light of the fire, they saw three men lolling on the ground, reclining comfortably against fallen logs. In the middle of the glade, a pig on a spit was roasting over bright embers. The men were gnawing great chunks of meat that they had carved off with their knives, washing them down with gulps of wine from their flasks. Periodically, when fat dripped from the pig onto the embers, the low-burning fire sputtered to life and flared anew in bright flame, clearly illuminating the three men. Two of them were fair-colored and blue-eyed, with long, blonde hair pulled back from their faces and tied with leather thongs. The third man, whom everyone had described as a giant, was almost literally so, though Arthur gauged his height to be closer to seven than the eight feet mentioned. Dark-haired, with a matching bushy beard that was greasy and fouled with bits of pig, the enormous, muscular man looked relaxed as he leaned back and took another long swig of wine, his broad shoulders resting against the log. An immense spiked war club was lying close to his hand. While Arthur hoped the gigantic man would be somewhat impaired by the effects of drink, he was under no illusion that he would not be a formidable foe. His two henchmen, both above average height and well armed with swords and shields, appeared to be in good fighting trim. Silently, Cei and Bedwyr indicated to each other which of the two men they would deal with. Earlier, Arthur had made it clear to them that he would fight the slayer of his kinswoman himself; only if he were to fall should his companions attack the giant, using whatever means necessary to rid the world of the brute. Although his friends had tried to dissuade him, he had remained adamant.

When Arthur signaled, he and his two companions took their shields from their shoulders, quietly drew their swords and stepped into the light of the fire. The giant immediately roared a command, and the two Franks were on their feet in an instant with weapons drawn. The spiked club, which would have been picked up with difficulty by two men, was easily snatched from the ground by the gigantic man. He looked around anxiously at first, but relaxed when he saw that there were only three men to be fought. Sneering a few words in contempt, the giant nodded towards the spit. One of the giant's companions, smiling broadly, obliged with a rough translation into the British language. "Plenty of room on the spit for three more squealing pigs."

Without wasting breath on a reply, Arthur and his companions attacked. Arthur had hoped to strike before the giant could swing his massive club, but the enormous man was surprisingly fast, and Arthur took a resounding blow on his shield. The spikes drove through and held there, and the shield was wrenched violently from Arthur's grasp. The giant immediately swung another blow, but the impaled shield made the club awkward. When the giant stepped on the shield to lever off his club, Arthur came in with a slashing cut across his enemy's forehead. The wound, though not deep, was stinging and the giant, bellowing with rage, dropped the club. Rushing headlong like a wild boar, he threw his arms around Arthur and lifted him off his feet as easily as if he were a child. The massive man then squeezed with all his might. Arthur gasped from the shooting pain as his ribs were compressed in the man's iron grip. He kicked and tried to wriggle free, but the giant only tightened his hold. Cei and Bedwyr, each battling his own formidable foe, saw what was happening but neither was able to help.

Unable to take a breath, Arthur felt darkness threaten. He knew he would lose consciousness if he did not break free soon. Both his arms were pinned helplessly to his side, but Caliburn was still in his hand. With a sharp twist of his wrist, Arthur managed to gash his foe's outer thigh with his blade's keen edge. Howling in pain, the giant slackened his hold just enough that Arthur was able to wrench himself free.

Furious, the giant wiped away the blood that was streaming into his eyes from the cut across his forehead. Snatching up his club, he swung it at Arthur.

The blow was well aimed and would have been fatal, but Arthur ducked under the club and came in with a quick jab to the man's exposed flank. The giant answered by trying to slam him with a backhanded recovery stroke, but Arthur, anticipating the move, had jumped out of the way. Blinded by the blood running continuously into his eyes, the giant now began flailing his club wildly. Any one of the mighty blows would have been lethal, but Arthur managed to avoid them. Meanwhile, many of Arthur's strokes were meeting their mark.

Cei and Bedwyr, having each dispatched his own adversary, watched as their king adroitly dodged blow after blow from the spiked club. When the giant paused to clear his eyes again, Arthur sprang behind him and swept Caliburn across the back of his knees, hamstringing him. The giant, stunned, swayed for a moment, then toppled forward stiffly like an uprooted oak. Lying face down on the ground, he moaned in pain.

"This is for Princess Helena," Arthur cried. Swinging his sword high, he brought it down hard on the back of the giant's corded and bull-like neck. But he had not brought the sword down quite hard enough. Wrenching the blade free, he lifted it a second time. "And this is for the old lady," he said furiously as Caliburn cleaved the air and then the giant's neck.

Chapter 11

Message from Isca

The British troops had been in Armorica for over two months when Rodarch and Ganieda received King Arthur's latest dispatch. Queen Gwenwyfar and Prince Mordred, the two regents, had been assiduous in seeing that copies were made of the High King's reports and distributed to the kings and queens of Britain. The news from Armorica, as usual, was mixed.

A month and a half earlier, the Franks had massed together in an attack upon Condate Riedonum, the Armorican capital. The siege of the city had been broken when King Arthur had led his cavalry in a surprise counter attack, repulsing the Frankish force. Since then, the Franks had changed their tactics, resuming small scale but savage raids on civilians. Kings Arthur and Hoel had answered by changing their own tactics, dividing their respective forces into smaller cavalry and light infantry units to quickly overtake the marauders, pursuing them into the forests. While the Franks continued to suffer greater casualties than the Britons, there seemed to be an unending supply of them. With no major battles, there had been no decisive victories, and the fighting continued to drag on. Meanwhile, work on constructing a chapel over the marble tomb that had been built for Princess Helena had begun. During the dedication, King Hoel had solemnly vowed that the island where his beloved niece had died, now named for her, would remain forever in the possession of the Armoricans of Little Britain.

After Ganieda finished reading the dispatch that her husband had given to her, she once again expressed her sorrow over young Helena's death. "I know how devastating it must have been for Arthur to have arrived too late to save Princess Helena. It must weigh heavily upon him to know that if he had arrived just one day earlier, he might have saved her."

Rodarch nodded gravely. "Indeed. Her death was a terrible blow to both kings. At least, thanks to our king, that monstrously evil brute will harm no more innocents, however small such consolation must be for Arthur." Opening the seal on the second letter that always accompanied Arthur's reports, Rodarch quickly scanned its contents. He said, with relief, "At least the enemies of Britain are remaining quiet and have not used our High King's absence as an opportunity to attack." He handed Ganieda the regents' latest report on the state of affairs in the kingdom.

After reading the report, she examined the document carefully, looking at the polite felicitations to her and King Rodarch and at the signatures of both regents. "I see that the regents' directives to you and Peredur are the same as before – to remain diligent in patrolling the northern border by keeping our joint forces along the wall."

"A sensible precaution, I would say, under the circumstances. As you know, the Scoti and the Picts stay within their borders only so long as they see a strong force poised and ready to oppose them."

"True," she said, thoughtfully. "And we know from Stater that he and Merlin's other loyal chieftains have been ordered to keep their men along Cambria's west coast to guard against Irish raiders. The regents' directives seem to be nothing but sensible precautions, and yet…"

"And yet?" asked Rodarch, raising his eyebrows at his wife.

"I'm not sure; it's just a feeling I have."

"A feeling upon which you would wish me to act?"

"No, Rodarch, I think not. Not at this point anyway. But meanwhile, with your agreement, I think I'll have some discreet inquiries made."

"Of course."

A short while later, Hermogenes entered Ganieda's study and knelt before his queen.

"Thank you for coming so promptly, Hermogenes. Please sit down," she said, waving him to a chair. "I have a mission in mind which could be potentially dangerous. I give you the option to refuse freely with no reproach to yourself."

"So when do I leave?" he replied with a smile.

Smiling in turn, Ganieda said, "As soon as possible. I'd like you to ride south to Isca, keeping your eyes and ears open as you go. I want you to determine what the true state of affairs in Britain really is. I must admit that I am sending you on this mission without having any evidence whatsoever that there may be reason for concern. It's merely a hunch I have – a hunch which may prove entirely groundless. Indeed, I hope I am proven wrong. But I know that I will remain uneasy until I can have the veracity of the regents' reports on the state of affairs of the kingdom discreetly and independently confirmed. Please take particular care when making inquiries around Isca. Cross the river at Burrium, rather than at Isca, and take the west road to the city. When you arrive there, I would suggest that you speak first with my brother's old friend Madog. I've kept in touch with Madog over the years, and you can trust him implicitly. He lives in town now, the second house down from the fortress on the same side of the street as the Church of Saint Aaron. Send me no messages; I shall be content to wait until I can hear your findings from your own lips. Also, if any actions need to be taken before you are able to consult with me, please take them; as always I have full confidence in your judgment."

"Thank you, My Queen. It is my honor to serve you. With your permission then, I shall be away within the hour."

"Thank you, Hermogenes, and good luck. Until I see you again."

Hoel and Arthur were sitting their horses on a height of land overlooking the peninsula which jutted like a spearhead to the northwest, far into the British Sea. This opportunity was the one toward which they had been working. A fortnight earlier King Hoel, having regained much of his strength, had used his cavalry to drive several large parties of Franks from the vicinity of the capital. As the Franks were withdrawing to the east to avoid an engagement, they were stunned when they came against King Arthur and his cavalry, who had circled around their position. Meanwhile King Cador, heading the joint Armorican and British infantry, had come up from the south, forming a bulwark between the two cavalry forces. To avoid battle, the Franks had turned north to elude their foes. By choosing to flee rather than fight their way through the British and Armorican lines, the Franks had made the tactical error that Hoel and Arthur had been hoping they would make. Keeping pressure on the enemy force, the Britons and Armoricans had pursued the Franks northward, clipping at their heels. As the Franks continued their flight, they seemed oblivious that the broad peninsula upon which they were fleeing was ever narrowing. Surrounded on three sides by the sea and with the joint armies cutting off any chance of escape to the south without their entering into a major engagement, the Franks realized, too late, that a net had been cast by Hoel and Arthur. Now that net was rapidly tightening.

Watching the distant enemy forces withdrawing helter-skelter across the patchwork of open fields and pastures before them, Arthur turned to his cousin Hoel. "I still can't understand why the Franks are continuing their flight to the north. Were I in their position, I would have long ago turned to fight. Even they must be aware by now that their position becomes less tenable with every passing day as the land upon which they have to maneuver becomes ever more constricted."

"I think, Arthur, that you are giving mindless brutes too much credit in believing that there might be some overarching plan to their flight. I believe that the Franks are completely ignorant of battle tactics; they have yet to demonstrate that they can fight as a cohesive force. We should only be thankful that their knowledge of military strategy is as poor as their knowledge of geography." Hoel glanced toward the sun. "About an hour before sunset. Perhaps, Arthur, we should call halt and make camp for the night."

Arthur nodded his agreement. Turning to his foster brother, cousin and uncle, sitting their horses at his side, Arthur said, "Cei, keep your cavalry positioned on the west coast to prevent the enemy from breaking through along the beach. Constantine, you will do the same on the east. King Cador, set pickets across the peninsula as before. Also as before, all our soldiers are to remain in battle dress. I suspect that when the Franks finally do make their move, they will do so at night when they hope to take us at a disadvantage."

"Then they will be in for a surprise," replied Cador grimly, patting the axe at his side.

Prince Mordred was writing at a table in the High King's private chamber off the great hall when there was a knock at the door. "Come in," he said setting down his pen. Lord Drustan entered and bowed to the regent. "You wished to see me, Prince Mordred?"

"Ah yes, thank you for coming so promptly, Lord Drustan. Please sit down. May I offer you some wine? No?" Mordred paused, clearing his throat. "Recently, word has been brought to me from Clausentum of violations being committed by Saxon traders."

"What sort of violations, Lord Prince?" asked Drustan, looking concerned.

Mordred smiled. "Nothing too egregious, Lord Drustan, but I wish to have this sort of thing nipped in the bud before it becomes ingrained and thus more difficult to stop. As you know, when King Arthur negotiated the trade agreement with Cerdic, he made certain concessions to the Saxon king. One of those concessions was in allowing two Saxon ships to enter any of the designated British trading ports together so long as they were traveling in tandem for the sake of safety. Recently, however, and on more than a few occasions, I have been informed that groups of three and even four Saxon trading vessels have entered the port at Clausentum to unload goods. While I know this may sound trivial, I suspect the Saxons may be testing us, seeing how much they can get away with while our High King is away."

Drustan nodded, his brow knitted, as he wondered why Lucius, his second-in-command who regularly patrolled those waters, had not brought these infractions to his attention. "How would you wish me to deal with them, Lord Prince?"

"Nothing too drastic, Lord Drustan. I don't want this to boil over, giving the Saxons an excuse to make an incident of the matter. I would simply give the captains of those vessels a warning, reminding them of the terms of our trading agreement. A second offense will incur a fine of, say, a tenth part of the value of the goods on board. I believe you have someone onboard your flagship who speaks Saxon well enough to act as translator?"

"Yes, Lord Prince. Conveying such a warning to violators should pose no problem. How many ships would you wish me to take?"

"Your entire fleet."

Drustan looked startled. "My entire fleet? But surely, Lord Prince, the entire fleet is not needed to deal with a violation which, as you yourself pointed out, is not too egregious?"

Mordred, momentarily annoyed, quickly recovered his composed visage. "I appreciate your opinion, Lord Drustan, and I thank you for expressing it, however, I must disagree. While I am aware that three or four of our ships could, no doubt, easily deal with the problem, an unspoken show of force is the best way to reinforce mere words. As I said, I suspect they are testing our resolve now that our High King is away. I believe that a massive display of strength is exactly what is required to put the Saxons back in their place again. When your entire fleet of…how many ships are in your fleet again?"

"Fourteen ships, Lord Prince."

"…fourteen ships arrives, we will be sending the strongest possible message to the Saxons that we are ready and able to enforce our laws and defend our shores even while our High King is away."

"And the co-regent? Is this her command as well?"

Mordred schooled his visage with difficulty. "Of course, Lord Drustan. The co-regent and I always consult with each other and make all our decisions jointly. Queen Gwenhwyfar and I discussed this matter at some length before you were summoned. Thank you, Lord Drustan, I shan't detain you any longer; I believe you will soon have the tide. I wish you success on your mission and look forward to receiving a report upon your return."

Ganieda was on the ramparts, pacing back and forth. The previous night she had slept only fitfully. For the sake of her husband's tranquility, she had quietly slipped from bed and tiptoed into the antechamber. Lighting a lamp, she had picked up a book but found she could not concentrate on reading. Finally giving up, she threw a few cushions on the floor and stretched out on them, covering herself with a blanket. Tired, yet unable to find sleep, she had waited for the square of night sky framed by the window to lighten so that she could begin what had so far been an equally restless day. Conscious that the guards were no doubt growing discomforted at the sight of their queen pacing restlessly back and forth on the ramparts, Ganieda decided to take a walk in the woods, hoping to find repose in some secluded glade. As she was turning to go, she caught sight of a royal messenger, riding posthaste up the hill toward the gates. She knew that the regular courier was not due until tomorrow. Immediately, she hurried down the steps and across the courtyard to the royal residence to learn what news he was bringing.

Ganieda found Rodarch in his study off the great hall. Alerting her husband to the imminent arrival of the messenger, she took a seat next to him, trying to still her feeling of foreboding. Moments later, Rodarch's steward announced the courier, and the man, still grimy from his travels and looking grave, entered the room. Bowing respectfully, he then fell to one knee as he proffered two documents. Rodarch could see that the usual dispatch from King Arthur was not among them. Concerned, Rodarch first opened the letter sent by the regents. As he read, the color drained from his face. He was quite ashen when the parchment slipped from his hand and fell to the floor. Reeling, he gripped the arms of his chair, seeking their support.

Ganieda, in alarm, said, "Rodarch, husband, what is it? What is the news?"

He turned to her without speaking, looking like a man stunned by a blow. Then, in a strained voice, barely above a whisper, he said, "King Arthur is dead."

Chapter 12

At Clausentum

anieda was dumbstruck. Then, in disbelief, she said, "Dead? King Arthur dead? No, no! It cannot be! How? When?"

"Our High King was killed in battle two weeks ago. He and King Hoel had been pursuing the Franks in a major offensive. They had been unaware that they, in turn, were being pursued by a second and much larger enemy force coming up from behind. When battle was engaged, they were caught between the two Frankish forces."

"Arthur caught unaware? How could such a thing be possible?"

"The regents put the blame on King Hoel," Rodarch began. He stopped and turned to the messenger. "Thank you, courier. You realize that this terrible news is distressing beyond words. You needn't wait; Queen Ganieda and I shall be sending our reply and a letter of condolence to Queen Gwenhwyfar by our own courier."

"If you please, Lord King, I have been instructed to carry back your reply myself."

Rodarch, frowning slightly, said, "Very well, but you will have to wait while we take a little time to compose our thoughts before writing our letters. I am sure you understand that this horrific news is a terrible shock for us both. My steward, whom you will find outside, will see that you have a meal and a room where you may rest before your departure."

"Of course. Thank you, Lord King," said the messenger, rising to his feet. Bowing courteously in turn to each, he said, "My Queen, Lord King." With another polite bow, he turned and left the room.

Ganieda waited until the door had closed. Then she said, "Rodarch, I can't believe that Arthur is dead."

"It is even worse."

"Worse? How worse?"

"King Arthur's heirs, King Cador and his son, Prince Constantine, were also killed during the battle, as was Prince Gawain. And over half of our British force was lost. The battle was a rout."

Ganieda gripped her chair. "This is horrific, beyond belief. How is all this known to be true?"

"Lord Cei, who survived the battle, sent a dispatch to Isca. This other missive is a copy of his report." Breaking the seal of the second document, he scanned it quickly. Shaking his head, he said sorrowfully, "Unfortunately, Lord Cei's report confirms everything in the regents' letter. Cei says that Hoel acted rashly, pursuing the Franks without considering that the enemy might have been leading them into a trap. Cei believes Hoel's desire for retribution following the murder of his niece clouded his judgment. King Arthur and our British soldiers fought valiantly, but they were overcome by the vastly superior numbers of the enemy army. Arthur was trapped behind the enemy line when he was surrounded by Frankish soldiers. Cei and Bedwyr were too far away to help when they sighted our High King, alone and fighting like a lion. But even King Arthur himself could not prevail against so many jackals. Though mortally wounded, our High King fought his way back to the British line so he could give his final directives to Cei and Bedwyr. He commanded that Prince Constantine's eldest son Arwel, now heir to the throne, should be crowned immediately, so that our enemies do not take advantage of a leaderless country, as they did following King Uther's death. Arthur's last words were, 'To Gwenhwyfar, my beloved wife, I give my eternal and undying love.'"

Rodarch's voice wavered, and Ganieda laid her hand on his arm. In a voice hoarse with emotion, he continued. "When Lord Cei wrote this report, our remaining British forces were retreating with King Hoel and the Armoricans back to Condate Riedonum. Arthur is to be buried in the capital, with full honors, next to the tombs of his Armorican ancestors." Through his own tears, he saw that Ganieda had begun to cry. He stood and held out his hands to her. Rising, she hugged her husband tightly as both gave vent to their profound sorrow.

Drustan was standing in the bow of the *Sea Eagle*, scanning the waters ahead as the island of Vectis passed to starboard. Running with the wind, the fourteen ships in his fleet were making good progress. Soon they would sail north into the inlet and then up the River Itchen to Clausentum. Once there, Drustan hoped to learn why Lucius, the commander of the eastern fleet that regularly patrolled the waters around Vectis and along the Saxon Shore, had failed to so much as report the violations being committed by the Saxon traders. Lucius had always been one of his most trusted and diligent captains, and it troubled him greatly that he might have to discipline a respected senior officer, whom he also considered a friend.

Several hours later the British fleet entered the mouth of the Itchen River on an incoming tide. After rounding a broad curve in the winding river, Drustan could see the town of Clausentum in the distance. He was shocked to observe numerous ships tied along the quay. He became even more disturbed when he recognized all ten vessels as Sea Hawk ships. That Lucius had allowed his entire fleet to remain idle, especially during these potentially perilous times, was a blatant dereliction of duty. There was now no doubt in Drustan's mind that he would have to relieve Lucius of his command.

As the flagship approached to dock, Drustan impatiently leapt from the gunwale to the quayside. He was amazed to observe Lucius walking toward him, looking equable and unperturbed. As Lucius saluted his superior officer, Drustan demanded angrily, "Captain, why have you allowed your fleet to be idle?"

Lucius was taken aback. "Lord Drustan, I beg your pardon, Lord, but I was obeying your order to cease patrolling the Saxon Shore."

"My order to cease patrolling the Saxon Shore! I gave no such order. Why on earth would I give such a daft command!"

"Begging your pardon, Lord Drustan, but I was told that, by your command, I was to immediately cease all patrols and await your arrival at Clausentum. Frankly, Lord, I was perplexed by those orders myself."

"Who told you those were my orders?"

"Why Lord Meliot himself, the interim commander of the King's Harriers."

"Meliot!"

"Yes, Lord Drustan."

"When was this?"

"It must be – let me think – eight days ago now. He arrived by ship. He told me that you yourself had spoken to him directly when you were at Isca. He said that, by your order, all ships under my command were to cease patrolling the Saxon Shore and gather at Clausentum for a naval operation. When I asked for details, he told me that everything would be made clear upon your arrival."

"Then Meliot told you a lie. I never spoke to him about any naval operation nor did I ever give him any order whatsoever to convey to you. Where is Meliot now?"

"He left soon after he arrived, Lord."

Drustan was mystified as he pondered this information. If Meliot had arrived eight days ago, he must have left Isca well before his own departure. Further, as interim commander of the King's Harriers, Meliot could hardly have vacated his post without Prince Mordred's permission.

Lucius broke into his thoughts. "Begging your pardon, Lord Drustan, but then why have you brought your entire fleet to Clausentum?"

Drustan seemed almost startled by the question. "By the regents' command," he said. "Prince Mordred informed me that on numerous occasions more than two Saxon vessels at a time have docked at Clausentum to unload their cargo, in clear violation of our trading agreement with them. He ordered me to come here with the entire fleet to demonstrate to the Saxons, by show of force, that such violations will no longer be tolerated."

Lucius looked utterly bewildered. "With respect Lord Drustan, there have been no violations at Clausentum or at any port under my watch. If more than two Saxon vessels had ever tried to dock here or anywhere else, they would have been turned away with a warning, and I would have informed you of the incident. Lord Drustan, there have been no such incidents. Though why you have been told such an untruth, I cannot fathom."

By Lucius's puzzled and ingenuous expression, Drustan was certain that his friend was telling the truth. With dawning awareness, Drustan realized that the British fleet, bottled up as it was on a narrow and winding tidal river, was in jeopardy. He spoke urgently. "Lucius, I believe there is treachery at work here. Get your men on board and away as soon as possible. Sail out into the channel where you can maneuver. I fear we may have been led into a trap."

A sailor in the rigging, who had been furling a sail, called down. "Lord Drustan, five vessels coming up the river." As Drustan and Lucius shaded their eyes to look, the man continued, "Ten, no wait, more!" The man above gasped. "Lord Drustan, at least thirty Saxon war boats, coming up fast!"

Drustan shouted, "Cast off men, and prepare for battle. Lucius, I'll try to hold them off until you can get your ships under way. Make for Tintagel at once. Tell Princess Elen to shut herself in the fortress with her two sons and trust no one, at least until it's known where loyalties lie. I pray your warning does not come too late. Send the rest of the fleet to Armorica to inform King

Arthur of what has happened here. Our High King will no doubt need as many ships as possible to transport his forces back to Britain to deal with this emergency. Good-bye and good luck, dear friend. Forgive me for ever doubting you."

"Thank you, Lord Drustan. Godspeed, Commander!"

Lucius ran down the quay, shouting orders to his men as Drustan leapt back onboard. Within minutes, the flagship was under sail and in the vanguard of his fleet. Meanwhile, the Saxon war boats, each holding some forty-five men, were sweeping swiftly up the river. Within the confines of the river, Drustan knew that the sleek Saxon rowing boats would be faster than the British ships, sailing against the tide. Looking ahead to the far distance, he suppressed a gasp when he saw a line of ten more Saxon vessels, blockading the river's mouth. Hopelessly outnumbered, Drustan resolutely ordered his men to take battle positions, and his command was relayed to the other thirteen ships in his fleet.

As the Saxon vessels drew near, Drustan was stunned when he recognized members of the King's Harriers among the Saxon oarsmen. His shock turned to disgust when he realized that every one of them was still wearing the red dragon badge of the High King of Britain. In the bow of the foremost Saxon vessel he spotted Meliot, looking back at him smugly. Smiling, Meliot gave him a mock salute. Suddenly, a Harrier archer stood. Taking aim at Drustan, he loosed the arrow. It missed the British commander by inches but struck a sailor standing just behind him. Even before the wounded man had fallen to the deck, Drustan and Meliot simultaneously shouted to their archers to shoot at will.

Arrows were flying as the Saxon vessels closed in on the British ships. Two war boats veered toward the flagship and collided hard against its starboard side. The *Sea Eagle* was still shuddering from the impact as Saxons whirled grappling irons attached to chains over their heads. Tossing them over the ship's gunwales, they quickly drew their vessels close and began climbing up the flagship's side.

The Sea Hawks were ready for them. Armed with long spears, they stabbed at their foes, heaving them backward onto their boats or into the water. But soon the sheer mass of enemy soldiers began to overwhelm the defenders. As the Harriers and their Saxon allies began swarming over the gunwales and onto the deck, the Sea Hawks tossed aside their spears and drew their swords. The close, hand-to-hand combat was fierce. Drustan was amidship, fighting with sword in hand, when he saw a Saxon strike his helmsman with an axe. As the mortally wounded man slumped to the deck, the now unguided flagship began to swing about heavily, propelled by the wind and tide. With the two Saxon vessels still attached to its windward side, the ship was being rapidly driven toward the shoals along the riverbank. Realizing that his ship was about to run aground, Drustan furiously fought his way through a gauntlet of enemy combatants. He was nearing the stern when the same Saxon swung the axe at him. Agilely, the British commander jumped back to dodge the blade. The powerful blow, meeting only air, swung wide, leaving the Saxon's right side exposed. Drustan lunged at the opening, and the Saxon went down with a cry. Leaping over the man's body, Drustan grabbed the tiller while shouting orders to his remaining crew in an attempt to forestall the ship's drift onto the shoal.

Meliot, meanwhile, had been calmly watching the action from one of the Saxon vessels fastened alongside. With deliberation, he plucked an arrow from his quiver and nocked it. Pulling back the bowstring, he took careful aim on Drustan. Then he let his arrow fly.

Chapter 13

The Regents

Gwenhwyfar was sitting at a small table in the courtyard of the royal residence at Isca, enjoying a mid-day meal with Annwr and Alys. So far it had been a damp and dreary September, but this day had dawned so bright and pleasantly warm that Gwenhwyfar had thought to make the most of the rare, balmy weather by eating outdoors with her friends. Elen, with whom they usually made a foursome, had left for Tintagel shortly after her husband Constantine had departed with King Arthur and the British troops. Elen's brother Efan, who had been named warden of that fortress while King Cador and Prince Constantine were away, had also been charged to continue the military training of Elen's two sons. Efan, a skilled soldier training his own son Conanus, had been well pleased to accept both commissions.

During their meal together, Gwenhwyfar shared with her friends the contents of a letter from Elen, which had arrived earlier that day. "Elen says we won't recognize Arwel when we next see him; in the few months since he's been away, he's been shooting up like a weed. She says both boys miss Delwyn. She was wondering, Alys, if you might consider sending him to Tintagel. She asked Efan if it would be all right, and he said he'd be happy to have him for training."

Alys thought for a moment but shook her head. "I don't know, Gwen. I don't think I could bear being parted from Delwyn, not now, while his father is away."

Gwenhwyfar nodded. "Of course, Alys. I'll let Elen know when I write back to her. I do understand," she said, patting her friend's hand.

She did indeed. All three women were under the same strain of being parted from loved ones fighting a brutal enemy in a distant land. Whenever a letter arrived, they felt the same anxiety, followed by the same relief when it was found not to contain any dread tidings. Even Elen's cheery little note had given Gwenhwyfar a momentary twinge of apprehension before she had opened it and quickly scanned its contents. Only after determining that Elen's letter bore no bad news had she allowed herself the luxury of reading it slowly and enjoying its pleasantly homely contents.

They had finished their meal when Gwenhwyfar glanced at the old Roman sundial mounted on a column near the center of the open courtyard. "Well, ladies, shall we take a quick turn around the ramparts to make the most of this sunny weather while it lasts? Prince Mordred and I have another enormous pile of parchment to go through which will, no doubt, take up the rest of the day. I never appreciated how many documents and petitions and reports my poor, dear husband had to go through just to keep pace with the work. Thank goodness for Lord Ulfin! Without the Chamberlain's help, we'd soon be overwhelmed by them!"

Annwr and Alys readily agreed, and the three friends walked from the royal residence to the nearest gate. Entering one of the towers that flanked the twin arched doorways, they climbed the stairs to the level of the ramparts and began strolling around the perimeter of the fortress, enjoying the views of the city beyond. As they were rounding the east corner and the river came into view, Gwenhwyfar stopped to look for Lord Drustan's flagship among the vessels tied along the quay. It had not yet returned. She was not overly concerned since Drustan had departed only the day before.

The previous evening, as she was taking her customary walk before supper, she had noticed that the *Sea Eagle* was missing. That Lord Drustan would have departed so suddenly and without seeking her leave was unusual conduct for the ever polite and conscientious commander. When she had asked Prince Mordred about Drustan's hasty departure, he had explained that the commander had received word from a man in a small fishing boat of a vessel in distress. Apparently, a British trading ship had struck a hidden reef off the coast of northern Dumnonia and was taking on water faster than it could be bailed out. Because of the emergency, Drustan had left without delay in order to render aid to the foundering vessel. Upon hearing Mordred's explanation, Gwenhwyfar had expressed concern for the crewmembers of the stricken vessel, earnestly hoping for their safe and speedy rescue. Although she had been satisfied as to why Drustan had departed so precipitously, she remained troubled that her co-regent had not thought to bring this news to her immediate attention. This was not the first time that he had neglected to keep her apprised of an important event. His recent and rather high-handed behavior had been bothering her greatly, and she felt that she should mention it to him, however uncomfortable such a conversation might be.

As she continued walking along with her friends, considering how best she might express her concerns to Mordred without giving offense, Annwr broke into her thoughts. "Look, Gwenhwyfar, isn't that an Armorican ship? The one that's just leaving the quay."

As Gwenhwyfar stopped to look back, the banner at the top of the mast of the departing ship unfurled in the breeze. It was emblazoned with the device of King Hoel. She exclaimed, "Yes, Annwr, yes it is! Arthur's latest report must have arrived. Please excuse me, ladies; I'll see you both later at supper."

Hastening down the nearest flight of stairs, Gwenhwyfar swiftly made her way to the old Roman headquarters building where the day-to-day business of the realm was conducted. She was now determined to confront Mordred and bluntly speak her mind about how he had been treating her of late as a less than equal partner in their co-regency. Before she had joined Annwr and Alys, she had specifically told him where she would be, stressing, as always, that she should be interrupted if anything of importance occurred. That he had not notified her immediately of the arrival of a ship from Armorica and, further, had allowed it to depart again before she could give the messenger the letter that she had written to her husband was unconscionable.

Normally, she would have knocked before entering the room where she and Mordred conducted business, but in her current frame of mind, she marched right in. As she entered, she was surprised to see him crumple a piece of parchment and toss it onto the brazier. When she looked at him questioningly, he smiled. "Only a letter from my mother," he said smoothly. "My dear mother's letters can be a bit embarrassing with their effusive love and kisses. I wouldn't want any of them falling into the hands of one of my men since my credibility as a soldier might be called into question," he said laughingly.

Just as the scorched parchment caught flame, Gwenhwyfar had a glimpse of the signature at the bottom. She thought it was her husband's. When she saw Mordred regarding her intently, she said lightly, "Please give your mother my best regards when you write back to her. Kindly tell her that I am looking forward to seeing her again when this ghastly war is finally over, and we can all celebrate peace together."

"Amen to that," he replied with a smile. "My mother shares your sentiments. I know she will not rest easily until she can hold her eldest and most beloved child in her arms once again. Oh dear! I hope that did not make me sound like a jealous second son."

Gwenhwyfar gave him a smile as reply. Seeing the burning letter had made her pause. If her observation had been correct, the implications of Mordred's action were almost too disturbing to contemplate. The more she thought about what she may have seen, the more convinced she became that she might have been mistaken about the signature. Indeed, she prayed that she was.

"Oh, by the way," said Mordred casually, "a dispatch from Lord Cei just arrived. I waited for you to return before opening it."

"Was there no report from Arthur? Nor a letter from him for me?" she asked anxiously.

"No, but I'm sure there is no reason for concern since the messenger didn't mention that anything was amiss."

She took the roll of parchment and broke the wax seal with trepidation. Until now Arthur had always written all reports himself, and he had never before failed to pen a personal letter to her. As she scanned Cei's report, her face grew pale. She was swaying unsteadily on her feet and might have fallen had Mordred not caught her around the waist. Solicitously, he helped her to a chair.

"Gwenhwyfar, what is it?" he asked, looking at her with concern.

She spoke with difficulty. "My husband," she murmured, "I cannot believe it. Cei says that my husband is dead."

"No, no, that cannot be," Mordred replied in a shocked voice. "King Arthur dead? Impossible! Why would the messenger have said nothing to me?"

"I don't know, I don't know. Oh my God, my God."

"Here, let me take a look, perhaps you are mistaken."

Gently he took the parchment from her hand. As he read, his brow furrowed. "Oh my God, you are right, Gwenhwyfar. Our beloved High King has been killed in battle. Oh my dearest, dearest Gwenhwyfar, I am so, so sorry for your loss." Continuing to scan the letter, he let out a cry of dismay. "I cannot believe it! King Cador and Prince Constantine were also killed during the conflict! As was my brother Gawain! Oh my dear, dear valiant, foolhardy brother! If only I had been there to have taken your place! I would have gladly exchanged my life for yours. My poor mother will be crushed by this horrific news. This is a nightmare, a terrible nightmare." Badly shaken, he sat on the chair beside her, supporting his head with both hands. After a moment of silence, he wiped his eyes and took up the letter again. "But I must force myself to continue." Reading further, he said, "King Arthur's death has not yet been made public. Ah, that explains why the messenger from Armorica didn't say anything about this tragedy! Cei says it was King Arthur's final command that Prince Constantine's son Arwel, as next in line to the throne, should be crowned immediately. King Arthur feared that otherwise our enemies might be tempted to take advantage of a leaderless country, as they did following the death of King Uther. I see that we are to continue our regency until Prince Arwel reaches majority." He paused and looked at Gwenhwyfar. "Cei ends his letter with King Arthur's final words: 'To my beloved wife Gwenhwyfar, I give my eternal and undying love.'"

Gwenhwyfar was sobbing uncontrollably when Mordred took her hands into his own. "Oh my dearest, dearest Gwenhwyfar, words cannot adequately convey how truly sorry I am for your loss. Yet we must try to make ourselves brave in these perilous times for the good of our country. Don't worry, my dear," he said patting her hand. "I'll see that Arthur's commands are carried out. I'll have an escort sent to Tintagel so that Prince Arwel can be brought back to Isca safely and without delay. Then, once Arwel has been crowned High King and our country has been made secure again, there will be time for both of us to mourn the loss of our loved ones."

Solicitously, Mordred escorted the grief-stricken Gwenhwyfar back to the royal residence. At the door to her chambers, he embraced her comfortingly, promising to look in on her soon. Then, before leaving, he kissed her hand.

Gwenhwyfar's movements were heedless and automatic as she made her way across the anteroom and entered the adjoining chamber. When she saw the bed that she had shared with her husband, tears began to pour from her eyes anew. Sick with grief, she was about to lie down when she heard a soft rustle coming from behind the wall hanging that covered a small alcove. Walking toward the sound, she gasped in surprise as a woman stepped out from behind the embroidery. The woman immediately gestured for silence with a cautionary forefinger across her lips and approached closely. "Where is Prince Mordred?" she asked softly.

"He said he was going back to the headquarters building. But Nimue, I must tell you the terrible news. A dispatch just arrived from Armorica, from Lord Cei. Cei says that Arthur has been killed in battle."

"Impossible. It's a lie. I would know, I would have *seen* if King Arthur had been killed."

"But why would Cei lie?"

"Not Cei. Mordred."

"Mordred!"

"Hush, Gwenhwyfar, hush," she whispered, her eyes darting to the door.

"I'm sorry," Gwenhwyfar said, lowering her voice. "But the dispatch that Mordred handed me was sealed."

"And you imagine Mordred not capable of forging a letter and putting a wax seal on it?"

"No, of course he would be capable," she said thoughtfully. "But, no, he couldn't have; I saw the seal. It was impressed with Lord Cei's signet."

"Another forgery, easily accomplished by a devious and ambitious man."

Gwenhwyfar face lit up. "Are you telling me, Nimue, that my husband is not dead!"

"Please, Gwenhwyfar, more quietly," whispered Nimue. "Yes, that is exactly what I have been trying to tell you. I am certain King Arthur is not dead. Though he is in grave danger. As are you."

"From whom?"

"From Mordred, of course. He is not to be trusted."

"But Nimue, Arthur trusted him implicitly. Even so far as naming him co-regent."

Nimue sighed. "I know, I know. And I blame myself for that. I had misgivings about Mordred, but I never expressed them to King Arthur because I had nothing but vague feelings. Lately, however, the scales have fallen from my eyes, and I have seen Mordred for what he is. It is as if he has had to let his guard down, now that his plan is coming to fruition."

"What plan?"

"To seize the High Kingship of Britain."

"Oh my God! Nimue, are you sure?"

"As sure as I have ever been about anything."

Gwenhwyfar considered for a moment, then nodded. "It is true. Lately he has changed his manner toward me. He has become high-handed, purposely neglecting to keep me informed of important news and events. Even today he failed to inform me of the arrival of the ship from Armorica. I saw it quite by accident as it was departing. Later, as I was entering the room to confront him, he tossed a letter on the brazier. He said it was from his mother, but just before it caught flame, I thought I saw Arthur's signature on the bottom. Then he handed me the sealed dispatch, presumably from Cei, which he claimed had just arrived from Armorica. The report said that Arthur, Cador, Constantine and Gawain had been killed in a disastrous defeat and that it was Arthur's final command that Prince Arwel be brought back to Isca and crowned High King as soon as possible. Mordred and I are to continue our regency until Arwel comes of age."

Nimue looked worried. "I doubt that Arwel will live long enough to come of age. In fact, I doubt that Arwel and his brother will survive the journey from Tintagel. I'm sure some sort of 'accident' will be arranged. Listen, Gwenhwyfar, you are in danger. You must leave Isca at once. Take Alys and Annwr and their children with you. Go to Tintagel and warn Princess Elen of Mordred's treachery. The fortress will be your safe haven until King Arthur returns. My husband and his loyal men will escort you there. Take as little with you as possible to avoid suspicion. If you are challenged at the gate, remember that you are the Queen. Be imperious, say anything, just get past the guards. If they try to stop you, Pelleas will deal with them. Once you are on the road, ride hard and put as much distance as possible between yourself and any pursuers. The younger children can ride with the adults. My husband is familiar with the lesser known routes; he will keep you safe."

"Will you come with us?"

"No. I intend to go to Armorica to find out what is really going on there and to inform King Arthur of the danger here. Meet Pelleas between the two granaries nearest the northwest gate, as soon as it gets dark. Pelleas and his men will bring horses and any necessary supplies. Good luck, Gwenwyfar."

"Good luck, Nimue," she said, embracing the other woman. "You have always been my husband's loyal advisor, and mine as well. Give my love to my husband when you see him. Please tell him that I shall wait, forever faithful, until he returns."

The Lord Chamberlain was sitting at a table in his office, neatly organizing petitions and other documents into tidy stacks so that they could be presented in order of their importance for the consideration of the regents. Hearing a knock at the door, he turned from his work and bade the person to come in. When he saw it was the regent, he rose and bowed politely.

Closing the door, Mordred looked at Ulfin gravely. "Lord Chamberlain," he said, "there is tragic news from Armorica. This dispatch from Lord Cei has just arrived. I'm sorry, but the news it contains will come as a shock. I regret to have to inform you that Arthur, our beloved High King, has been killed in battle."

"Oh my God!" exclaimed the elderly man, clutching a hand over his heart.

Mordred nodded grimly. "I'm afraid you must brace yourself, for there is even more bad news to tell. King Cador, Prince Constantine and my own brother were also killed during the conflict, along with half of our soldiers. The Franks routed our army in a surprise attack."

"I can't believe it. King Arthur killed? Our army defeated? How could this have happened?"

"I know, I know, this is terrible news. Terrible beyond words." Mordred shook his head, overcome with grief. "I'm sorry, Lord Ulfin, but it is a little hard for me to speak just now. Cei's report will explain everything," he said, handing over the document. The old man, his hands shaking, took the parchment and unrolled it on the table.

When Ulfin had finished reading, Mordred said, "Copies will need to be made of Cei's report, of course, and distributed to every kingdom. I will also need to have copies made of a letter which I shall write to accompany the report. I want to reassure the people of Britain during these troubled times that Prince Arwel will be crowned High King, as soon as possible, to ensure a prompt and peaceful succession to the throne."

While Mordred was speaking, Ulfin had continued to study the document on the table. After lifting the parchment to his eyes and closely examining the seal, he said, "Prince Mordred, until we can have the information contained in this report verified, I would strongly advise against distributing copies of it. In my opinion, this document is a forgery."

"A forgery! Are you certain?"

"Quite certain, I am very familiar with Cei's signature and his signet."

"What a relief! I was hoping against hope that the letter might prove a forgery and the news it contained false. I was suspicious of it myself, yet the source seemed too impeccable to question."

"Do you have any idea who might have done it?"

"Actually I do. And he is surprisingly close. Do you remember, Lord Ulfin, many years ago when you and Merlin went to Tintagel on one dark and stormy night?"

Ulfin started. "Whatever would that have to do…"

"Please, just wait and listen. All will be revealed in due time. Now who was the third man with you that night? I'm trying to recall his name."

"You must know."

"Kindly answer the question. I wish to hear it from your lips."

Ulfin looked at Mordred apprehensively. "High King Uther Pendragon."

"That's right! High King Uther Pendragon, made to resemble King Gorlois by Merlin's craft. And for what purpose was this deception done?"

Ulfin, who had grown quite pale, didn't answer.

"Come, come, Lord Chamberlain, you must know. Don't be ashamed. After all, you and Merlin are honorable men so surely it must have been done for some noble cause. No? Nothing? Must I remind you? Very well. *So that Uther could rape Gorlois's wife!*" he exclaimed. "Then you and Merlin, panderers to the High King, had Gorlois murdered so that Uther could continue to satisfy his lust."

The old man was shaking, but forced himself to reply. "That's not true. King Gorlois was not murdered; he died in battle. Neither of us imagined he would leave the safety of his fortress that night."

"And how else might you and Merlin have 'imagined' that a truly honorable man would act but by fighting to protect his family and reputation! And I frankly find it rather hard to believe that Merlin, the renowned prophet, could have somehow failed to have foreseen my grandfather's death. But why dwell on the past? Why dredge all this up now? If I may answer my own questions: because, my dear Ulfin, I want you to understand the reason for what I'm about to do. Oh, and by the way, in case you're still wondering, it was I who forged the report. But of course you've probably already figured that out. Goodbye, Lord Ulfin," he said. "I'm sorry, but I really can't say that it's been a pleasure knowing you."

When Mordred pulled a knife from his belt, Ulfin cried out in fear. He tried to run to the door, but the younger man adroitly blocked his escape and pushed him back into the room. With lightning speed, Mordred lunged forward and grabbed the fabric at the neck of Ulfin's tunic in a choking hold. Keeping him at arm's length, Mordred smiled while he watched the old man struggle ineffectually. Then, abruptly, he yanked Ulfin close with one hand. With the other he plunged his knife into the old man's stomach. When he released his grip, Ulfin staggered backward, striking his head on the edge of the table as he fell onto the stone floor. Blood was bubbling from his mouth as he continued to gasp for breath.

"Really, Lord Chamberlain, no more from you," said Mordred. Stooping, he swept his blade across the fallen man's throat. After meticulously cleaning his knife on a bit of Ulfin's tunic that hadn't been bloodied, he straightened and surveyed the scene. "Well, my dear Lord Chamberlain, you've certainly made a mess. I hope you're not expecting me to clean up after you. But I will, at least, try to make you a little more decent." Walking around the table, he tipped it up onto two legs, sending the tidy piles of parchment flying to the floor. When the last sheets had finally settled, Ulfin's body was covered by a shroud of petitions. "There," said Mordred, dusting his hands, "that's better. So much for those tedious things."

It was dark when Gwenhwyfar opened a little used door of the royal residence and looked cautiously from side to side. Seeing that the way was clear, she stepped out and signaled to her friends. Behind her came Alys and Annwr, each cradling a baby held in a sling, followed by their six other children. Annwr's eldest daughter Meleri was holding the hands of her two sisters, while Delwyn had charge of his two younger brothers. Earlier, the women had warned the children to make no sound. So far they were behaving, but the women could only pray that the babies would not begin to cry.

As they made their way in the dark to the granaries, Gwenhwyfar continued to rehearse in her mind the tale she would tell if they were challenged at the gate. She knew her story – that she and the others were going to visit a sick friend not expected to survive the night – was feeble, especially with all the children along. Normally the guards would not presume to question her, but now she was less certain about where their loyalties might lie. She was well aware that most of the soldiers in the garrison were members of Mordred's own military unit.

When they reached the granaries and turned down the narrow alleyway between the two massive stone buildings, Gwenhwyfar was disappointed not to find Lord Pelleas there, waiting for them. Silently, she motioned to the others to line up against the wall behind one of the buttresses to avoid being detected by the guards walking periodically along the ramparts above.

As time passed, Gwenhwyfar began to fear that something must have gone wrong. The moon, just past full, had already risen, and by its light she could see the babies squirming in their mothers' arms. The toddlers were becoming equally restless. She knew that if Pelleas did not arrive soon, she would have to come up with another plan. With young children along and no horses or supplies, their options were limited. Just as she decided to leave the others and go to the stables to try to find out what had happened, she heard the hoofbeats of an approaching horse. With relief, she saw Lord Pelleas ride up. He halted his mount at the front of the granaries and quietly slipped from the saddle. After glancing around, he drew his sword and lurched clumsily down the passageway toward her. Before he could reach her, he stumbled over the base of one of the buttresses and fell face forward onto the ground. Gwenhwyfar's surprise turned to horror when she saw three arrows protruding from the back of the motionless man. Her mind was still reeling as a troop of soldiers approached. Any hope that they might be men loyal to her was dashed when she recognized Mordred, striding at their head.

Chapter 14

Besieged

Gwenhwyfar said, "Quick, to the gate!" Rushing forward, she stooped and picked up Pelleas's sword. Then she turned and ran as fast as she could. She soon caught up with Alys and Annwr who were behind their children, exhorting them to run faster. Delwyn had a brother under each of his arms, while Meleri was pulling her two young sisters along. Annwr snatched her second youngest into her arms, and her baby began bawling loudly in complaint. Alys's baby began answering with equally loud howls at being jostled.

As they neared the gate, Gwenhwyfar could see two guards standing in front of the barred doors. In the most imperious voice she could muster while approaching at a run, she ordered them to open the gates. Neither soldier moved. When she commanded them again, this time in the name of King Arthur, their response was the same. Looking back, she saw Mordred and his men, only moments away.

Desperately, she said, "Quick, into the tower!" As the mothers and their children ran to the closer of the two towers that flanked the gates, Gwenhwyfar, who was behind them, heard Mordred call out to the guards, "Stop her, you fools!"

She had nearly reached the tower when one of the guards grabbed her arm. Spinning around reflexively, she struck him with the sword. He was startled rather than hurt by the ringing blow to his helmet, but he relaxed his grip enough so that she was able to twist free. She dove through the open door and into the tower. Delwyn was inside, waiting for her. He slammed the door shut and dropped the oaken beam across. "Where's Annwr and your mother?" Gwenhwyfar asked breathlessly as she peered around the darkened room.

"They went upstairs to bar the other doors."

Gwenhwyfar nodded, and they climbed the steep flight of stairs to join the others. Annwr and Alys had already secured the doors on either side of the room so the tower could no longer be entered by way of the ramparts. Gwenhwyfar quickly swept her eyes over the stone projectiles, armaments and other supplies kept stockpiled in every tower. Then she cautiously peered through one of the narrow windows facing the interior of the fortress. Below, she could see Mordred, angrily shouting orders. With alarm she heard him call for a battering ram.

Turning from the window she said, "Delwyn and Meleri, gather any ropes you can find and see what's in that keg over there. Alys, stay here with the children. Keep them seated on the floor, and don't let them go near the windows. Annwr, let's bring these arrows and some bows to the roof. But first help me secure the hatchway." After fastening down the door, the two women began carrying the heavy stones from the pile and stacking them on top. They were still working when Delwyn and Meleri came over to see if they could help.

"Queen Gwenhwyfar, we couldn't find any rope, but the keg is full of these," said Delwyn, holding up a fistful of lead shot."

"Good. Are there any slings?"

"Right here," he said, pulling one from the bag at his belt.

"And here," said Meleri, pulling one from hers.

Annwr had to smile. "Her aim is almost as good as Delwyn's."

"Better!" said her daughter.

"All right you two," said Gwenhwyfar, "bring as much shot as you can carry up to the roof. But remember, this is no game. The soldiers below will be shooting back. Keep your heads down and stay out of sight!"

"We will," said Delwyn as he and Meleri began filling their bags full of the lead pellets.

After placing a final stone over the trapdoor, Gwenhwyfar straightened, wiping with her forearm damp strands of auburn hair from her face. "There," she said, "that should keep them out if they manage to break in downstairs."

Alys, with two squalling babies in her arms, was sitting on the floor with the younger children. Looking up, she asked anxiously, "Gwenhwyfar, what are we going to do?"

"Escape," replied Gwenhwyfar resolutely.

"But how?"

Gwenhwyfar thought for a second. "Since there's no rope, we'll have to make our own." She took off her cloak and handed it to Alys. "Do you have a knife?"

"No," Alys replied, looking frightened.

"Here, take mine. Tear everyone's cloaks, the children's too, into strips and knot them together to make a rope. We'll lower the babies and children to the ground from the roof and then climb down after them."

Alys was horrified. "But the soldiers will stop us."

"Not if we keep them busy with arrows and lead," said Gwenhwyfar with far more confidence than she felt.

When the men returned with the ram, Mordred immediately ordered them to batter down the door to the tower. The soldiers were advancing when a sudden hail of arrows and lead shot began raining down on them from the roof. Not anticipating any resistance, they retreated precipitously. Even Mordred, who had been standing some distance away with his captains, was forced to retreat when a lead pellet struck his helmet with a blow that made his ears ring. Angrily, he ordered the soldiers to fall back beyond the range of the missiles.

Mordred was considering how best to proceed when one of his captains ventured, "Lord Prince, we could shoot a barrage of arrows and have them cleared from the roof in no time."

Mordred turned on the man in fury. "And have Queen Gwenhwyfar killed in the process? You know she is up there with the others. Were you asleep when I explained to everybody that the Queen is to be taken unharmed?"

"Yes, Prince Mordred…I mean no, Prince Mordred, I wasn't asleep. I'm sorry, Lord," replied the captain, withering under his commander's ire and the mocking looks of his fellow soldiers.

After summarily demoting the captain back into the ranks, Mordred turned his attention to re-forming his men for a second attempt on the tower. He positioned the soldiers into four columns, with each man in the outer ranks gripping two shields to protect both himself and the adjacent man holding the ram. On Prince Mordred's order, the soldiers raced forward at speed. As soon as they came within range, a renewed flurry of missiles began raining down on them. Several were struck by arrows and shot which found their marks through gaps between the shields. With mounting casualties, the soldiers retreated again. Mocking the soldiers for running away from women and children, Mordred reorganized his force and ordered another assault. This time they reached the tower and immediately began pounding the door with the ram. On the fourth blow, the door gave way with a screech of rending wood. As soon as the door had been breached, Mordred and a select group of his men raced forward, holding their shields over their heads. Reaching the tower, Mordred nimbly leapt over the splintered boards of the rent door and peered around the darkened room. Seeing no one inside, he ordered two of his men to open the hatchway door. Mounting the steps, the burly soldiers pushed against the door with all their might, but it did not budge.

"Prince Mordred, should we try to break through with the ram?" asked one of them.

"And have whatever heavy objects the women have piled on top fall on your heads?" replied Mordred. "No, I think not." With an oath he ordered the soldiers to pick up the ram and follow him.

Before the soldiers could hurry beyond bow range, three more of Annwr's arrows had met their mark. Meanwhile, Delwyn had returned to the roof with two toddlers in his arms. Crossing over to where Queen Gwenhwyfar was waiting with the fabric rope, he helped her secure it around one of the children. Then, while he held the rope, Gwenhwyfar lifted the child up and over the parapet. Swiftly, the frightened boy was lowered outside the fortress walls into the awaiting arms of Meleri, who had been the first to be lowered to the ground. Once Meleri had freed the boy, Gwenhwyfar quickly pulled up the rope and tied it around the other child. As soon as she saw the little girl safe in Meleri's arms, she hurried over to join Annwr. Seeing but a single arrow in the quiver slung over her friend's shoulder, Gwenhwyfar asked, "How many arrows are left?"

"This is the last one," said Annwr.

Gwenhwyfar replied grimly, "Then make it count."

Annwr nodded as she fit the arrow to her bow. She had positioned herself at the inner corner of the tower, to gain a better angle for a shot aimed down toward the ramparts. Behind her, to the southeast, the moon had risen high above the fortress walls. By its light she could easily discern a troop of soldiers on the ramparts, rapidly approaching the tower. Just behind the soldiers holding the ram, she spotted Mordred. He was holding a shield in his left hand, but from her vantage, she had a clear shot to his right flank. Taking careful aim, she drew back the bowstring and loosed the arrow.

Mordred had been striding briskly when the pace of the men carrying the ram suddenly slowed, forcing him to pause. At the same instant, an arrow came winging toward him. He flinched when the arrow struck the man just ahead of him. As the soldier cried out and tumbled from the ramparts, Mordred looked up to the roof of the tower. He caught sight of Annwr just before she withdrew behind the battlements.

Delwyn had gone back down the stairs to help his mother bring the infants to the roof when a thundering blow shook the entire tower. The walls were still reverberating when a second blow split the oaken beam, and the door flew open on its hinges with a crash. As the door recoiled from striking the wall, Delwyn slipped behind it and quietly drew his knife.

On Mordred's order, the soldiers moved aside so he could be first to enter the tower. He paused at the threshold while he searched the dim, moonlit room. He smiled when he saw Alys, backed into the far corner with two infants in her arms. "The Queen would be on the roof with the others, I presume?" he said, taking several steps forward. No sooner had he spoken those words than a shadowed figure silently darted out from behind the door. As moonlight flashed on the uprising blade, Mordred caught the movement out of the corner of his eye. He could only half turn before the knife came down, taking him in the flank. As Delwyn was raising his knife for a second blow, Mordred grabbed the boy's wrist. Twisting the boy's arm back, he slammed Delwyn's hand against the edge of the door. The boy cried out in pain as the knife spun to the floor.

Alys was begging Mordred not to hurt her son as soldiers rushed into the room after their commander. "Hold him," said Mordred, shoving the boy into the hands of two of his men. Stooping, he picked up the knife and tucked it under his belt. Then he touched the gash to his side. His thick, leather cuirass had saved him from what would have been a debilitating blow. As it was, the wound, though not deep, had drawn blood. Mordred wiped his sticky fingers on his sleeve.

"A scratch," said Mordred dismissively, in answer to his men's worried looks. "You and you, hold his mother. Budoc, you and your men follow me. The rest of you, see that no one escapes."

Mordred climbed the steep flight of stairs that led to the roof. At the top, he stopped and looked around warily. When he saw Annwr standing next to Gwenhwyfar on the opposite side of the roof, he quickly raced up the last few steps. As he strode across, he ordered the men running up the stairs behind him to seize the two women. Leaning over the wall of the parapet, he saw four of Annwr and Alys's eight children standing on the ground below. The fifth child was dangling from the end of the rope that Gwenhwyfar was still quickly playing out. With a curse, Mordred tore the rope from the Queen's hands and began hoisting the little boy back to the roof.

When Meleri saw what was happening, she jumped up and seized the rope. Gripping it with one hand, she drew her knife with the other and began hacking at the thick fabric. She and the boy had been lifted some ten feet in the air when it finally severed. As Mordred staggered backward awkwardly, the children fell tumbling to the ground. The little boy rose unhurt, but Meleri gasped in pain when she stood. In spite of her twisted ankle, she took both toddlers in her arms and exhorted with the other two children to follow as she limped toward the woods. Meanwhile, the troop of soldiers sent by Mordred rushed from the tower and out through the gates in pursuit of the children.

Gwenhwyfar and Annwr were struggling to break free as they were forced down the stairs and into the room below. The Queen's repeated commands that she and her friends be released at once fell on deaf ears. On Mordred's order, torches were brought, and the room was soon ablaze with light. Delwyn and the three women, each held by two soldiers, were lined up against one of the walls. The two babies, wrenched from Alys's arms, had been roughly set on the stone floor on the opposite side of the room. Mordred, regarding the babies, seemed annoyed by their incessant bawling.

"Please," said Gwenhwyfar to Mordred, "at least let me put something soft under them."

He smiled at her anxious look. "Of course," he said, removing his cloak. At a nod from Mordred, the men holding Gwenhwyfar released her.

The Queen took the cloak from his hands. Folding it, she put it on the floor next to the infants and placed them on top, carefully tucking the fabric around them. She cooed at the babies, but they continued to cry.

"Your attentions do not seem to be working," observed Mordred.

"They are cold and hungry," she retorted. "They will not stop crying until they are back in their mothers' arms."

"How soon those precious little babes can be returned to their mothers' arms depends entirely upon you."

"Immediately, then."

"Not quite so fast. First I must have a certain promise from you."

"What promise?"

"Your promise to wed me."

"Wed you! You must be mad to think that I would wed you after what you have done!"

"And what is it that you think I have done?"

She looked at him incredulously. "Why this! Everything!"

"Must I remind you that all this…unpleasantness…was entirely your doing. Had you not attempted to leave the fortress by stealth, none of it would have happened."

"Who are you to presume to bar me and my companions from leaving the fortress to visit our ailing friend who is not expected to live the night."

"Really! Was that the best story you could come up with? I should have thought that you were capable of spinning a more convincing tale than that."

"I am Queen of Britain. How dare you question my authority!"

"The king's consort, more exactly. And as you know, the king is dead. What power you may have had is gone with him."

"Our High King is not dead!" she said fiercely. Drawing herself up, she looked around the room and into each man's face as she spoke. "Loyal men of Britain, King Arthur is alive! His latest report from Armorica arrived earlier this very day. I saw my husband's signature on the parchment just before this traitor Mordred threw the document on the fire and handed me a forgery, falsely reporting King Arthur's death. Through his falsehoods, this traitor means to depose our rightful High King and usurp the throne of Britain! Do not believe any of the lies he has told you! In the name of High King Arthur Pendragon, I, Queen Gwenhwyfar, as the High King's Regent, order you to seize this man and keep him in custody until he can be brought to face justice as the traitor that he is!"

Not one of the stony-faced soldiers moved. Mordred laughed lightly. "A fine little speech, madam," he said. "But I'm afraid that you have not revealed anything that my loyal men don't already know."

"They know?" she said, looking around aghast.

"Of course they know. I hold nothing back from my men. And we are all of like mind. We believe that a king who willingly and thoughtlessly abandons his responsibilities to embroil and endanger his country in some frivolous overseas escapade is a king whom we are no longer obliged to follow. In effect Arthur abdicated his throne the moment he stepped off British soil to fight on behalf of some sickly distant relative too unfit to protect his own country. We must remember that Arthur's grandfather Constantine was from Armorica and his father Uther Pendragon was brought up there; perhaps Arthur considers himself more Armorican than Briton."

"That is not true," she retorted. "No one is more committed to protecting Britannia and her people than King Arthur."

"Yet where is he? Is he here among us? What sort of protection can our High King afford the British people when he is on the other side of the British Sea? Perhaps the same sort of protection he is affording you now?"

Gwenhwyfar was about to reply when she heard the doors of gateway below swing open, followed by the clatter of a troop of soldiers marching through. Beneath the clank of metal and the tramp of heavy boots she could hear the faint and fearful whimpers of children.

Mordred smiled. "Queen Gwenhwyfar, unless I'm very much mistaken, I do believe that we are about to witness the touching reunion of your two dear friends and their beloved children."

Minutes later, Budoc entered, followed by five of his men. Each of the soldiers was carrying a child. Meleri, whose hands had been bound, was thrashing forcefully in the arms of her captor. Mordred ordered another soldier to help hold the girl as she and the other children were lined up against the wall opposite their mothers. Annwr and Alys were struggling in vain to free themselves from their captors and to rush to the aid of their children.

"What a touching scene!" observed Mordred. "Truly, there is nothing stronger than the bond between a mother and her children."

"Let them go, Mordred. They have nothing to do with…with what you want. I promise I will not try to escape if you let my friends and their children leave the city."

"That is not the promise that I have been waiting to hear, Gwenhwyfar."

"What promise?"

"Your promise to wed me."

"You must be insane! You yourself admitted that my husband is alive!"

"A trifling and inconvenient detail, soon to be corrected. I ask you one more time, Gwenhwyfar. Will you wed me?"

"No! Never!"

"Good! I was actually hoping that would be your answer."

Pulling the knife from his belt, Mordred walked to where Delwyn was being held. He ignored the pleas of the women as he grabbed the boy's ear and twisted it cruelly. Then he hacked it off with the knife. Mordred paid no heed to Delwyn's screams as he tossed the ear to the floor and calmly wiped the blade clean across the front of the boy's tunic.

Nonchalantly, Mordred turned to Gwenhwyfar and asked, "Shall we alternate between Alys's and Annwr's brats?"

The women were begging Mordred to stop as he walked to Meleri. Positioning himself so they could see, he held the knife above the girl's ear. For a moment he stood, poised with the knife. Then he began lowering the blade. Meleri did not cry out, but her face became ashen as the knife cut into her skin. Gwenhwyfar was screaming to him to stop when he paused. A thick line of blood rose as he lifted the blade. "I'm still waiting, Gwenhwyfar," he warned.

"Yes! Yes! Anything! You have my word. I promise to marry you!" cried Gwenhwyfar.

"Good!" he said. As the women looked on in horror, he grabbed the girl's earlobe and sliced it off with a flick of the blade. "For your hesitation," he said, tossing it at Gwenhwyfar's feet. "As my wife you will learn that it is not a good idea to keep me waiting."

Chapter 15

Chase

A stooped and elderly white-haired man, standing in the moon-cast shadow of an outbuilding, was looking nervously toward the roof of his house. He started when he heard a sudden snort and then the light footfalls of someone coming up rapidly from behind. Turning around fearfully, he saw it was only his neighbor's dog, snuffling as she searched for tidbits along the street. With a sigh of relief, he turned his gaze back to the roof of his house.

Ever since King Arthur had left Britannia, there had been a feeling of unease among those living in the capital. That feeling had grown earlier that day when the gates of the fortress and the bridge leading into the city had been inexplicably closed, with no exceptions made or explanations given by any of the King's Harriers, the soldiers who now mostly garrisoned the fortress. Then, some time after dark, there had been shouts of men and women coming from inside the fortress, followed by thundering crashes, sounds of combat and cries of pain. The tumult had brought him and most of his neighbors out into the streets. Unlike his neighbors, however, he had remained outside long after the others had retreated into their homes and fearfully extinguished their lamps.

The sounds had ceased for some time when the man lying flat on the roof of his house began slowly backing away from its peak. When he reached the edge, he agilely lowered himself from the eaves onto the sloping roof of an attached shed before quietly slipping to the ground. When Madog peered at him questioningly, he put a finger to his lips. Nodding, the old man led his visitor back inside. Neither spoke a word until the door was closed.

"What did you see?" whispered Madog.

"It was as you feared," replied Hermogenes quietly. "The woman's voice that you heard was Queen Gwenhwyfar's. I saw her on the roof of the tower with another woman, along with a girl and a boy. They were shooting arrows and slingshot at their attackers. Then the Queen and the others began lowering children to the ground outside the walls of the fortress. Unfortunately, all five children were later recaptured after Prince Mordred and his men gained the tower and seized the Queen and her companion."

"Mordred! Then my fears about that man were correct! I warned Merlinus to beware Mordred the last time we spoke together. That was years ago now, of course. I've lost track of how many," said Madog. He paused while counting on his fingers. Then, impatiently, he waved his hands. "Anyway, however long ago it was, I told Merlinus then about my suspicions. Merlinus said that he shared my misgivings but refused to impeach a man on suspicions alone. I'm afraid that my dear friend's scruples, while admirable, were misplaced, as we have seen this very day. Yet, it is true; as Merlinus himself had observed to me all those years ago – how can one indict a criminal before he commits his crime? Then again, on the other hand, would it not have been better, for the greater good, to have prosecuted this traitor for his contemplated crimes rather than to have waited for him to have actually committed them and thus have innocents suffer and, indeed, have our very country put into jeopardy as a result?"

"Be that as it may, Mordred has now committed his crimes, and it is up to us to act. The woman on the roof with Gwenhwyfar, might she have been Bedwyr's wife Annwr?"

"She might have been either Lady Annwr or Lady Alys, both women are close companions of the Queen. But did you say she was shooting arrows? Why then yes, yes, that would no doubt have been the Lady Annwr – she's quite handy with a bow."

"And the boy and girl? I'd say they were both about thirteen years of age."

"About thirteen, you say? A boy and a girl? Let me think now," said Madog, pulling on his beard. "Ah, yes, yes, I know whom you saw. Actually they are both eleven, I believe, though they do appear a bit older than their age. The girl was, without doubt, Lady Annwr's daughter Meleri. A most lively girl she is. And the boy would have been Delwyn, Lord Cei's eldest son. Delwyn and Meleri can rarely be found if not in each other's company."

Hermogenes nodded, looking worried. "Do you think Princess Elen and her two sons could be with the Queen?"

"The Lady Alys could be, but not Princess Elen or her sons, praise the gods! Princess Elen took both boys to Tintagel shortly after her husband left for Armorica. Her brother, Lord Efan, is warden of Tintagel while King Cador and Prince Constantine are away."

"Praise the gods indeed! But Princess Elen must be warned. She and her sons will be in grave danger if Mordred's men reach the fortress before word is received there of his treachery. I must make for Tintagel at once."

"But you have only just arrived. Surely you will stay the night after your long journey?"

"No, I thank you, but I fear I cannot. I must reach Tintagel before Mordred's men do. Hopefully they won't be leaving until daybreak."

"Which way will you go? The bridge, as you know, has been closed."

"Fortunately, I came by way of Burrium. I left my horse hidden in the woods outside of town."

"Fortunate indeed!"

"Actually more than just good fortune. Queen Ganieda warned me to be cautious as I approached Isca. I'm glad I took her always prudent advice."

"How is Queen Ganieda? I have not seen her in many a year now, though we do still correspond."

"The queen is well, but concerned about the true state of affairs of our country. Rightly so as we have seen. That's why she sent me here."

"Most perspicacious, as usual. Although she protests that she lacks her brother's gifts, I do believe that she shares more than a little of his prophetic ability. Has there been any news of dear Merlinus?"

"Sadly no, he has not been seen in over two years. Queen Ganieda is convinced, however, that her brother still lives. But my dear sir, I really must be off. Though I hesitate to leave you here on your own with the capital in turmoil."

"I'll be fine; I assure you. My daughter and her husband live nearby. And if it is my time to go, well, I've lived a good long life. May the gods speed you on your way, good Hermogenes. When you next see Queen Ganieda, kindly tell her that old Madog keeps her and her brother always in his prayers."

"I will, sir; I thank you."

Hermogenes was some hours from Tintagel when he stopped at a stream to water his horse. While the horse drank, he looked back up the road toward the rising land over which he had just ridden. Seeing no one, he slipped to the ground. His legs were shaking as he unsaddled the gelding and tied it where it could graze.

Although he had ridden hard for the past three days, he still had the unshakeable feeling that Mordred's men had not been far behind. He was well aware that he had lost precious time when he had had to make his way back through the woods to retrieve his horse and then ride all the way north to Burrium in order to cross the River Usk. Mordred's men, he knew, would have taken the shorter route, crossing the river at Isca and riding directly to Glevum.

After drinking deeply at the stream himself and filling his empty flask with water, he walked back up the road. At the top of the rise, he scanned the open and desolate lands to the east. He gasped when he saw a cloud of dust rising above the road, no doubt marking the approach of a large group of mounted men. Not two miles away, they were coming up fast. Turning, Hermogenes raced back down the road and hurriedly saddled his horse. Vaulting onto the saddle, he scanned the barren, treeless terrain stretching out for miles before him. With concealment impossible and on a tired horse, he decided that his only recourse was to allow himself to be overtaken. The likelihood that he would be recognized by any of Mordred's men was small. Further, as a precaution, he had brought with him two saddlebags full of small useful items – brooches and buckles, ribbons and hairpins, salt and spices, needles and thread and the like to provide himself a cover story as an itinerant merchant should he be challenged. With any luck his story would be accepted. Then, once the soldiers were out of sight, he would ride cross-country to the lesser-used coastal route and try to reach Tintagel before they did.

Setting his horse off at a walk, Hermogenes soon heard the approaching hoofbeats. He turned in the saddle and watched as a troop of some hundred soldiers, wearing the colors of the King's Harriers, crested the height of land. The officer riding at their head was a man well known to him. Before Budoc's promotion as third in command of the King's Harriers, he had regularly traveled to Brocavum in his capacity as royal messenger. Although Hermogenes had allowed a beard to grow, he realized that Budoc would no doubt recognize him as Queen Ganieda's agent. Quickly, Hermogenes untied his saddlebags and tossed them to the ground to lessen the weight that his mount bore. Ignoring Budoc's command to halt, he spurred his horse to a gallop. The Harriers replied by thundering down the hill in pursuit.

Princess Elen had been watching her sons Arwel and Aled practice their sword fighting skills with her nephew Conanus when she decided to take a short walk before dinner. Although she had been one of Queen Igraine's handmaidens at Tintagel for many years, she now found the fortress confining, having become used to the comforts and freedom of Isca. After speaking a few words of her intentions to her brother Efan, who was supervising the boys, she walked up the path to the walled garden that had been created for Queen Igraine's enjoyment. While she was picking a bouquet of the late summer blooms, she decided that after laying the flowers on Queen Igraine's grave, she would walk a little further along the sea cliff to the spot where Prince Constantine had proposed to her. She smiled as she remembered how deliriously happy she had been that day. So happy, in fact, that his proposal had left her quite speechless, and she had only been able to accept him with a passionate kiss. What had precipitously followed still made her blush. Constantine had later quipped that he had not at all minded how his proposal had been accepted. Her smile faded as she contemplated where her husband was now. She resolved then and there that instead of taking a walk, she would go into the church beside the graveyard and pray to God that He watch over and protect the man whom she loved.

After leaving the garden, Elen made her way down the hill to the fortress gates. There, the captain of the guards politely offered to assist her in making the crossing. She was happy to accept his help. Clutching the bouquet in one hand, she tightly held his arm with the other as they passed through the gate and stepped out onto the knife-edged neck of land that connected the fortress to the mainland. The gusty wind and the incessant waves crashing far below against the base of the rocky citadel never failed to make her feel giddy and unsteady on her feet. Once on the other side, they walked across the outer ward of another fortification that had been built behind a deep defensive ditch. The only exit was along a narrow and vertiginous path that had been cut into the side of a cliff. Elen dreaded this second crossing almost as much as the first. As she and the captain were nearing the gateway, one of the guards standing on the ramparts above called down that a rider was rapidly approaching. Hurriedly excusing himself, the captain left the princess and quickly climbed up the flight of stone steps.

Joining the guards on the ramparts, the captain could see a civilian galloping his horse toward the fortress at breakneck speed. When the rider reached the great ditch, he did not dismount but instead urged his foaming and sweat-covered horse onto the narrow path. The exhausted animal, its legs shaking, teetered dangerously close to the edge as it advanced. The captain could not imagine why the rider was taking such a risk when he sighted a large number of cavalrymen galloping their horses in pursuit. By their colors, he recognized them as King's Harriers. Meanwhile, the fugitve had reached the gateway and was shouting to be let in.

"Should I open the gates for him, captain?" called the porter.

"No! Not until I find out why the Harriers are chasing him."

When the man heard the captain, he looked up and cried, "Please, no! Then it will be too late! Please listen to me. My name is Hermogenes; I am Queen Ganieda's agent. Prince Mordred has usurped the throne! I was in Isca when I witnessed Mordred seize Queen Gwenhwyfar and her companions by force. These Harriers who are pursuing me are Mordred's men. They'll silence me and tell you only lies. Please, open the gates now."

"Prince Mordred usurp the throne? And seize the Queen by force?" scoffed the captain. "What kind of story are you trying to spin? I'll wager it's you who's telling the lies! Seems to me that you're a fugitive, hoping to escape justice with some wild tale."

"No," exclaimed Hermogenes breathlessly, "I'm telling no tale. Please, listen to me! These soldiers mean to harm Princess Elen and her sons! Please open the gates! Look," he said, drawing his sword and tossing it to the ground, "I come unarmed. At least let me speak to Princess Elen!"

"Porter, open the gates immediately," a woman's voice commanded.

The captain turned, surprised to find the princess standing next to him on the ramparts.

"But Princess Elen, this man is clearly a fugitive. He could be dangerous. We should first speak to the commander of the Harriers."

"Did you not hear Hermogenes? And see him toss away his sword? Captain, I know this man. He is who he says he is, and I trust him and Queen Ganieda explicitly. Porter, admit Hermogenes at once. Then bar the doors again. Do not admit any of the Harriers."

The captain had opened his mouth to countermand her order but closed it again when she shot him a pointed look. The porter had begun pushing the massive beam into a recess in the wall to open the gate as the Harriers came thundering up to the edge of the great ditch. Budoc, who had been riding at their head, spurred his mount forward onto the narrow path, but his horse jibbed sharply at the precipitous crossing. Thrown from the saddle, Budoc saved himself by wrapping his arms around his horse's neck. With his feet dangling some thirty feet above the sharpened stakes set into the bottom of the ditch, he held on for dear life. As the frightened animal backed up, Budoc gained his footing on the path. Cursing his mount, he wiped his sweaty palms on his sleeves and drew his sword. Racing on foot across the narrow path, he reached the gate just as the massive oaken door slammed shut in his face.

大Chapter 16

Beyond Doubt

Lucius was standing in the bow of the *Fulmar* as it rounded a curve on the river, and Drustan's flagship came into view. Two Saxon war boats were attached to the *Sea Eagle's* side, and the ship was being driven by the wind and tide onto the shoals along the river's east bank. Lucius immediately ordered his steersman to head for the beleaguered ship but had to belay his command moments later when he sighted three enemy vessels swiftly approaching his own on the incoming tide. As soon as the closest vessel came within range, Lucius ordered his soldiers to shoot at will. The Britons' barrage of arrows and lead pellets was so intense that the Saxons gave up the chase and veered off. Jeering loudly at their cowardly comrades, the Saxons in the other two vessels made for the Britons at speed. Lucius's steersman managed to outmaneuver the second vessel and sail past it. The sleek, narrow Saxon boats, some seventy-five feet long, were swift but difficult to turn, and the *Fulmar* soon left it in its wake. The third boat, however, anticipating the Britons' change of tack, came up at speed and slammed against the ship's port side. Throwing grappling irons and pulling their vessel close, the Saxons began swarming on board. Lucius and his men drew their weapons and fought back in the close, hand-to-hand combat. When the short, brutal battle was over, not a Saxon remained alive, though the victory had not been without cost to the Britons who had lost nine men with five more badly wounded.

Once the *Fulmar* had been freed from the Saxon boat, Lucius ordered his steersman to make for the *Sea Eagle*. As they were nearing the ship, Lucius could see Lord Drustan in the stern, holding the tiller. Even with an arrow buried deeply in his shoulder, the Sea Hawks' commander was still shouting orders to his men. Just then, Lucius spotted a lone figure in one of the boats fastened to the flagship. It was Meliot, calmly nocking an arrow. Lucius ordered his archers to shoot the traitor, but at that distance their arrows fell just short of their target, striking the water. Standing, Meliot took aim and loosed the arrow at the Sea Hawks' commander. It struck Lord Drustan in the chest. Overpowered by rage, Lucius ordered his steersman to ram Meliot's vessel at speed.

Drustan, who was still managing to stand, though barely, shook his head when he saw the *Fulmar* approaching. Although he could no longer speak, he signaled clearly to Lucius that he was to continue down the river. Lucius, with tears in his eyes, saluted and called out that he understood and would obey his superior officer's command. Satisfied, Drustan nodded and returned the salute. A second later, the *Sea Eagle* lurched to a halt on the shoals. Drustan stumbled, then collapsed out of sight onto the deck. No other Briton on board the flagship remained alive to render aid to his commanding officer. The last thing Lucius saw before he turned away was a ring of Saxons, their swords and axes flashing, as they raised them against the fallen British commander.

Wiping his eyes, Lucius looked back up the river to count how many Sea Hawk ships had come through. He was shocked to discover that none were following his own. Not far behind, the two Saxon vessels had turned and were once again closing on the *Fulmar*. Ahead, he saw a line of ten Saxon vessels, blockading the river's mouth. With bleak acceptance, Lucius realized it would be impossible to break through the enemy line. But at least, he decided grimly, he and his men would take more than a few Saxons with them before going down themselves. Then he remembered his mission. If he failed to carry out Lord Drustan's final command to him, King Arthur and Princess Elen might not receive word of Mordred's treachery until it was too late. The urgency of that charge made Lucius determined not to fail. And when he looked into the firmly set faces of the men around him, he knew that these last of the Sea Hawks shared his resolve.

It was dawn on the sixth day of the siege when Budoc strode up under a white flag of truce and stopped before the shut gates of Tintagel. As usual, Princess Elen and her brother Lord Efan stood side-by-side on the ramparts to listen to what he had to say. With each passing day, Budoc's demands had become more and more strident. Today, he delivered a final ultimatum to Princess Elen: by order of the regents of Britannia, Princess Elen was to release the two princes into the care of the King's Harriers, to be escorted safely back to Isca for the coronation of Prince Arwel as High King of Britain, or both of her sons' claims to the throne would be forever forfeit. Princess Elen's answer remained the same: she would not be deceived by a lying henchman who would kill her sons and put the traitor Mordred upon the throne.

Upon hearing her words, Budoc angrily tossed the white flag into the ditch and stalked back to the barricade which his men had built across the road leading to the fortress. As soon as he stepped behind the barrier, four Harrier archers, who had concealed themselves during the night within bow range of the fortress, stood and loosed their arrows at Princess Elen and Lord Efan. Grabbing each other, the siblings threw themselves behind the parapet, and the arrows flew harmlessly over their heads. By the time their guards shot arrows in reply, the four archers had darted back to safety behind the barricade. This overt display of treachery dispelled any doubt that may have been remaining in anyone's mind about the Harriers' murderous intent and the veracity of Hermogenes's account.

A fishing boat, making its way back to its homeport, had just entered the Solent, the narrow strait between the mainland and the island of Vectis, lying off the southern coast. The two men on board the boat were brothers who regularly plied those coastal waters, delivering their catches on market days to towns along Britain's southern shores. Today, they were returning after having sold a particularly large and lucrative haul at Lacuna, the harbor town not far south of Vindocladia. Normally, with so many coins jingling in their bags, the brothers would have been in a merry mood, looking forward to putting more than a few to good use at the quayside inn at Clausentum. But now, after having learned the terrible news, the two were silent as they contemplated what this calamity meant not only for themselves but also for their entire country. It was still almost impossible for them to comprehend that King Arthur was dead.

As children growing up on the south coast of Britannia, their lives had been fraught with danger. During the turbulent years following King Uther's death, Saxons had often breached the boundaries of their treaty lands, raiding British homesteads and villages with impunity. Their own father, a master boat builder, had been killed during one of those raids. The boys had escaped their father's fate or a life of slavery only because they had been out fishing at the time. Years later, during the wars with the Saxons, when King Arthur's advisor, Merlinus Ambrosius, had quietly sought the help of fishermen to spy on enemy troop movements, the two had eagerly enlisted. Although they had been partly motivated by the prospect of adventure and excitement, thoughts of vengeance had never been far from their minds. After the war the two brothers had been lauded by King Arthur in the great hall at Isca in front of thousands of people. The High King had declared that if not for their courage and diligence, the invading army from Germania would never have been detected and the entire British cause lost. Then the king had placed over each of their heads, a silver chain bearing a gold medallion emblazoned with the image of the Red Dragon of Britain, the highest honor a civilian could achieve. The brothers had proudly worn them every day since. Now, sailing on in silence, they fingered their medallions unconsciously as they brooded darkly on an uncertain future in a Britain without King Arthur.

The brothers were torn from their gloomy reveries when the mouth of the Itchen River came into distant view. Their worst fears suddenly seemed realized when they sighted a line of Saxon war boats, blocking the river's entrance. Heading downstream toward the enemy blockade was a single British ship. By its familiar shape and size, they recognized it at once as Captain Lucius's vessel. Without a word or a second thought, the brothers sailed resolutely onward.

They were still some distance away when they saw the *Fulmar* suddenly veer toward the river's west bank. When the two Saxon boats that had been closely following the ship turned back sharply into the main channel to avoid running aground, the brothers only smiled at the British captain's maneuver. Between the shoals and the riverbank was a narrow channel, navigable only toward high tide. By the time the Saxons in the two boats realized that they had been tricked, the intervening shoals were already blocking their pursuit.

Meanwhile, the commander of the Saxon blockade, not understanding why the two boats were not closing in on the British ship, angrily signaled his fleet forward. The commander's vessel was in the forefront, set on a direct course to intercept the British ship. Eagerly, the Saxon leader stood in the bow as his great war boat's prow sliced through the water toward this last of the Sea Hawks' ships. Close by, to either side, sped the other boats of the fleet, whose occupants were just as anxious for their share of the glory. Suddenly, the steersman in the lead boat shouted "halt" to the rowers. Furious, the Saxon commander countermanded the order and turned to upbraid the steersman. A second later he was flying though the air. At the same instant, the rowers in the boat were thrown violently backward, head over heels, landing sprawled on the bottom of the boat. Only the steersman, anticipating the jolt and holding on tightly to the tiller, managed to remain upright. A moment later, the four vessels that had been jockeying closely for second place, also came to a dead halt, with similar results to their crew, while the other boats of the fleet were crashing together as they swerved to avoid running aground on the hidden shoal.

Meanwhile, the Saxon commander, who had been pitched overboard, was screaming for help as he flailed in the shallow water. After trying to stand, he was sinking fast in mud that was already reaching his hips. By the time an oar had been extended to him, and he had been pulled from the mud with great effort and a loud sucking noise, the British ship had already sailed out into the inlet.

As the brothers neared the *Fulmar*, cheering and waving their arms, the jubilant Sea Hawks returned the fishermen's cheers and grins. Only Lucius looked back anxiously at the Saxons during this brief moment of triumph. Although the enemy was still in disarray, Lucius called out to the brothers that he needed to speak with them, but would not do so until they were safely out in the open waters of the channel. Understanding the captain's caution, the fishermen saluted and brought their boat about in order to follow.

Even after his ship had exited the inlet, Lucius remained wary. Rather than setting a westerly course along the Solent, where another ambush might lie at its constricted western end, Lucius set his ship on a southeasterly course. Not until the *Fulmar* had entered the calm waters on the leeward side of the Isle of Vectis did he have the sails struck. Striking their own, the two brothers came up alongside, within easy hailing distance.

Quickly, Lucius explained the circumstances leading up to the battle and the treachery of Prince Mordred, Lord Meliot and the Harriers. The brothers gave exclamations of shock and dismay when they heard the account of Lord Drustan's death and learned of the full extent of British losses during the calamitous battle. That the Saxons were capable of such treachery the brothers could easily fathom, but that the King's Harriers and the regent himself were complicit was hard for them to grasp.

"Do you mean Prince Mordred and the King's Harriers have joined with the Saxons?" asked Gallus, the younger brother.

"I fear it is beyond doubt. It was the regent who ordered Lord Drustan into a trap, and with my own eyes I saw numerous Harriers in the Saxon boats and witnessed their leader, that coward Meliot, use arrows to cut down our noble commander."

"What about the other regent? Could Queen Gwenhwyfar have known?" Gallus had openly voiced the question that had been niggling at the back of Lucius's mind.

"I can't believe that the Queen could in any way be involved," stated Lucius firmly, though he spoke with more confidence than he felt.

"What's to be done now, Captain?" asked Mori, the elder brother. "Is there anything we can do to help?"

"Yes. Yes, there is, and I thank God you arrived when you did! Lord Drustan's final command to me was to warn King Arthur and Princess Elen of Mordred's treachery. I have been torn since both need to be informed without delay. But now my mind is at ease, knowing that as I go to Tintagel to warn Princess Elen, you and Gallus will be taking this urgent news to King Arthur."

The brothers were aghast. Finally the elder brother said, "Captain, haven't you heard? About King Arthur?"

"What about King Arthur?" said Lucius, with growing dread.

The two brothers hesitated, looking at each other. Then Mori said, "King Arthur…our High King…is dead!"

For a moment Lucius was not able speak. "King Arthur…dead? How? When? How do you know?"

"We were in the market square at Lacuna early this morning when a royal herald arrived. He read a report that had been sent by Lord Cei from Armorica. Lord Cei said that King Arthur had been killed in an ambush by the Franks. King Arthur, King Cador, Prince Constantine and Prince Gawain were all killed. And over half our army was lost."

Lucius had to grasp the gunwale for support. He looked stunned, as if by a blow. After some time had passed he said, "No, I had not heard. No word had been brought to Clausentum. This is terrible! Terrible beyond belief!" He paused to think. "Yet this horrific news explains Mordred's actions. Learning that King Arthur was dead, the regent decided to make a bid for the throne while our country is vulnerable. Even going so far as forming an alliance with our enemies! I pray to God I reach Tintagel in time. It's clear that Mordred would not hesitate to murder the two princes or anyone else who stands in his way."

"What do you want us to do, Captain? Should we still go to Armorica?" asked Mori.

Lucius considered. "Yes. Lord Cei must now be in command of our forces. He needs to be informed of Mordred's treachery. Go to Armorica and find out where our army is. Take care that you do not fall into the hands of the Franks. Let Lord Cei know what has happened at Clausentum. As soon as I have delivered my message to Princess Elen, I will join you at Armorica. Lord Cei will need every ship he can get his hands on to transport our troops back to Britain. If Mordred is to be stopped, our army must return to Britain at once!"

Chapter 17

Journey to Tintagel

After bidding the brothers farewell, Lucius had put in briefly at a nearby harbor town on Vectis to place his wounded men into the care of a trusted doctor. Since then, during the days-long voyage, the captain had had much time to reflect. He now realized that the likelihood of Mordred having not already seized and taken the two remaining heirs into custody was virtually nil. Most likely, the two princes were already dead. Nevertheless, he continued to pray for a miracle while a glimmer of hope remained, determined to obey Lord Drustan's final command to him.

Lucius had kept the ship close to shore as it made its way up the Sabrina Estuary toward Tintagel. The fortress was still over an hour away when the *Fulmar* put in beneath the towering cliffs of a sheltered cove. As the ship approached the sandy beach in the fading light of the setting sun, two men dressed in dark clothing jumped over the gunwales and into the water. After swimming through the surf to the shore, they began scrambling up the cliff face. When Lucius saw them reach the top, he moved the ship further out into the cove and dropped anchor to await his scouts' findings.

It was well past nightfall when the two men, proceeding cautiously along the coastal path, sighted a small church, silhouetted darkly against the star-filled sky. Beyond the church and rising steeply from the sea to their left was the brooding hulk of land upon which the fortress Tintagel stood. Even from this distance, they could hear the dull thump of waves, pounding ceaselessly against the citadel's rocky base. Ahead, the flickering glow that they had detected earlier resolved into a small campfire, built directly on the path. They froze when they saw a figure cross in front of the flames and disappear into the darkness. Moments later, the figure returned and added some sticks to the fire. Signaling silently to his fellow, one of the

Sea Hawks began circling around the back of the church toward the lane leading to the entrance of the fortress. Meanwhile, the other scout stealthily advanced. When he came adjacent to the church, he stepped through the gateway and entered the cemetery. Inside the ancient enclosure, he had to tread carefully on ground uneven with sunken graves and scattered tumuli, the final resting places of generations of Dumnonian nobility. More than once he stumbled over a low, eroded mound, hidden by darkness and high grass. As he was walking past the tallest and most recent burial mound, he crossed himself, as much for protection as for reverence. After the death of her son, he feared that the shade of Queen Igraine would no longer be resting peacefully.

At the far end of the cemetery, he crouched behind a stonewall, heavily furred with lichen. Slowly raising his head, he could see the campfire, now less than fifty feet away. A soldier standing next to it was soon joined by two others, hiking up their breeches after having relieved themselves. All three threw themselves comfortably on the ground and began passing around a flask. Then one of them pulled out knucklebones, and they began to play. Although they were apparently picket guards, and Harriers by their dress, they had the indolent air of soldiers bored by days of inaction during siege warfare. Their commander, whoever he might be, must have been just as complacent as his men to allow such dereliction.

The scout continued to watch and listen, but the guards' conversation was mere gutter talk, broken occasionally by guffaws over a crude joke. At one point he heard one of them mention Princess Elen's name. He tried to catch the gist of what he was saying, but the soldier had his back to him and, of the three, was the least loud. So intent was the scout on trying to make out the words that he failed to hear the soft footfalls coming up from behind him. When a twig snapped and he turned, a tall, dark figure was just paces away. He gasped before he could stop himself. The other Sea Hawk put a finger to his lips, but it was already too late. The picket guards had jumped to their feet.

"Where did it come from?" said one of them.

"Over there, in the cemetery."

Looking toward the wall, the men drew their swords. Just then, leaping from her perch on the roof of the church, a white shape swooped low over the heads of the scouts. Screaming loudly, she flew at the three soldiers, her angry, hissing cry sounding like a Fury's. The ghostly apparition circled twice around the guards before vanishing into darkness.

"It's only that blasted owl again," said one of the Harriers with bravado, though his hand was still shaking as he thrust his sword back into its scabbard.

One of the other guards was doubled over, laughing at him. "You should see your face. You're just as white as that owl."

"You should see your own stupid face. I swear I'm gonna put an arrow through that damned bird."

"I'd like to see you try. You'd be shaking too hard."

"Are you calling me a coward? 'Cause if you are, we can settle that right here and now."

"Hoi! Will you two jus' shut it and get back to the game. Don't think fightin' over nothin' made me forget tha' both o' you owe me money."

Once the soldiers had resumed playing, the scouts quietly backed away from the wall. Before leaving the churchyard, they turned to make sure they were not being followed. As they did, a ghostly white shape silently materialized from out of the darkness and alighted on top of Queen Igraine's tomb, her large, brown eyes fixed directly upon them. Giving each other a frightened look, both men crossed themselves and hurried away.

Captain Lucius was thoughtful after he heard his scouts' report.

"How many men did you see near the fortress?" he asked one.

"About a dozen, but from the number of tents and campfires I saw, there must be a hundred, maybe more. And they've built a barricade across the road leading to the gate. It looks like they've been there for a while."

"I think we may also gather that from the lax behavior of those picket guards," said Lucius. "Their complacency is going to be to our advantage since they're apparently not expecting any opposing forces to break their siege."

The scouts looked at each other apprehensively. Then one of them said, "May I speak, Captain."

"Of course."

"You're not planning on attacking them, are you, Captain?"

"Thirty-four against over a hundred? No, I think not. Even with the element of surprise, the odds would be in their favor. There is a way, however, to enter the fortress without confronting Mordred's forces."

The two scouts looked at the captain quizzically.

"Gather everyone on deck and I'll explain."

After leaving the cabin, one of the scouts whispered to the other, "Do you think we should have told the captain about that owl?"

"Naw, I don't think so. Makes us sound a bit daft. Besides, if it is the shade of Queen Igraine, it looks like she's on our side."

After sailing around the jutting fist of land upon which the fortress Tintagel stood, the *Fulmar* put into the narrow cove on the leeward side of the promontory. Under the dim light of a crescent moon, the crew maneuvered the ship into the deep water alongside the sheer cliff face. Lowering anchors at both bow and stern, they moored the ship so that it was beneath the crane used to hoist heavy cargo directly into the fortress. The great arm of the crane reached out from a platform built into the cliffside, over a hundred feet above. The ship, anchored behind the rocky point projecting into the cove, could not be seen by besiegers positioned at the fortress's entrance on the mainland. Even so, Lucius remained silent as he mimed his intentions to the two soldiers standing on duty there. A third was already hurrying up the precipitous path to the fortress, no doubt to alert the garrison commander of the ship's arrival. Some minutes later, the soldier returned with three others, one of whom was a woman.

Lucius gave a signal to those above. Indicating that they understood him, one of the men began lowering a massive iron hook that was fastened by a thick rope to the pulley block at the end of the crane. When the rope came within reach, Lucius grabbed it and stepped onto the hook. Soon, he was swinging high over his ship as he was hoisted up. Using his vantage to scan for signs of the enemy, he spotted a distant campfire that had been built on the cliffs northeast of the fortress. He could only hope that the picket guards stationed there were just as lax as their fellows to the south.

When he had been lifted high enough, another soldier began hauling on a line that drew the swinging arm of the crane inwards on its pivot. As Lucius was brought near, he was helped onto the platform. Giving thanks to them all, he turned to the woman. Quite overcome with emotion, he fell to one knee before her. "Princess Elen, I thank God you are well."

"As I thank God that you are also well, Captain Lucius," she replied. "Please rise, sir, and tell us your news."

"Thank you," he replied. "But, please, first tell me; how are the Princes Arwel and Aled?"

"Both are safe and here in the fortress, thanks to this man," she said. "Captain, have you met Queen Ganieda's agent, Hermogenes? It was he who warned us of Prince Mordred's treachery, arriving only seconds before the Harriers. If not for him, neither I nor my sons would be alive today."

"Please let me shake your hand, sir," said Lucius with great feeling.

"It is an honor to meet you, Captain."

"Captain Lucius, have you met my brother, Lord Efan?"

"It is an honor, Lord."

"Mine too," replied Efan briskly. "But since time is short and your ship's position perilous, tell us your news. And can you tell us where Lord Drustan is? We saw his fleet pass by some time ago, but until your arrival, we have not seen his or any other Sea Hawk vessel since."

"Alas, Lord, that is my news, and I fear it is grave. Lord Commander Drustan lost his life in a naval engagement five days ago. We were ambushed at Clausentum by the Harriers and their Saxon allies in a trap set by Prince Mordred."

"The Harriers and their *Saxon* allies!" said Efan, shocked.

"I fear it is true, Lord. There were numerous Harriers on board the forty Saxon war boats that attacked us. And with my own eyes I witnessed that coward Meliot use an arrow to cut down Lord Drustan from afar."

As the others became increasingly distressed, Lucius briefly recounted the battle and its disastrous outcome. There was silence when he finished.

"Then it is even worse than we imagined," Lord Efan finally said. "King Arthur, King Cador and Prince Constantine dead, our fleet destroyed, Mordred on the throne, and now we learn that the Harriers are allied with the Saxons."

"Mordred on the throne?"

"Yes. Just this morning we were informed by that treacherous windbag Budoc that Mordred has 'reluctantly' accepted the throne. And he has taken Queen Gwenhwyfar as his wife."

"Then the Queen is complicit!"

"No, sir, the Queen most certainly is not," broke in Hermogenes. "I had been sent to Isca by Queen Ganieda, who had became suspicious of Mordred. I had only just arrived when sounds of combat were heard coming from inside the fortress. Since the gates had been shut, I climbed on the roof of a house to see what was happening. With my own eyes I saw Queen Gwenhwyfar on top of one of the towers, fighting like a lioness. Then, using a rope, she began lowering her ladies' children to the ground so that they could escape. Unfortunately, the Queen and her ladies were overwhelmed by Mordred and his forces and taken into captivity and the children later recaptured. I can assure you, Captain, that any so-called marriage was coerced."

"I thank you for your correction, sir. I should have realized that Queen Gwenhwyfar would never…"

"Look there!" said Efan abruptly. Turning to where he was pointing, Lucius could see two men on the other side of the cove, running toward the main encampment.

Urgently, Lucius said, "Princess Elen, if you and your sons come with me, I will take you to safety."

"Safety? And where is that, Captain? Not at Isca, nor at Clausentum and certainly not at Armorica where my dear husband…" she broke off. "No, Captain, I thank you with all my heart for your offer, but my sons and I shall stay here and take our chances. This place is as safe as any other – safer perhaps – and we are well-provisioned."

Lucius nodded. "Then I will cross the British Sea and do what I can to help Lord Cei bring our remaining troops back to Britain. With the help of God, we shall defeat the usurper and put Prince Arwel, King Arthur's rightful heir, on the throne."

"Amen to that prayer. May God always guide and protect you, Captain," said Elen.

"As I pray that He always guides and protects you and yours, Princess Elen."

As Lucius turned to leave, Hermogenes said, "Captain, if I may, I would come with you – to refute Mordred's lies and to do what I can in Armorica."

"Certainly, Hermogenes. Your help is most welcome. Come down after me then."

Once Lucius had returned to his ship, the hook was quickly lifted again. When it came within reach, Hermogenes grabbed the rope.

Looking at him anxiously, Elen said, "God go with you, good Hermogenes."

"And may God go always with you and yours, Princess."

Agilely, he pulled himself up and stepped onto the hook. As he was swung out high over the ship, Hermogenes caught sight of soldiers assembling along the far side of the cove. Before he could open his mouth to alert those below, he heard Lucius shout, "Get down!" as Budoc bellowed, "Loose!"

Dozens of arrows came winging toward him and the ship. With relief, Hermogenes watched them strike the water, short of their intended targets. Just then, he saw several archers clambering out onto the rocks directly opposite the ship. He shouted a warning to the Sea Hawks. A moment later, he felt searing pain as an arrow tore through his arm and another struck his shoulder. Losing his grip, he began to fall backwards. Desperately, he clawed for the rope, but it was already beyond his grasp. Plummeting, he came to a jarring halt when one of his boots became wedged in the hook. Stunned and bleeding freely as he hung suspended, upside down, he felt himself growing increasingly light-headed. Coming distantly from somewhere, he could hear a woman, frantically urging someone to hurry. The sound of concern in her voice made him smile. Far below him, he could see tiny sailors scrambling about in a toy ship. Hovering over them, he felt quite calm and detached while he watched them. This, he thought, must be how the dead observe the living. When he saw them looking at him anxiously, he wanted to call down to them, to let them know that he was no longer in any pain, but found that he no longer had a voice. Curiously, the men appeared to be growing ever larger, though they still seemed no bigger than dolls when he felt his foot slip from his boot. A woman's scream was the last thing he heard before slamming onto the deck.

Chapter 18

In Armorica

Lord Cei was standing with his companions on a height of land, watching as the enemy withdrew once again to avoid battle. Although the Franks had continued their northward flight for many days, Cei knew that on the ever-narrowing peninsula, they would soon be forced to stand and fight. There was no doubt in his mind that in an open, pitched battle the Britons would be victorious, and they would all soon be going home. He smiled as he thought about the triumphal homecoming they would be receiving from their grateful countrymen, and he smiled even more broadly when he thought about the greeting he would receive from his wife. With concern, he suddenly realized he would need to bring home gifts for Alys and his four sons. After some thought, he decided he would give his wife a nice piece of jewelry, maybe the kind with a design made of cut garnets set into little cells of gold. To his middle sons he would give good Frankish daggers and to Delwyn, his eldest, who was now almost a man, he would give nothing less than a fine Frankish sword. But he was at a loss as he pondered what to give to his youngest who was only a baby when he left. Some sort of toy, he concluded, which he could easily find in Condate Riedonum. No doubt there would be a victory celebration for them back at the Armorican capital before they returned to Britain. Silently, he began counting on his fingers to figure out how many months old his youngest must be now, but his calculations were suddenly cut short by the approach of two guards. He was surprised when they addressed him rather than the man standing at his side.

"Lord Cei, two Britons from Clausentum who are most insistent on seeing you have arrived. They say they bear important news for you."

Cei turned to the other man in bewilderment. That man shrugged, smiling.

"Er, yes, well, bring them over."

Cei was still mystified as two men who were strangers to him came forward and bowed respectfully. "Lord Cei, we bring you urgent news from Britain," said one.

"For me?"

"Yes, Lord," replied the other.

Recognizing them, Cei's companion stepped from the group. When the two brothers saw him, they gasped and fell to their knees. Looking up in amazement, they said simultaneously, "You're alive!"

A jocular reply leapt to Arthur's mind, but he checked it, knowing that only a serious matter could have brought them to Armorica. After embracing each in turn he said, "Mori and Gallus, tell me what has brought you all the way here."

"News from Britain, Lord King, and none of it good," replied Mori.

"Tell me quickly then. Hold nothing back."

"Treachery, Lord King."

"Whose?'

"Prince Mordred's."

"That's a lie!" someone shouted. Balling his hands into fists, a tall, brawny man, his face as flaming as his hair, strode threateningly toward the brothers.

"Hold off, Gawain. I know these men." Turning to Mori, Arthur said sharply, "Do you know what you are saying!"

"We know, Lord King."

"How do you know?"

"Lord King, we can only tell you what we were told by Captain Lucius, what we have heard, and what we have seen with our own eyes," replied Mori, looking cautiously at Gawain glowering down on him. "My brother and I were sailing back to our homeport at Clausentum when we spotted ten Saxon war boats blocking the mouth of the Itchen River. Heading downstream toward them was the *Fulmar*, Captain Lucius's ship. The Saxons attacked the ship, but the captain outmaneuvered them and broke free. Later, Captain Lucius himself told us that Prince Mordred had ordered Lord Drustan and the entire Sea Hawk fleet to sail to Clausentum. The regent had said that a large show of force was necessary to stop the Saxons from making some trade violations, but in truth he was sending the Sea Hawks into a trap. Captain Lucius saw many of the King's Harriers in the Saxon boats that attacked them."

"How did he know they were really Harriers?"

"They were wearing Harrier uniforms, Lord King, and the captain recognized some of them, including Lord Meliot who killed Lord Commander Drustan from afar, using a bow."

"Drustan? Drustan is dead?" said Constantine, shocked.

"Yes, Lord Prince," replied Mori. "We are very sorry to have to bring such terrible news."

"Do you know how many ships were lost?" said Arthur.

Mori paused for a moment, his eyes downcast. "As far as we know, the *Fulmar* was the only one that came through, Lord King."

"What of Queen Gwenhwyfar?"

"We have no direct news, Lord King. But while we were in the market at Lacuna, a royal messenger from Isca arrived. He read a dispatch that he said had been written by Lord Cei. The dispatch reported that our High King had been killed in battle. Praise God it was not true."

Cei, looking confused, said, "Arthur, I sent no dispatch."

"What else did this false dispatch say?" asked King Arthur grimly.

"That half the British army was lost, defeated in a major battle, and that King Cador, Prince Constantine and…and Prince Gawain were also dead," said Mori, looking up warily, but the big man remained motionless.

"Queen Gwenhwyfar. You said you have some news of the Queen?"

"No direct news, Lord King, only that a proclamation also read to us by the messenger had been sent in the name of both regents."

"This proclamation, what was in it?"

"That Prince Arwel, as the rightful heir, would be crowned High King of Britain as soon as he could be brought from Tintagel to Isca for the coronation."

"Why didn't Captain Lucius bring me this news himself?"

"He would have, Lord King, but because he believes the two princes are in grave danger, he went to Tintagel himself to warn Princess Elen of Mordred's treachery. He believes that Prince Mordred means to…to do away with the two princes and seize the throne for himself."

Constantine roared, "I swear by all the gods in heaven and on earth that if Mordred harms a hair on the head of either of my sons, I will track down that filthy, lying traitor and tear the bastard apart, limb from limb. I never trusted Mordred, but because everyone else was so worshipful toward him, I never said anything against him, more fool I. Now, too late, everyone can see his true colors."

"And the people of Britain? Are the people of Britain simply allowing this to happen?" asked Arthur incredulously.

The brothers looked at each other. "Lord King, the people of Britain think you are dead," said Gallus.

Arthur fell silent, looking as stunned as the rest of the group. King Cador now spoke up. "Arthur, we must return at once! My son's children, your heirs, are in danger! This a matter of life or death, and seconds may count."

"What about my sons? And my wife?" said Cei. "I left them in Isca, thinking they would be safe there."

"And now you realize that you have left your loved ones in a viper's nest," spat out Constantine. "As have we all."

King Hoel said, "King Cador is right, Arthur. You must return to Britain to throw down this usurper and reclaim your throne."

"But cousin, how can I leave now when we are on the brink of battle? If I withdraw my forces, the Franks will not only become emboldened but will also hold the numerical advantage."

"It is true that this is the very worst time for us to leave," mused Cador. "If we withdraw all our soldiers now, we will simply be handing Armorica to the Franks."

"Then some of our troops must stay," said Arthur firmly. "We have about fourteen hundred men fit for duty, six hundred ninety of those mounted. One cavalry unit and two infantry units will remain here in Armorica. The rest of our troops will return with us to Britain."

"That's…what? Only eleven hundred men going back with us, Arthur," said Constantine.

"Almost three times the number of Harriers that Mordred has."

"But that's not enough, now that Mordred has Saxon allies," said Constantine. Turning to Mori, he asked, "How many Saxons were at Clausentum?"

"We saw ten boats, but Captain Lucius told us there were about forty in all."

"Forty!"

"Yes, Lord Prince."

"How many men can one of their boats hold?"

"Up to forty-five, Lord Prince."

"That's…wait a moment, let me think…how many is that, Arthur?"

"Eighteen hundred."

"Eighteen hundred Saxons!" exclaimed Constantine. "Add all the Harriers, and that's…what? That's well over two thousand men! The enemy will outnumber us by two to one."

"No doubt many were killed during the battle at Clausentum," said Arthur.

"And no doubt Mordred will recruit more. There always seems to be an unending supply of Saxons."

"But once we are back, the people will rally around us," said Arthur. "I know we can count on the kings and chieftains of Britain to send us troops."

Under his breath Constantine muttered, "Just don't count on any Lothians coming to our aid."

Gawain, whose face had slowly drained of its color, flushed red again. Bedwyr put a hand on his arm, but Gawain shook it off.

Arthur glanced at his nephew anxiously. Briskly, he said, "If no one has anything further to say, we will start setting up camp for the night. The second cavalry and the second and third infantry will be staying in Armorica. I put those units and their officers under your command, King Hoel."

"I thank you, King Arthur," said Hoel. "Of course I put my ships at your disposal."

"Thank you, King Hoel. We will need them." Arthur glanced up at the sky. "It looks to be a clear night. Cei and Bedwyr – after nightfall, inform the men of our plans. Tell those coming with us that they will be quietly striking their tents and withdrawing to the south once the moon sets. Stress that everyone is to remain completely silent. Moreover – and this is important – tell no one, not even the officers, until after nightfall. I don't want the Franks detecting any changes, even inadvertent, in our behavior as we set up camp."

"Yes, Lord King," both replied.

Turning to the brothers, he said, "Mori and Gallus, will you be my eyes and ears once again and find out where Mordred and his Saxon allies are and what they are doing? I need not remind you to be cautious."

"It is an honor to serve you, Lord King," replied Gallus, as both brothers bowed.

"Thank you. When you have information to report, make for Aleth, where our troops will be embarking for the crossing."

"We will, Lord King," said the brothers, saluting.

Arthur addressed his officers. "That will be all for now, gentlemen, thank you. Please return to your regular duties. This evening, King Hoel and I will review our plans with you in my tent."

After saluting their High King, Constantine and Gawain glared at each other before departing. Arthur thought to call them back, to try to reconcile the two, but the emotions now swirling in his mind precluded making the attempt. Over and over, he berated himself for his lapse of judgment. How could he have been so naive, so blind, so stupid? How could he have misread his nephew Mordred so badly that he had blithely left Gwenhwyfar in the hands of such a scoundrel? And how could he live with himself if, because of his folly, anything should happen to the woman he loved more than life itelf?

A week later at Aleth, the Britons were loading supplies and armaments onto the Amorican vessels. Arthur was leading a skittish horse from the quay over a gangway when a long horn blast from the nearby watchtower sounded, indicating that an approaching ship had been sighted. The horse started and might have fallen, but Arthur checked the gelding sharply and quickly brought it on board. After handing the animal to a soldier to secure, he ran back across the gangway and down the quay, shouting orders to his officers and men to prepare for combat. With a strong wind blowing from out of the north, he knew that the Armorican ships would be unable to sail out of the harbor. Besides, even if they were able to row out into the channel in time, Arthur was well aware that his soldiers were cavalry and infantrymen, unused to fighting at sea. After stationing a troop of soldiers onboard each of the docked ships, he ordered the sailors to bring up buckets and wool blankets onto the decks to smother flames should the enemy attempt to set fire to the fleet. Then he positioned the remainder of his force along the quay, ready to respond wherever enemy attacks should occur.

With helmets donned and weapons in hand, the men waited anxiously, their eyes trained toward the entrance to the harbor. After many tense minutes, one of the scouts stationed at the watchtower came running down with the news that the single ship approaching from across the channel had been followed by no others. Even so, Arthur had his men maintain battle readiness. Only after the *Fulmar* had entered the harbor and Arthur could see for himself that those on board were indeed Sea Hawks did he finally rescind his order. As the soldiers relaxed and proceeded with the loading of the ships, Arthur called Cador over, and together they walked to the empty berth where the pilot was leading the ship. As it neared the quay, a somber-looking Lucius leapt ashore. When the captain recognized the man standing before him, he gasped in disbelief and fell to his knees. Exclaiming, "You're alive," he took one of Arthur's hands to kiss.

Raising Lucius to his feet, Arthur embraced him.

"Yes, King Cador and I are alive, as are Prince Constantine and Prince Gawain. Set your mind at rest, captain, there was no defeat, and our army remains intact. Mori and Gallus were here and informed us of that false dispatch, forged by Mordred in Lord Cei's name."

"Ah, Lord King, thank God, thank God! God be praised that you are alive and for all these good tidings!"

"God be praised. But Captain Lucius, please tell me quickly: how are the two Princes and their mother, Princess Elen?"

"All three are well, Lord King. But I must inform you that Tintagel is under siege."

"Under siege? By whom?"

"By Budoc and some hundred Harriers, sent there by Prince Mordred."

"And Mordred? Do you have any news about him?"

Quickly, the captain recounted the events at Tintagel. At one point Arthur interrupted him. "Budoc said Mordred *married* Gwenhwyfar! How could that be possible?"

"Mordred is completely without scruples, Lord King. He may call it a marriage, but in fact it is really…" Lucius stopped, embarrassed.

Cador broke in. "Lord King, I know that Queen Gwenhwyfar would never have consented to this marriage. It is a sham, a ruse by Mordred to try to give legitimacy to his supposed kingship." Although Cador had made this statement boldly, he was, in fact, worried. Might Gwenhwyfar, who had been his ward and whom his sister Igraine had raised as if her own child, been tempted to marry that suave scoundrel? Cador recalled a day, many years ago now, when he had caught sight of the two, exchanging admiring glances. Gwenhwyfar had blushed prettily under Mordred's gaze, even though the occasion had been a solemn one – Queen Igraine's funeral. Cador had never forgotten the incident, though he had kept it at the back of his mind – until now.

As if reading Cador's thoughts, Lucius said, "There is no doubt whatsoever that this so-called marriage was coerced. I know this because of what Hermogenes saw at Isca. As I have already said, it was thanks to Queen Ganieda's agent that Princess Elen had been forewarned of Mordred's treachery. If not for him, well…Princess Elen herself declared that she and her sons would not be alive today." Lucius went on to describe how Hermogenes had hoped to come to Armorica to refute Mordred's lies, how he had been wounded, and how he now wished to speak to King Arthur.

"He survived? That terrible fall?"

"Yes, praise God, though he dislocated one of his ankles and is unable to walk. He's in my cabin and is most anxious to tell you himself what he witnessed at Isca."

"Of course. Please lead the way."

Arthur and Cador followed Lucius onto the ship and entered the darkened cabin. Inside, lying on the captain's bunk, a man was propped up against some stuffed sacking. His left leg was splinted, his right arm was in a sling and his shoulder and chest were bandaged. His face was so swollen and bruised that Arthur would have never recognized him as Queen Ganieda's agent. When the injured man saw the king, he winced as he tried to raise his free arm in a salute.

"Please, that is not necessary. How do you feel?" asked Arthur with concern.

"I've felt better," Hermogenes replied with a slight smile. "But thanks to Captain Lucius and his men, I am alive and, I trust, will soon be mended."

"I pray that you have a speedy recovery, good Hermogenes."

"Thank you, Lord King."

"I understand that you wish to tell me what you saw at Isca."

"I do, Lord King, and I thank you for this opportunity. To begin, I must tell you that I had been sent to Isca by Queen Ganieda, who had become suspicious of Prince Mordred. The queen had warned me to be cautious and to seek information from a friend of King Merlinus's, an older man named Madog. Perhaps you know him?"

"Yes, I know good Madog and consider him my friend as well."

Hermogenes nodded. "I had only just arrived when Madog and I heard sounds of combat and the shouts of men and women, coming from inside the fortress. The gates of the fortress had been shut, so I climbed onto the roof of Madog's house to see what was happening. His house lies close to the northeast gate."

"Yes, I know it."

"It was after nightfall, but the moon was bright, and I could see Queen Gwenhwyfar on the roof of a tower, fighting like a lioness. A woman and two children were with her, whom Madog later identified as Lady Annwr and her daughter Meleri and Lord Cei's son Delwyn. The Queen and Lady Annwr were shooting arrows while the children were hurling slingshot at their attackers. For a long time, they held Mordred's men at bay. Then, while Lady Annwr kept up a steady barrage, Queen Gwenhwyfar began lowering the children outside the fortress walls. She had lowered four children to the ground before Mordred's men finally gained the tower. They had only been able to do so because the defenders had run out of arrows."

"How did Mordred's men get in?"

"They used a ram, Lord King. I couldn't see it from where I was, but I could hear pounding and then the sound of a door being rent."

"Did you actually see Mordred?"

"I did. He came up onto the roof with some of his men."

"What did he do?"

"The Queen had been lowering a fifth child to the ground when Mordred tore the rope from her hands. He began hauling the child back onto the roof but stumbled backward and pulled up a shortened end. Lady Annwr's daughter Meleri must have cut the rope so the child could escape."

"Were the children able to get away?"

"They fled into the woods, but unfortunately all five were later recaptured and brought back to the fortress."

"And Gwenhwyfar? What happened to Gwenhwyfar and Annwr?"

"They were seized by Mordred's men and forced from the roof, Lord King." Hermogenes glanced up at the king's face. Seeing Arthur's expression, he fell silent, not sure if he should go on.

"What else, Hermogenes? I must know everything. Do not hold anything back from me."

"Yes, Lord King. I'm sorry, Lord King, for the rest is hard to tell. After several minutes passed, lights appeared in the upper room of the tower. Then…then I heard a boy scream – in pain – and the cries and pleadings of the women. Mordred was…was obviously ill-using the children to compel the Queen's compliance. I'm sorry, Lord King, to bring you such horrific news."

"No, good Hermogenes, I thank you for bringing me this news. Until now, I was still unsure if I could kill my own sister's son. Now I know I can. And I will. Even if it costs me my own life, I will. I swear I will rid Britain of that monster who would destroy all that is good and honorable and virtuous…" Arthur stopped, fighting to keep his emotions in check. He went on. "You said that my Queen fought like a lioness. Who would have ever thought that my gentle wife could be so fierce in battle? My dearest Gwenhwyfar…I have never been more proud of you than I am right now. My dearest wife…I left you in his hands…I have only myself to blame, Cador… why did I ever trust him?…I swear I will kill him…by all the gods, I swear…" Arthur broke off abruptly, for he had begun to weep.

Chapter 19

At Aleth

The ships had been loaded and the fleet was ready to sail, but the wind continued to hold stubbornly from out of the north. Although both man and beast chafed at their confinement on board the ships, there was no remedy but to wait for more favorable conditions. After speaking once again with the harbormaster, who could only offer a shrug about the recalcitrant wind, Arthur allowed the soldiers to return to shore as long as they stayed within sight of the quay. As the morning wore on and it became obvious that they would not be departing any time soon, Arthur called for another war council with his military advisors. Certain key issues had remained unresolved since their previous meeting and, while the decision would be ultimately his to make, Arthur had hoped to achieve at least a degree of unanimity among his officers before he made it.

As the men were gathering in the tower room, Arthur walked to a window and peered out. In the harbor below he could see the banners on the mast tops flapping vigorously in winds still coming from out of the north. Turning from the window, he shook his head in answer to his officers' inquiring looks. As soon as everyone was seated, Arthur once again queried how Mordred could be countered without endangering Queen Gwenhwyfar and her companions.

King Cador was the first to speak up. "We must make for Isca at once and take the fortress by storm! Yesterday, many here advocated waiting at Glevum until the kings and chieftains of Britain send us reinforcements," he said, looking around the table. "But I say waiting will only give Mordred time to strengthen his position. Strike now," he said, pounding a fist for emphasis, "while the numbers are still to our advantage!"

Agreeing with his father, Prince Constantine added, "We know that Mordred sent—what?—maybe a hundred Harriers to Tintagel with Budoc and another hundred to Clausentum with Meliot. He must have two hundred at most at Isca. With so few men, he will never leave the safety of the fortress. But if we show, say, only a hundred soldiers of our own on the field of battle, Mordred will be lured into combat by the prospect of an easy victory. Then, once he and his men are outside the fortress walls, the rest of our troops that will have been hidden in the hills to the north will swoop down and defeat Mordred in open combat."

Rolling his eyes, Gawain said, "Mordred would never be tricked by such an obvious ploy."

Constantine replied, "Oh? But didn't King Arthur himself use this tactic? When our High King and his cavalry came charging out of the old Roman amphitheatre, didn't they trounce your father, King Lot?"

"Just why it won't work again. Whatever Mordred's faults are, he's no fool."

"Faults? You call your brother's heinous actions *faults?* Call them for what they are: crimes, atrocities, treason!"

Gawain remained silent, glowering at Constantine as reply. When Arthur asked Gawain for his opinion as to how best to proceed, he muttered that he would do whatever he was told. Arthur chose not to press him. After having privately cautioned Constantine and Gawain that their mutual antagonism was bad for morale, Arthur had hoped that at least their open display of animosity would have ceased. Obviously, he needed to talk to them again, using stronger terms, but would not do so before their peers.

Turning instead to Cador he said, "While I, too, want nothing more than to free Queen Gwenhwyfar and her companions as quickly as possible, I fear that a direct attack on the fortress could imperil their safety. Judging by Mordred's foul and cowardly actions, he has shown that he would not hesitate to threaten the hostages and, moreover, be prepared to carry out his threats."

Cei now spoke up. "I agree with our High King that a direct assault on the fortress could endanger the hostages. And I also agree with King Cador that waiting will give Mordred time to strengthen his position with more Saxon allies. But I think I've come up with an idea. What if we block all accesses to the city so Mordred can't bring in more troops while we besiege the fortress? That will force Mordred to make a move."

"And what if his move," said Constantine darkly, "is to drag the hostages, including your own wife and sons, to the top of the ramparts and murder them one by one before your very eyes? We all know Gawain's brother is capable of doing it."

Cei bowed his head. When his shoulders began to shake, Bedwyr, sitting next to him, gently patted his friend on the arm. Cei looked up, wiping his eyes. "I'm sorry, Arthur. I didn't mean to stop the meeting. But it's hard, you know, feeling all this rage inside me against a bastard I can't get my hands on without seeing my family hurt. Or worse."

Bedwyr, who rarely spoke at meetings, now quietly offered, "Lord King, what if we freed the hostages by stealth?"

When Arthur asked him to elaborate, Bedwyr said, "Maybe a small group of us could climb the walls on a stormy night when any sounds we make would be covered. Also, the guards on patrol might be less careful during a rainstorm. Then, once we're inside, some of us could find and protect the hostages while the rest of us could open the gates and let our soldiers in."

Shaking his head, Constantine said, "How on earth would you be able to locate the hostages? And remain undetected yourselves? Besides, even if you do find them, how could you and a small group of men be able to protect them once the alarm is raised? It seems to me your plan is just as likely to put their lives in danger. Besides, I'm sure the hostages aren't all in one place, or in places easy to get to. As Mordred's brother Gawain here has pointed out to us, the traitor is no fool."

Under his breath, but loud enough for all to hear, Gawain muttered, "Constantine is always the naysayer, but he can't come up with a proper plan of this own."

Expecting a retort from Constantine, Arthur was relieved when Captain Lucius interjected, asking if he might speak. "Yes, Captain, please," urged Arthur.

"Thank you, Lord King. Thank you for inviting me to this council meeting. And thank you, gentlemen, all. Listening to the proposals being put forward, I can certainly understand the concern that Mordred might use the hostages as bargaining chips. But what if none of us were around to witness his heinous acts? It is unlikely that he would harm valuable hostages if there were no gain in it for him." Seeing their blank faces, he went on. "What I am proposing is that our objective should be Clausentum, not Isca. If we blockade the Saxon fleet at Clausentum, Mordred will be forced to leave the fortress to join his allies. Mordred has to realize that the Saxons will not obey the commands of an absentee leader for very long – and a British one at that – particularly when they're under attack themselves."

There were nods of agreement and sounds of approval from around the table. King Arthur himself was nodding. "Thank you, Captain Lucius," he said. "Your idea certainly merits consideration. Gentlemen, I open the captain's proposal for discussion."

Most eyes instantly turned to Constantine, but before that man could open his mouth, a horn blast sounded. As everyone jumped to his feet, Arthur shouted, "One short blast – a small vessel approaching – but more could be coming. Officers, return to your units and prepare your soldiers for combat. Same positions as before. Captain Lucius, please return to the *Fulmar* and see that your men have buckets and blankets on hand. We may need to protect the fleet against firing."

"Yes, Lord King," Lucius replied, as he and the rest hurried after their king.

Arthur and the others were halfway to the harbor when one of the scouts from the watchtower intercepted them. Puffing for breath, he saluted the High King. "A small vessel approaching, Lord King," he said. "Looks like a fishing boat."

"Only one vessel?"

"Yes, Lord King."

"Thank you, scout," said Arthur. "Return to the tower and report back at once if any more are sighted."

"Yes, Lord King."

Arthur turned to his men. "With luck, it could be Mori and Gallus. The information they may be bringing could change everything."

As the boat neared the quay, Arthur was relieved to see that it was, indeed, the two brothers who were on board. "What news?" he shouted.

"The Saxons have left Clausentum, Lord King," called back Mori as both brothers saluted. Jumping to the quay with a line, Mori continued to speak as he secured the craft to a bollard. "We sailed to Clausentum, thinking to spy on the Saxons, but by the time we got there, they were already gone."

"Gone, but not before they had plundered the place, Lord King," interjected Gallus as he threw a second line to his brother and began furling the sail.

Mori nodded. "It's true, Lord King. Our town is a shambles."

"I am very sorry to hear it. Do you know if any lives were lost?"

"Thankfully none. Some townspeople had already returned, and they told us that everyone had been able to get away while the battle was still waging. Most went to Calleva to seek shelter. One of them – he's a neighbor and good friend of ours – told us that while he was in Calleva, he saw about thirty Harriers skirt around the city walls. They were heading southeast, toward the Saxon treaty lands. Lord King, Prince Mordred was riding at their head."

"Mordred! At Calleva! How did your friend know it was Mordred? Had he ever seen him before?"

"He had. He went to Isca last summer for the games. He said he was certain it was Prince Mordred."

"This friend of yours. Is he reliable?"

"Very. We've known him since childhood. You can trust what he said he saw, Lord King."

Considering this information, Arthur said, "So it appears that Mordred has already left Isca to join his Saxon allies. Do you have any idea where the Saxon fleet may have gone?"

"We do, Lord King," said Gallus as he joined his brother on the quay. "After we left Clausentum, we headed east along the coast. We figured the Saxons might have returned to their treaty lands to make repairs to their boats. At that old Roman fort in the bay, the one called Anderida, we counted twenty-seven war boats moored in the harbor there.

"Twenty-seven? Do you think the rest of the fleet may have gone further east?"

"No, Lord King, those twenty-seven are all the boats they have left. My brother didn't tell you that on our way to Clausentum, we saw five boats half-sunk in the river and another eight lying abandoned along the riverbank."

"Good news, indeed!" said Arthur. "That evens the odds. If twenty-seven boats could now hold them, they must have – what? – twelve-hundred men at most, maybe less."

"Actually, Lord King, maybe a lot less," said Mori. "Those eight boats that were abandoned still looked seaworthy. They must have been left behind because they didn't have enough men to row them back."

Arthur nodded. "Thank you, gentlemen both. This information that you have brought is invaluable. Turning to the others, he said, "It is now up to us to ensure that the Sea Hawks' sacrifice was not made in vain. I say we take this fight to Mordred and his Saxon allies!"

To a man, his officers shouted their agreement.

Mori and Gallus were pleased when they received new orders from the High King to continue their surveillance work and watch for any vessels that might be making the crossing from Germania to augment the Saxon forces. Captain Lucius also received new orders from the High King though he was not so pleased when he heard them. He and his fellow Sea Hawks had been eager to avenge their fallen comrades. But now, instead of joining the fight, he and his men would be returning to Britain, acting as glorified messengers to bring word that King Arthur lived. Although disappointed, Lucius understood why he and his men had been chosen for the assignment. The *Fulmar* had always been renowned as the fastest ship in the British fleet. In addition, he himself was a well-known commander, and his authority to issue directives on the High King's behalf would not be questioned. Once news had been brought to Tintagel, Lucius had been charged by the High King to cross the estuary to Moridunum so that riders could be sent to raise the men of Cambria. Following that stop, Lucius was to drop off scouts near Isca, so that they might learn what they could about the hostages and the strength of the garrison that had been left there. While the scouts were thus engaged, the *Fulmar* was to sail further up the Sabrina to Glevum where messengers would ride out to rally support from the other kingdoms of Britain. Finally, after returning to a prearranged location to pick up the scouts, the Sea Hawks were to join forces with King Arthur. By that time, however, Lucius could well imagine that the fighting would be over and the war won. Or lost.

Chapter 20

Battle on the Beach

Lurching across the deck, Arthur was trying to keep his balance as the ship pitched sharply upward to ascend another enormous wave. Although the sail had long since been furled and ropes let out into the sea to slow the ship's momentum, fierce gale force winds from the southwest were propelling the ship rapidly forward. Only minutes before, two soldiers, who were with the many others vomiting over the rails, had been swept away when a sudden violent gust caught the stern and turned the ship broadside to the waves. The ship had rolled and almost overturned as men frantically grabbed whatever they could. Fighting hard, the steersman had managed to right the ship and bring it back around, but Arthur was appalled when he counted two fewer men on board. In such monstrously high seas, however, he knew there was no possibility of even attempting a rescue. Deeply regretting that he had not done so before the tragedy, Arthur had ordered the soldiers to tie ropes around their waists and secure themselves to the mast or the rails. Now, however, he was exempting himself from his own order as he made his way to the horses. Tethered by their halters in stalls that had been built for them amidships, all eight had fallen when the vessel had heeled over. Arthur's own horse Llamrei was among them. Hooves were flailing as the panic-stricken animals screamed in terror, frantically trying to regain their footing on the slippery and steeply inclined deck. Cresting the wave, the ship began flying down the steep ridge of water, its bow poised to plow into the back of a gigantic wave looming ahead. As the foredeck plunged underwater, Arthur was swept off his feet. Seemingly doomed, the entire ship shuddered violently. Then, slowly, the bow began to rise, sending water sluicing furiously from the deck. Caught in the inescapable flow, Arthur was being carried along with it. About to be swept overboard, he desperately plunged his arms into the water. Feeling the gunwale, he grabbed it and held on while the relentless current tried to drag him into the sea. As the bow continued to rise and the water dissipated, Arthur was finally able to heave himself over the rail. Tumbling onto the deck, he lay prone, coughing up water and gasping for breath. Then, clambering to his feet, he waved to the steersman, who was looking at him with concern, and stumbled back to the horses.

The previous morning at Aleth, the wind had finally shifted, and with a freshening southerly breeze, all had agreed that the conditions appeared favorable for the crossing. Although brisk, the wind was holding steadily from the southwest, and the ships had made swift progress. The fleet was almost halfway across the channel when the wind speed began to increase. Observing the lowery skies and rapidly worsening conditions with alarm, the sailors had scrambled to drop the sails and secure them as the swells began to build. The High King's last shouted order relayed between the ships had been to do whatever it took to survive and proceed to the landing place only when possible. Since then, propelled by heavy seas and gale force winds, the ships in the fleet had become separated as they struggled against the overwhelming forces of wind and water.

By using ropes and the ever changing pitch of the deck, Arthur and the only two cavalrymen who had not been incapacitated by seasickness helped roll the horses back to their feet while dodging blows from the frightened animals' hooves. Several of the horses had sustained minor injuries, including Llamrei who had suffered a gash to her flank. Stroking Llamrei, Arthur spoke soothingly to her and the other horses. As the ship was cresting another wave, Arthur used the vantage to scan the turbulent seas all around. No other vessels were in sight. Then, when the ship pitched sharply downward again, he and the two cavalrymen grabbed the top rail of the stall to steady themselves. With the next wave looming, Arthur tried to keep the dread that he felt from his voice while continuing to try to calm the frightened animals. Suddenly, without warning, a rush of cold air from the northwest hit the ship broadside. As waves began breaking over the ship's port side, the steersman fought hard and turned the vessel into the wind. Now, the full fury of the storm could be felt as wave after wave came crashing over the bow in seemingly endless succession.

After enduring many more fraught hours at sea, the storm-battered ship was at last approaching Britain's southern coast. Between a leaden sky and an equally gray sea, a line of cliffs suddenly appeared, gleaming brightly when the sun finally broke free from the clouds. Jutting out into the channel and higher than the rest, one particular white chalk cliff, rising over five hundred feet straight from the sea, was prominent. Some four miles west of this notable landmark lay the inlet that was the British fleet's destination.

Standing in the bow, Arthur strained his eyes to see if any other ships had already arrived. He could see none. With a growing sense of dread, Arthur contemplated the horrifying possibility that the entire fleet had been lost at sea. The thought sent a chill up his spine. Continuing to scan the line of undulating white cliffs, he called out to the steersman when he spotted what appeared to be three British ships beached beyond the headland. Although they were some five miles past the chosen landing place, he could easily imagine that they had been blown further east by the storm. Some distance away from where the ships had landed, Arthur could also see the old Roman fortress Anderida, standing conspicuously on a low peninsula in the bay. Although the long, sloping ridge paralleling the shore was now effectively blocking any view of the beached ships from the fort, Arthur could only hope that they had not been sighted before making landfall. As his own ship was approaching the shore, Arthur was heartened by the sight of British soldiers, happily waving from the cobbled strand. He was further heartened when he picked out three particular individuals among the men. Gawain, Cei and Bedwyr had all come through. With relief, Arthur vigorously waved back.

His ship was just entering the surf when movement caught his eye. To the east, Arthur watched as two men came scrambling down from the top of the ridge onto the beach below. Although still some thousand yards from the ships, they were gesticulating wildly and shouting something which Arthur strained to hear but could not make out over that distance and above the din of the crashing breakers. Hearing their exact words proved unnecessary, however, as hundreds of Saxon warriors began pouring over the ridge behind them.

Arthur had already given orders to his soldiers to arm themselves as he stood poised to leap over the gunwale. Most of the men were ready to follow, but a few, who had not yet recovered from the effects of seasickness, were moving sluggishly. Shouting to the captain to have the others help bring those men off, Arthur leapt into the surf and ran to where Gawain, Cei and Bedwyr had already formed their soldiers into a line to defend the ships, now stranded by the outgoing tide.

"It's no good," shouted Arthur, pointing to the adjacent slope as he came up to them. "We don't have enough men. They can come around and trap us in a pincer. We have to abandon the ships and withdraw to the base of the cliffs where they can't outflank us."

"But Arthur, our horses are still on board," said Bedwyr.

Arthur grimaced. "I can't endanger men to save the lives of horses."

Saluting their High King, Cei and Bedwyr immediately ordered the soldiers to retreat to the cliffs while Arthur ran back to his ship to see that all the men had been brought off. Seconds after the Britons had reached the narrow strip of land exposed by the ebbing tide, a second enemy force appeared on the top of the ridge adjacent to the ships. Five mounted men were at its forefront. The man in the middle, obviously the leader, pulled up his horse and halted his troops with a gesture. Irritated that his tactic had been anticipated, he watched intently as the Britons quickly and efficiently formed a line of men four ranks deep, extending from the base of the vertical cliff face to the waves breaking against the narrow white chalk shelf. While he would never make the mistake of underestimating the ability of those battle-hardened Britons, he knew that two hundred soldiers, however capable, could not stand for long against a thousand Saxon warriors. Even if their leader were King Arthur.

Arthur, standing in the frontline with his men, easily recognized the enemy commander. That man, seeing he had caught Arthur's eye, gave the High King a sardonic salute. Then, raising his sword, he signaled the Saxon forces forward. Arthur was appalled to see the enemy advancing, not toward his own position but to the now undefended ships. Agonized, Arthur watched as the Saxons began boarding the first ship. Within seconds, the screams of horses could be heard, carried clearly over the tumult of the crashing waves. Cei and Bedwyr and the other soldiers begged their High King to counterattack, but Arthur brusquely ordered them to hold their position. He was well aware that the enemy leader was trying to incite that very response.

Methodically, the Saxons proceeded from one ship to the next, tossing firebrands into each as they left. Thick, black clouds of smoke were billowing into the air when they approached the last vessel. As the enemy soldiers began climbing up the sides of the ship, Arthur silently berated himself for not having had the foresight to untie Llamrei and the other horses. Now, instead of having at least some small chance of survival, she and the other horses would be utterly defenseless.

Three Saxons in the forefront were just clambering over the gunwale when Arthur heard a familiar, bloodcurdling bellow. Shocked, he realized that the battle cry had come, not from one of the men around him, but from the direction of the ship. Suddenly, in quick succession, three Saxon warriors went flying backwards off the ship, their hacked bodies landing sprawled over their comrades below. Giving another defiant bellow, an enormous man with flaming red hair and bristling beard leapt onto the top rail of the ship. Waving an enormous, bloody battleaxe over his head, he welcomed the other Saxons to come aboard. The fearsome warrior's sudden, terrifying appearance brought the entire Saxon army to a standstill.

Turning his piercing blue eyes on the enemy leader, still sitting his horse on the ridge, he shouted, "Come down and fight me, you damned coward!"

"No, I refuse to have my own brother's blood on my hands. Or clothes," the other called back coolly.

"Filthy lying traitor! You're no brother of mine!" he roared. Then, looking down at the hundreds of Saxons standing on the beach below him, Gawain shouted, "Well, what are you bastards waiting for?"

Although few understood his words, all understood their meaning. Shouting fierce battle cries of their own, the Saxons once again began climbing up the sides of the ship. The first man to reach the gunwale tumbled backward, his helmet and skull cloven by a single blow from Gawain's axe. The second, third, fourth, and fifth man met similar fates. Then, as more and more Saxons began swarming onboard, Gawain jumped back down onto the deck. Swinging his battleaxe, he fought like a man possessed. Or rather like a man who no longer cared whether he lived or died. Soon, every Saxon unlucky enough to have climbed onboard had been cut down and tossed back onto the heads of his fellows. Now believing that a significant British force must have remained concealed on the ship, the Saxon army once again halted.

"One man! He's only one man," screamed Mordred from the ridge, his words bellowed in translation by one of the Saxon leaders at his side. "Where is Saxon courage that a single Briton is able to stop an entire Saxon army!"

With that taunt ringing in their ears, the Saxons began boarding the ship en masse. Moving amidships, Gawain used the row of horses to protect his back. Llamrei and the other warhorses, trained to use their rear hooves in combat, brought down any Saxon warrior foolish enough to attempt circling around Gawain from behind. Gawain, fighting with the uncontrollable fury and abandon of a berserk man, was holding off the entire Saxon army.

One of the Saxons, dodging out of the way of Gawain's battleaxe, fell backward over a cache of oars that had been stowed on deck. Jumping to his feet, he untied one of the long ashen oars and waited. Just as Gawain was turning to exchange blows with three enemy soldiers to his right, the Saxon approached him from the opposite side. Safely beyond reach of the lethal battleaxe, the Saxon warrior swung the heavy oar high in the air and brought it down as hard as he could on Gawain's helmet. The crack could be heard all the way to the Britons' position.

Arthur was watching through tear-blurred eyes as the Saxons tossed firebrands into the last ship. He cleared them with his sleeve when the enemy began advancing on the British position. At his command, the men in the frontline briskly overlapped their shields. At another, the soldiers in the second and third ranks lifted their shields to cover those in front of them. Like the other men standing in the forefront, Arthur was bracing his spear and shield for impact as the enemy soldiers came pelting toward them. The Saxons were racing full tilt when they collided with the Britons in a violent clash of arms. Pushed back, the British center began to buckle. Fighting furiously, Arthur shouted to those around him to press forward, and the British line slowly straightened. The battle then became a shoving match between two opposing forces as soldiers on both sides jabbed their spears into any openings while at the same time they tried to keep themselves covered with their shields. Whenever a Briton received a debilitating wound, he was moved behind the lines and replaced by the soldier standing in back of him. Meanwhile, any Saxon unfortunate enough to fall after being wounded was trampled underfoot by his fellows who were eagerly pushing forward.

As time passed, the ranks of the badly outnumbered Britons inevitably began to thin. While most of the Saxons were well-protected with mail, there had been no time for the Britons to don their own mail shirts, left in the holds of their ships. Knowing their advantage and egged on by their leaders, the Saxons redoubled their efforts to break the British line. As the Britons were pushed back, a handful of soldiers who had been holding the line nearest to the sea found themselves cut off. Bedwyr was among them. Surrounded on three sides by the enemy and forced further and further into the surf, the small band of Britons fought on, though desperately. Bedwyr was the last man standing when a Saxon thrust a spear into his leg. Wrenching out the weapon, the Saxon struck Bedwyr on the back of the head with the butt of his spear and left him floating face down in the water.

Seeing what had happened, Cei furiously dispatched the soldier he had been fighting and splashed through the surf to his friend. Waves were pummeling Bedwyr's body when he reached him. Lifting him out of the water, Cei shook him and cried his name, but he did not respond. Finally, in desperation, he gave him several mighty thumps on the back, and Bedwyr suddenly came back to life, coughing up water and gasping for breath.

Grabbing hold of Bedwyr by his tunic, Cei was making his way through the surf toward the British line when two Saxon swordsmen attacked him. He was managing to fend off the swordsmen when a spearman joined the fight. Just as Cei was parrying a sword stroke, the spearman thrust his weapon into Cei's now open right side. Yanking out the spear, the Saxon was lunging with the finishing blow when the shaft he was holding cleft in two. His cry of surprise was silenced as Caliburn rebounded and peremptorily slashed across his throat. The swordsmen scarcely had time to react before they, too, fell to King Arthur's blade.

Wrapping an arm around his brother, Arthur splashed through the surf back toward the British line. Cei was grasping Bedwyr just as tightly. Spotting the vulnerable men, one of them King Arthur himself, several Saxons rushed to attack them but were thwarted by a score of Britons who came running to the aid of their High King. Once behind the British line, Arthur gently laid his brother down on the wave-smoothed chalk next to Bedwyr. His hands were shaking as he fumbled to remove his brother's leather cuirass to examine the wound.

Cei shook his head. "No, Arthur, no. There's nothing you can do. Just promise you'll tell Alys and my children that I love them. Let them know I was thinking about them right to the end."

"Please, brother, don't speak of your end. Let me look at your wound."

Grabbing Arthur's arm, he gasped, "Just tell them that, won't you?"

"Of course, brother. Now please…"

"No, Arthur, listen. It's too late for me. Look to Bedwyr now. Don't worry about me," he said, smiling wanly. His grip was slackening as he murmured, "I love you, Arthur."

"I love you, too, Cei," replied Arthur, gently closing the eyes of the man who could no longer hear him.

Bedwyr, having witnessed the terrible scene, was weeping uncontrollably, berating himself for being the cause of Cei's death. Turning to aid him, Arthur ripped a sleeve from his own tunic and began binding Bedwyr's wound. "No, dear friend" he said consolingly, "you are not to blame. You must never think that. But listen, Bedwyr, I must leave you now. If it is not our fate to meet again in this world, I hope I shall see you in another and far better place."

Stooping, he kissed Bedwyr's brow. Then he hurried back to where the battle was still waging. When a soldier on the frontline was wounded, Arthur quickly stepped forward to take his place. Fighting with uncharacteristic savagery, Arthur seemed determined to cut through, single-handedly, the hundreds of Saxons who were standing between him and the smug-looking man watching the battle from the ridge. But against such overwhelming numbers, Arthur knew that he and his men could not prevail. Unable to reach the murderous traitor and seeing his fellow Britons falling all around him, Arthur was despairing, not for himself, but for the loyal men who had stood faithfully beside him, battle after battle, year after year, and who were to die with him that very hour. Yet even greater was his despair in knowing that he would be leaving his country – and his beloved wife – in the hands of a monster.

The battle's end was near when the Saxons finally broke through the thin British line. Expecting that he and his soldiers would be quickly enveloped, Arthur was amazed to see the enemy falter. When he heard Mordred and the Saxon leaders shouting to their men to withdraw, Arthur quickly glanced over his shoulder. Coming along the shore from out of the west, a British cavalry force was fast approaching and King Cador and Prince Constantine were galloping their horses at its head.

By the time the cavalrymen arrived, the Saxons had already disappeared over the ridge. Cador and Constantine were eager to follow but reined in their horses and saluted their High King. When they asked for orders, Arthur hesitated. The eighty-some British soldiers who, with him, had survived the battle were exhausted and desperately thirsty. In addition, the tide had turned, and the wounded needed to be moved to higher ground and given care without delay. Although he wished more than anything to pursue Mordred and the fleeing army, Arthur knew it would be folly to advance into unfamiliar and hostile territory with less than his full cavalry and no infantry. Explaining his reasoning, Arthur gave orders to set pickets and establish a beachhead on higher ground.

After seeing to the immediate needs of the wounded, Arthur consulted with his men to determine an honorable method for the disposition of the dead. To ensure that their bodies not be desecrated, the Britons decided to place their slain countrymen in the ships. Reverently, King Arthur carried the body of his brother into the charred hulk where Gawain had perished and placed him on top of one of the stacks of driftwood that had been piled inside. Once the last body had been positioned, the wood that had been carefully arranged both inside and out of the blackened hulls was ignited and the brands tossed into the ships. As the smoldering hulks caught fire once again and the consuming flames leapt high into the air, most of the soldiers were weeping for their fallen comrades. Others, looking steely-eyed, were vowing vengeance.

The next morning, Prince Constantine informed the High King that none of the twenty-eight wounded Saxons had survived the night. Arthur frowned but asked no questions. Tersely, he ordered that their bodies be added to the row of enemy corpses that had been placed above the debris of the strandline along the shore. The Saxon people, it had been decided, would be responsible for dealing with their own dead.

Chapter 21

Decision

The ships and the British dead had been reduced to little more than embers and ash when the tide came in, washing over what remained. As it receded again, most of what had been left was carried out to sea. Once a wide enough strip of land below the chalk cliffs had been exposed again by the ebbing tide, Arthur withdrew his forces westward along the shore to the inlet where the British fleet was now moored. Three vessels remained unaccounted for and were presumed to have been lost at sea. When a lookout on top of the nearby cliff shouted down that he had sighted the ships, beating their way back from the east, the entire camp erupted with shouts of joy. As the errant ships entered the inlet, the rousing cheers greeting those onboard dispelled any apprehension that they might have felt about their tardy arrival. The soldiers from those ships were still disembarking when a scout came riding in with his latest report: Mordred and his allies remained ensconced at Anderida.

To bring the new arrivals up to date on the current situation, the High King called together his officers and military advisors. Once the battle and other recent events had been recounted, the discussion turned to what their next course of action should be. As usual, there were differing opinions. One idea broached by several officers to lay siege to Anderida was immediately rejected by others who contended that their own numbers were insufficient to repel the counterattack that was sure to follow inside hostile territory. In addition to that concern, more than a few called attention to the more obvious reason why a siege would fail: the twenty-seven war boats moored in Anderida's harbor in which the Saxons could easily make their escape.

While everyone agreed in principle that the Saxons should be met in open combat before reinforcements bolstered their numbers, the more practically minded pointed out that such a plan would be impossible unless Mordred could somehow be coaxed from his present, secure location. Given that man's shrewdness, none of the proposals that were then put forth seemed likely to achieve that goal. Ultimately, all discussions and debates and deliberations reached the same conclusion: everything would depend upon what Mordred did next. At the meeting's end, the High King directed his officers to maintain their men in a state of readiness so that they could respond at a moment's notice to any new developments.

The Britons did not have long to wait. Just after midnight, two scouts galloped their horses into camp with the news that the enemy was on the march. Mordred and his allies had left the fortress under cover of darkness. They were heading, not toward the British position, but to the northwest, through the Saxon treaty lands.

During the emergency war council which followed, Prince Constantine and more than a few others loudly advocated attacking the enemy immediately and at all costs. Others, including Constantine's own father, King Cador, were urging caution. Pursuing the enemy deep inside Saxon territory with so small a force would be extremely risky. Besides, knowing Mordred's devious ways, he could well be enticing the Britons into a trap. While the men continued their debate, Arthur remained silent, listening to what each of them had to say. Although he was just as eager as Constantine to pursue Mordred, Arthur knew that a major defeat inside Saxon territory would spell the end, not only of his army, but of the entire British cause. He was also aware that, as always, the final decision rested upon him. The weight of that responsibility brought to his mind another war council, now many years ago. Just before the final battle at Badon Hill, Arthur had also been listening to his military advisors, weighing all his options, and vacillating between the many choices he could make. He recalled how he had longed to ask Merlin for his counsel, but his chief advisor had been giving medical care to the wounded, and pulling him away would have been unconscionable. Arthur remembered how, at that time, he had been bolstered by Merlin's earlier prophetic words: "Decisions must be made, and none but you can make them." Somehow those words had given him the confidence to make the correct choice. Today, he hoped that Merlin's words still applied. Looking around at the men's expectant faces, he realized that they must have stopped speaking some time ago and were now awaiting his command. Decisively, he ordered, "Officers, inform your men that we will be breaking camp at first light and have them prepared to board the ships on the tide. We are making for Tintagel."

A few seemed satisfied. More looked confused.

The High King explained. "Princes Arwel and Aled and their mother, Princess Elen, remain at Tintagel, besieged by some hundred traitorous Harriers. I mean to break that siege. Then, we will continue on to Isca to free Queen Gwenhwyfar, her ladies, and their children. When we meet Mordred in battle, it will be on British soil. I don't yet know where it will be, but I do know this: Mordred cannot remain inside Saxon lands forever. Whenever and wherever he emerges, we will fight the murderous traitor and defeat him. Men of Britain, are you with me?"

King Arthur's words were met with a roar of approval.

Later that day, as the British fleet was beating its way west past the towering white cliffs of Britain's southern shore, King Arthur was standing in the bow of the leading ship. He found the wind, whipping his hair and sending spray onto his face, invigorating. Otherwise, alone with his thoughts, he might have easily been overcome by grief. Or rage. With difficulty, he did his best to beat down his sorrow and the dark and vengeful feelings that were roiling his mind. For the sake of those who were depending upon him, whose lives were now hanging in the balance, he knew that he had to keep those crippling emotions under control. Later, once the storm of battle was over, he prayed that there would be time enough to mourn the loss of those he loved. For although he had spoken boldly to his men, Arthur knew that the outcome of the pending battle was far from assured. But he had made his decision. Now, he could only hope that he had made the right one.

Chapter 22

Return

After the news of King Arthur's death had been made known to the people of Cumbria, a pall of gloom descended over the entire kingdom. Even the always festive market days in Brocavum, its capital city, had become subdued as people huddled in groups, speaking quietly and anxiously about what the future might hold. Although some were hopeful that Prince Arwel might prove a worthy successor to King Arthur, others pointed to the heir's young age as cause for concern. While Arthur himself had been youthful, he had been almost sixteen years old at his coronation. Prince Arwel had just turned fourteen. Knowing that Queen Gwenhwyfar and the popular Prince Mordred would be continuing in their roles as co-regents during Arwel's minority, many remained confident. Others, particularly those old enough to remember the dark and turbulent times that invariably followed the death of a High King, were far less optimistic. Cumbria's queen was among them.

Ever since she had learned of King Arthur's death, Ganieda had been filled with a strong, though inchoate, sense of foreboding. Immediately after she and Rodarch had sent off their formal letter of condolence and support via the regents' messenger, Ganieda had written a more personal expression of sympathy to Queen Gwenhwyfar. She had found the reply to her letter troubling. Queen Gwenhwyfar, the very model of propriety and decorum, had always sent thoughtful and carefully written letters in her own neat hand. The rather perfunctory note which Ganieda received in return had been penned by a different hand. Even the signature, while appearing genuine, seemed to lack the Queen's customary flair. When Ganieda had shown the note to her husband, he had attributed the uncharacteristic signature to Queen Gwenhwyfar's state of profound grief. As to the rather short reply having been written by a scribe, Rodarch explained, no doubt correctly, that the Queen must have received dozens, if not hundreds, of letters of condolence. It was hardly surprising that in her current frame of mind, the Queen would have tasked the work to a scribe. Ganieda, however, remained unconvinced. She was also troubled for another reason; Hermogenes had not yet returned. If all had been well in Isca, her always reliable agent should have long since returned to Brocavum. Even more troubling was the latest dispatch from the capital. Included with the regular report was a copy of a letter which the regents had received from Princess Elen. In it the princess related that a serious illness which had been sweeping through the garrison at Tintagel had been contracted by her sons. Until Prince Arwel and his brother recovered and were able to travel again, the coronation at Isca had been indefinitely postponed. Ganieda and Rodarch, alarmed by this news, had immediately written to Princess Elen, expressing their concern and extending their best wishes for her sons' speedy recovery. The messenger they had sent to Tintagel to deliver their letter was also long overdue. King Rodarch, now as worried as his wife, discussed with her his idea of traveling to Isca himself to find out what the true state of affairs was in the capital. Ganieda, fearful for her husband's safety, suggested sending an agent instead, someone unknown to anyone there, who could make some discreet inquiries first. At the end of the day, they left the matter unresolved, deciding to continue their discussion in the morning.

A man lying on the top of a mountain with his arms behind his head was staring up at the stars. Although it was a chilly night and his feet were bare, he seemed habituated to the cold. When the wolf stretched out at his side gave a little yelp to gain his attention, he reached over and stroked her just behind the ears, her favorite spot. He smiled when her rear leg began to thump with pleasure. Then, yawning, he resumed looking up into the night sky. He was staring at Mars, setting in the west, when the wandering star suddenly blazed luridly red. Then, just as quickly, the bright flare of light was extinguished, like a candle snuffed by a breeze. A low, dark cloud, invisible in the moonless sky, had scudded across it, obliterating the planet's warm glow.

In alarm, the man instantly sprang to his feet and began racing down the side of the mountain. Giving an excited bark, the wolf leapt up to hers and loped after him.

The young guard on duty above the gate at Brocavum could scarcely believe his eyes. In the first dim light of dawn, he could have sworn that the oddly attired man who had come riding up to the gate had leapt from the back of a stag. Just as he was almost certain that the animal running at his side had been a wolf and not a dog. Whatever they were, both animals were now gone, but the barefoot and wild-looking man was still there. Shouting loudly up to him, the strange man was imperiously demanding to see the king and queen. When the guard refused to admit him, the crazed lunatic began pounding furiously on the door.

Hearing the commotion, the captain of the guard came hurrying over. Peering down at the fur-clad man, the captain identified him as the queen's brother. Chuckling at the young guard's reaction, he said, "Don't worry, soldier, your caution is commendable. But it must be something important to bring *him* out of his precious woods. Hurry over and inform our king and queen that King Merlinus Ambrosius has returned and is anxious to see them." Saluting, the guard dashed away as the captain called down to the porter to open the gates.

The massive beam had scarcely been withdrawn before the wild man pushed open the heavy door and bounded past the startled porter toward the royal residence. Rodarch and Ganieda, with cloaks thrown over their nightclothes, came rushing down the stairs to meet him. The prophet's face was streaked with tears, and the color of his eyes was wavering as he cried out, "They, go, Barinthus!"

Ganieda begged her brother to make his meaning more clear. "Who? Who should go? To Barinthus?"

"They, them, Barinthus, they," he said, muddling his words. "Taliesin…" He struggled to speak. "Listen, listen, ship Luguvalium, Tintagel, Avalon. They. Barinthus, Taliesin and." At that point his words became incomprehensible. Through sheer force of will he managed two final words, "Arthur wounded." Frantic with frustration, he began pounding his chest with his fist.

"Merlin, brother, please calm yourself," said Ganieda, grabbing his arm. "I think I know what you are trying to say. Please nod if I understand you correctly. You want Taliesin to go to Luguvalium where he will find Barinthus waiting with his ship. From there they should sail to Tintagel. Is that correct?"

Merlin nodded to his sister encouragingly.

"To find Arthur?"

He nodded again.

She looked at him gravely. "Alas, dear brother, I am so very sorry. You must brace yourself, my dear, for I have terrible news to tell you. Merlin, King Arthur is dead. Our High King and most of the British army fell in a terrible battle in Armorica."

Vigorously, he shook his head.

"What do you mean, brother? Do you think that Arthur is alive?"

He nodded.

"Are you sure, Merlin?"

Fiercely, he flashed her a look that brooked no contradiction.

"I see, I see, I'm sorry, Merlin, I didn't mean to question you. This comes as a shock, though a happy one." She paused. "But you said 'Arthur wounded.' Has Arthur been wounded?"

He half shook his head.

"Will be wounded?"

He looked at her encouragingly.

"All right. Do you mean that after Arthur is wounded, he will need to be taken to Avalon? To be healed by Morgen?" Merlin looked infinitely relieved as he nodded to his sister.

After a glance at his wife, Rodarch opened the door and invited his brother-in-law to come inside and share a morning meal with them. Nervously, Merlin turned and looked toward the now closed gate. Understanding Merlin's reluctance, Rodarch assured him that he would be free to leave at any time. After a moment's hesitation, Merlin nodded and stepped inside. He was peering around apprehensively as Ganieda and Rodarch led him to the comfortable room which they used when they wished to dine privately. Once the door was closed and Merlin had been seated at the table, Rodarch pulled Ganieda aside to speak with her. While keeping an eye on Merlin, he said quietly, "Ganieda, can this possibly be true? That King Arthur is alive?"

Ganieda, surprised by her husband's skepticism, replied, "Husband, can you still have doubts about my brother? You have seen how Merlin's prophetic powers have remained intact even after Morwen's poison had otherwise damaged his mind. You do recall Archbishop Kentigern's visit and how Merlin predicted a threefold death for someone in the room? Merlin's prediction sounded absurd to everyone at the time yet, just days later, it came to pass."

"Yes, Ganieda, of course I recall it. But did you yourself not just doubt your brother?"

"Yes, foolishly for a moment, I did. But what my brother has revealed has finally opened my eyes. It is now my belief that in Arthur's absence, Mordred is attempting to seize the throne. I believe all these reports that we have been receiving from the capital have been nothing but a tissue of lies."

"Are you suggesting that Queen Gwenhwyfar is complicit?"

"No, I am suggesting that our Queen is being coerced by an evil and duplicitous man who is not above using intimidation and perhaps even threats of violence to force her to comply. Frankly, I never trusted Mordred. Nor did my brother. He often said as much to me; although having nothing but vague feelings, he was reluctant to express publicly his suspicions about the man."

While they were talking, Merlin had quietly slipped from his chair. When Ganieda saw him making for the door, she cried, "Wait, Merlin, please! The meal will be here shortly, and I've sent for Taliesin to join us. Taliesin has been staying with us for a while. But of course you must already know that," she added, a bit confusedly.

As if on cue, the door opened, and Taliesin stepped into the room. Opening wide his arms, he exclaimed, "King Merlinus! Surely you are not leaving already? And before having a delicious meal? I've just passed the kitchen, and I must tell you that the smell of bread coming fresh from the oven is more than enticing! Please, please, my dear prophet, let us sit down so that we may enjoy a meal together. Really, my dear Myrddin, words truly cannot express how good it is to see you again! It's been far too many years!"

Putting his hand lightly on Merlin's arm, Taliesin led him back to the table. Visibly relaxing, Merlin sat down just as the cook and her staff came bustling in, bearing loaves of hot, steaming bread, blackberry jam and butter, fried eggs and cheese, apples and nuts, and pitchers of milk and fresh cider. With a bit of a flourish, the cook placed a large plateful of honeyed nut cakes on the center of the table. When Merlin grabbed one and began eating contentedly, the cook said, with a smile at King Rodarch, that she had decided to serve the cakes now rather than saving them for later. After thanking the cook and her efficient staff, Rodarch informed her that they would be able to serve themselves. With curtsies and bows, she and her helpers swept from the room.

During the meal, Ganieda recounted to Taliesin the mission that Merlin wished him to undertake. Without hesitation, Taliesin declared, "It would be my privilege and honor to help bring our High King to Avalon to be healed by the Lady Morgen. Though I wish the circumstances could have been happier, I have no doubt that King Merlinus will be proven correct. But Queen Ganieda, you were saying that you thought your brother was about to name a third person before he was rendered unable to speak."

"Yes, I believe so."

Turning to Merlin and seeing a glint of comprehension in the prophet's eyes, he asked, "Myrddin, is Queen Ganieda correct in believing that you wish another person to accompany King Arthur to Avalon?"

At first staring at Taliesin quizzically, Merlin then seemed to be engaged in an inner struggle as he fought to express himself in words. But the sounds he was at last able to mouth were incomprehensible. Frustrated, he struck the table with his fist.

"No, Myrddin, please," said Taliesin, gently laying a hand on Merlin's arm. "But I can see that you understand what I am saying. Let me speak a few names. Please nod if I hit upon the correct one." He thought for a moment. "Well, perhaps you would want Queen Ganieda to accompany King Arthur on the voyage?"

Merlin shook his head.

"Then King Rodarch?"

Again he shook his head.

"Hmm, let me think. Perhaps your nephew, Prince Gwyn? King Peredur then? Chieftain Stater? Or maybe your steward, Marius?"

Each, in turn, received the same negative response.

"Well then, well then. Let me think harder. Aha! I believe I may have it! A skilled doctor would be needed to tend to our High King's injuries during the voyage. Myrddin, do you want King Peredur's physician, Machaon, to accompany our High King to Avalon?"

Smiling, Merlin nodded. Then he closed his eyes. The effort to remain cognitive appeared to have utterly exhausted him. Slipping from his chair, he curled up on the floor next to the hearth and immediately fell asleep.

Taliesin studied him thoughtfully. "I wonder if yet another person should accompany us to Avalon. If anyone can heal Merlin's troubled mind would it not be Lady Morgen, the most skillful healer of all?"

Ganieda exclaimed, "Yes, yes! You're right! Of course! If anyone can cure my brother's affliction, it would be the Lady of Avalon! Ah, my dearest Taliesin, thank you for your brilliant suggestion!"

Ganieda's face had become radiant at the bard's proposal. Rodarch, however, appeared troubled. Surprised by his reaction, she asked, "Is something the matter, husband?"

"Ganieda, you do remember the promise I made to your brother – that I would never again suffer him to be fettered or restrained in any way. Ganieda, I intend to keep my promise."

"But, Rodarch, taking Merlin to Avalon will be for his own good. And you know that if my brother is not restrained in some way, he will simply run back into the woods, never to be cured, never to be himself again."

"Then that is what will happen! I'm sorry, Ganieda, but I shall not break the vow that I made to him."

"If I might interject?" asked Taliesin politely.

"Of course."

"If I may say, it does seem as though King Merlinus is greatly calmed by no more than my touch upon his arm."

"Yes, yes," said Ganieda eagerly. "Surely a mere touch cannot be considered a restraint?"

Rodarch frowned as he considered this. But seeing the imploring look on his wife's face and the bard's earnest expression, he at last relented.

"Thank you, husband!" she said joyously.

"But no more than a touch!" he warned. Turning to Taliesin, he said, "If at any time Merlin wishes to part from your company, you must allow it, no matter the circumstances. Even so much as your taking his arm to hold him back, I should regard as a breach of the solemn vow which I made to him."

"Yes, Lord King. I understand your command and I shall obey it," replied Taliesin, deferentially bowing his head. "With your permission, Lord King, if I might have leave to make my preparations for the journey?"

"Of course."

"Thank you, Lord King, My Queen." Walking to the door, he turned and politely bowed his way out.

Rodarch and Ganieda had remained seated at the table. Both were now regarding Merlin, sleeping peacefully on the floor.

"See, Ganieda. If your brother is not forced, he seems content to stay."

"But the floor is so cold and hard. Do you think he might prefer a bed?"

"Please, dear wife. Let him be. You must allow Merlin to do as he chooses."

"I know, I know. You're right, Rodarch. If my brother does go to Avalon, it should be by his own choosing, not mine. And if he would rather live forevermore in the woods as he is now, well…"

"I realize this is hard for you, dearest. Just as I know that you only want what is best for your brother. As do I."

She nodded and kissed her husband's cheek.

Chapter 23

Misgivings

King Rodarch dispatched a letter with a fast rider to Luguvalium to inform King Peredur of Merlin's return and all that had transpired. At the same time, he sent a score of messengers to ride out to every corner of his kingdom to rally the fighting men of Cumbria. Based on what Merlin had revealed, Rodarch judged that the coming battle would take place at or near Tintagel. Since the army could travel no faster than the speed of its infantry, Rodarch knew the march to that distant fortress could take almost a month. As soon as the civilian soldiers had gathered to bolster his regular standing army, he would lead his Cumbrians south, in anticipation of receiving King Arthur's call. Rodarch knew he was taking a risk. As soon as he set foot beyond the boundaries of his own kingdom at the head of an army, his action could be considered treasonable. An added concern was that he and his army would have to cross Brigantia, the kingdom which lay directly south of his own. Although he had tried to maintain a reasonably cordial relationship with Brigantia's king, the two men were hardly close. King Marin was most notable for his frequent and sometimes violent bursts of anger. Once, after severely beating his own steward for committing a minor infraction, he had been summoned to the capital and reprimanded by King Arthur. Although Marin had apologized for his offense, a man of his nature would be unlikely to forget or to forgive such a rebuke. Further, his middle son Meliot was an officer in the King's Harriers. In the coming conflict, King Marin's loyalty to King Arthur would be dubious at best.

Meanwhile, Ganieda had set off with Taliesin on the short journey to Luguvalium to see her brother off. Although Merlin had so far proved amenable to the bard's gentle guidance, she believed that her presence might further help to calm her unpredictable brother. As the three rode up to the city gates, King Peredur's steward came forward to greet them. After having grooms see to their horses, he escorted them to a private chamber in the royal residence. Peredur and Machaon were already there, and both men rose when they entered. After the steward was dismissed, he courteously bowed his way out of the room, shutting the door behind him. As soon as the door had closed, Merlin became visibly nervous. He would have followed the steward from the room had Taliesin not intervened. Gently touching his arm, the bard led him to a chair. Mutely obedient, Merlin sat, but his eyes were darting around the room fearfully. Fur-clad and with long, unkempt hair and beard, he resembled nothing so much as a trapped, wild animal.

Remorsefully, Peredur said, "Seeing Merlin again after so many years should be one of the most joyous occasions of my life. Yet seeing him like this…ah, my dearest Ganieda, words cannot express how truly sorry I am for your brother's continuing affliction, for which I bear much responsibility. If I had only listened to him and waited for reinforcements as he had suggested, rather than thoughtlessly charging into battle, Merlin would still have his wits. And I would still have three brothers." He stopped abruptly, unable to suppress a sob.

"Dearest Peredur, please know that you are not responsible for Merlin's affliction. Morwen, the person who poisoned him, is solely to blame. And please remember that Gwenddolau's heinous depredations on innocent civilians had to be stopped. It was Gwenddolau, and Gwenddolau alone, who bears the responsibility for Arfderydd."

"Thank you for your comforting words, Ganieda. They mean so much to me, more than I can say. But please, I have kept you and Taliesin standing. Please, please sit down and allow me to offer you some refreshment after your long journey."

They were seated around the table, sipping their drinks, when Peredur continued. "Through your husband's letter, Ganieda, I understand that Merlin wishes Machaon to accompany Taliesin on a voyage to Tintagel. I have told Machaon here as much as I know."

With a polite inclination of his head, Machaon said, "Queen Ganieda, first let me say how good it is to see you again. From what King Rodarch has written, it is my understanding that a physician will be required to tend to our High King's injuries. I would, of course, be most eager to help in any way I can."

"Thank you, Machaon. I know you are the very best man for the job. There is a certain Cumbrian queen who can personally attest to your medical skills," she added with a smile.

"You are too kind. I also understand that Taliesin has suggested that your brother be brought with us, so that he might be examined and his condition evaluated by the Lady Morgen. I have, of course, heard of Lady Morgen's healing skills and would be most pleased to meet her."

Here Peredur interjected. "I should mention, however, that King Rodarch was most emphatic that Merlin should not be forced or restrained in any way but be free to do whatever he chooses. I shall, of course, honor your husband's wishes."

"I also honor my husband's wishes, and, as you have seen, I am hopeful that Taliesin's gentle touch will be sufficient to guide my brother during the voyage to Avalon."

Surprisingly, Peredur seemed somewhat discomforted by her words. She could not imagine why.

With a glance at the doctor, Peredur said, "Which brings us to the crux of the matter. As I was saying to Machaon just prior to your arrival, there may be a problem. Shortly after I received your husband's letter, I went to the quay to speak with Barinthus. Three vessels were moored there – a Hibernian trader, my own ship, and a local fishing boat. Ganieda, I fear that Barinthus is not presently at Luguvalium. When I spoke to the harbormaster, he informed me that Barinthus has not been in Luguvalium for well over fifteen years."

Even before Peredur had finished speaking, Ganieda felt her mind reel. Could Merlin be mistaken? Could the poison which damaged his mind have finally destroyed the most elemental of her brother's abilities – his powers of sight and of prophecy? Might Merlin even be wrong that King Arthur still lived? The turmoil of her thoughts must have shown clearly on her face because Peredur quickly added, "Of course I would be happy to provide my own ship to carry Taliesin, Machaon, and your brother to Tintagel. And if it indeed proves true that our High King is alive and has been wounded, it would be my privilege to have him come to Luguvalium to convalesce. But a voyage to Avalon…" He trailed off. "Well, quite frankly, from what I have been able to gather, no mariner, other than Barinthus, appears to have ever gone there or, indeed, to even know exactly where it lies."

Taliesin was giving Ganieda a troubled look when the chair next to his overturned. Before he could react, Merlin was already up and rushing across the room. Merlin flung open the door but paused on the threshold. Turning to the others, he gave a slight beckoning gesture. Then he disappeared.

"I think he means for us to follow him," exclaimed Ganieda, jumping to her feet. Determined to keep her brother in sight, she ran from the room, with the others trailing behind her. After leaving the building, Merlin began striding confidently through the streets of Luguvalium. Although he was moving briskly, he was walking at a pace so the others could keep up if they hurried. Ganieda knew that had her brother wished, he could have easily outrun them all.

As they wended their way through the city streets, the people they passed all stopped to stare at the bizarre sight of the bard Taliesin and their doctor Machaon trotting breathlessly behind King Peredur and Queen Ganieda who were, in turn, hurrying to keep up with what appeared to be a wild man. Pointing and speaking to each other excitedly, they came to realize that the strange-looking man in the lead could be none other than Merlin himself, and they were soon buzzing with speculation.

At the north gate, King Peredur called to the porter to unbar the door, and Merlin walked through without breaking stride. When he reached the old Roman bridge, however, he stopped. Ahead, on the other side of the River Eden, Hadrian's Wall extended to the east and to the west for as far as the eye could see. Beyond the wall's gate was the road which led north into the wild and trackless forests of Caledonia. Merlin stood motionless, looking longingly to the north while Ganieda waited anxiously to see what he would do. When he turned west and began walking downstream toward the quay, she breathed a sigh of relief. Following her brother, she stepped up onto the stone platform that ran along the edge of the river and looked ahead eagerly, expecting to see Barinthus's ship. But the only vessels there were the three that Peredur had described.

Ganieda was devastated, her bitter disappointment almost more than she could bear. Turning to the others, she said, "For a little while, I thought all would be well, that we would see Barinthus's ship moored here with the others. But now…now I no longer have hope. I think my brother is mistaken, mistaken about everything. I believe the poison has finally destroyed his powers of sight and prophecy. I fear that all is now lost, and King Arthur is in Armorica, lying cold in his grave." She began to weep.

Peredur said, "Dearest Ganieda, I am so very sorry, but I fear you may be correct in your assessment of your brother's condition. Frankly, until we receive confirmation about our High King, one way or the other, I think it only prudent that we not mobilize our forces."

"This is all my fault, Peredur. I should have realized that my poor brother can no longer be trusted. Just look at him! Who else would have believed him! And now, because of my lack of judgment, I have put my husband and my children and our very kingdom at risk."

While they were speaking, Merlin had furtively sidled away from them and was now standing on the furthermost corner of the quay. Ganieda gave a deep sigh. "Taliesin, could you kindly go over to my brother with me? If nothing else comes of this shambles, perhaps we might at least coax him to return with us to Brocavum where he can be properly cared for. Though I very much doubt that we will succeed."

"Of course, My Queen. We can but try."

As they approached him, Ganieda said, "Please, brother, I have to return home now. I will not try to force you, but I hope you might willingly come back with me. It would give Rodarch and the children and me the greatest joy if you were to live with us. Rodarch has pledged that you would be free to leave at any time, and I make that pledge to you as well."

When Taliesin touched his arm to lead him from the quay, Merlin shook him off. He remained standing with his back to them, his eyes fixed to the west. After waiting for many minutes, Ganieda found herself growing increasingly impatient with her brother. Because of her foolish faith in him, she had put her husband's honor and integrity in jeopardy. A king unilaterally raising an army following the death of a High King and before the coronation of his successor could be accused of sedition. She needed to return home as soon as possible, to let Rodarch know that he should immediately call off the mobilization of his troops. Even so, word was sure to reach the capital, putting him at risk of being summoned to explain his action before the regents. He might very well be publicly censured by Prince Mordred. The thought of her husband being subjected to such humiliation made her feel almost physically ill. All because of her own stupid naivety and unquestioning belief in her brother.

"I'm sorry, Merlin, but I must go. You are free to come with me or to do as you please." Abruptly, she turned and walked away from him. He did not follow. Looking at Merlin sadly, Taliesin turned and walked after the queen. They had rejoined the others and were about to make their way back to the city gates when Machaon shaded his eyes. Pointing downstream, he said, "Look, isn't that a ship just rounding the bend?"

Turning to where the doctor was pointing, they could see a distant ship, being born upstream on an incoming tide. For a moment, Ganieda felt her heart soar. Then, sternly, she silently reminded herself to remain cautious until the vessel could be identified. As the small, graceful craft drew near,

Ganieda could have cheered. She and the others actually did cheer as the short, bow-legged man at the tiller expertly maneuvered the ship into an empty berth along the quay. The steersman appeared quite nonplussed by their exuberant greeting. Ganieda smiled. She knew that Barinthus was a shy man of few words, more comfortable on water than on land. As soon as he and a younger man had secured the craft to the mooring rings, they came over and bobbed bows to the queen and king.

Joyfully grabbing Barinthus's hands, Ganieda exclaimed, "How good it is to see you again! I cannot begin to tell you how relieved I am! And might this young man at your side be your son?"

"He is, Queen Ganieda. Another Barinthus," said the proud father.

"I am so pleased to meet you, Barinthus," she said, extending her hand. Blushing, the younger Barinthus gave her another little bow and then shook the queen's hand.

After introducing Taliesin and Machaon, Ganieda caught sight of something that made her smile: her own name, painted neatly on the bow. "So this is the *Ganieda*!"

The elder Barinthus looked worried. "You don't mind, do you, Queen Ganieda? Myrddin thought you wouldn't mind."

"Mind? No, not at all! On the contrary, I am honored. She's a beautiful ship."

"Thank you, Queen Ganieda. Oh, Myrddin, there you are! I'm sorry I'm late. We came as fast as we could but got caught out in the estuary by the tide."

Merlin, who had quietly come over to join the others, gave a silent nod.

Ganieda explained. "Barinthus, I don't know if you are aware of my brother's condition. Eight years ago, during a battle with the warlord Gwenddolau at Arfderydd, my brother almost died after he was given poison, guilefully slipped into a flask of wine by a vengeful woman. Physically he has recovered, but because of the effect of the poison on his mind, he is usually incapable of speech."

"I did hear what happened, Queen Ganieda, and it pains me greatly to see him like this. But you needn't worry; Myrddin and I have other ways to communicate."

Machaon broke in. "I'm sorry to have to interrupt, but I need to retrieve my medical kit, and Taliesin and I both need to fetch our bags. Barinthus, since I know next to nothing about sailing and tides, could you please tell us how much time we have before we depart?"

"It'll be high tide soon, and it goes out again fast, so about an hour."

"Just enough time if we hurry. With your permission, King Peredur."

"Of course. But actually, let me return with you both. I'll have my people help you with your bags."

After the others had left, Ganieda remained standing with her brother on the quay. As if sensing her thoughts, Barinthus suggested to his son that the two of them go back onboard to wait. When they were alone, Ganieda said, "Merlin, I need to make an apology. I am sure you were able to read my thoughts before Barinthus arrived, and I apologize for them. I'm so very sorry for ever doubting you. Can you find it in your heart to forgive me?"

Silently, he nodded. Then, with great emotion, he opened his arms, and brother and sister embraced lovingly.

Chapter 24

Farewells

The courtyard inside the royal compound was bustling with activity as the civilian soldiers who had gathered in Brocavum were being mustered for inspection. Walking through their ranks, King Rodarch and his military advisors were examining the troops and seeing that additional equipment was issued where needed. Meanwhile, the smaller group of civilians who had arrived on horseback were being inspected by the cavalry officers. With the civilian soldiers, Cumbria's regular forces, and the additional troops provided by King Peredur, Rodarch would have at his back an army of some six hundred strong.

Previously, it had been decided that King Peredur would remain in the north with a sizeable army of his own to repel any opportunistic attacks by Picts, Scots, Hibernians or fellow Britons. Ganieda was particularly concerned about the latter possibility. Although Queen Anna of Lothian had given her pledge of support to King Arthur, Ganieda had no doubt that Mordred's mother would back her son in the coming conflict. Since Rheged and Cumbria were well known bastions of support for the High King, an attack on either or both kingdoms by the Lothians could be a real possibility.

Ganieda, standing on the ramparts, was anxiously viewing the preparations for war when she caught sight of her son Gwyn. Always rather quiet and restrained among his peers, Gwyn had become even more subdued after his discreditable behavior at the battle of Arfderydd. When he had sought his father's permission to accompany the army, not in a position of privilege, but as a common soldier in an infantry unit, he had received it. Ganieda knew that Gwyn was seeking redemption, not only in the eyes of his father, but in the eyes of the men he would some day command as their king. She had not stood in his way. Yet now, seeing him standing in the ranks with the other infantrymen, she felt nothing but trepidation for his welfare.

Once the civilian soldiers had been incorporated into the regular military units, Rodarch and his officers mounted their horses. At the king's command, the doors of the palisade were swung open. As King Rodarch rode through the gates, he was met by the thunderous cheers of people lining the streets of Brocavum. The cheering continued as the foot soldiers came marching out beneath the colorful banners which identified each infantry unit. When the cavalrymen emerged, riding jauntily under flags held aloft by their bannermen, the joyful clamor became even more boisterous. Finally the wagons, loaded to capacity with food, fodder, munitions, and the myriad other necessities that an army on the march required, began rumbling through the gates. The long baggage train was still rolling past as the cheering faded, and people began to disperse.

Ganieda, however, remained standing on the ramparts. Although she was looking at the wagons as they made their way down the hill and across the market square, her thoughts were elsewhere. The four men whom she loved most in the world – her brother, her husband, her son, and her king – were all heading to the same place, a place of danger. One of them, she already knew, would be wounded. What might happen to the others, she dared not contemplate but could only hope and pray and wait.

As the last distant wagon lumbered across the market square and then out of sight, the young woman standing by her side began to weep. Pulling her daughter close, Ganieda could no longer hold back her own tears.

Acknowledgments

I wish to thank my friends, Robert Shay and Donna Shay, without whose continuing help and encouragement I would have stopped writing years ago. My thanks also to Sean Murtha for, once again, literally donning Merlin's mantle and for his many helpful suggestions. My heartfelt thanks to Millie Goswell for providing a snug harbor in the UK and for taking me to nooks and crannies that I never would have discovered on my own. Many thanks also to Matthew Stewart and Gina Matarazzo for their superb artistry, to Petrina J. Hughes for her excellent photography, and special appreciation to Liz McGeary Stragis for her invaluable suggestions and commentary. Finally, I most humbly wish to express my gratitude to Geoffrey of Monmouth, whose works are the ultimate wellspring of enduring tales that continue to fascinate and inspire generation after generation of storytellers and their readers.

Author's Note

Was Merlin Scottish? Although it may come as a surprise, early Welsh poems place Myrddin, the legendary and possibly historical bard and prophet, in what is today southern Scotland and northern England. It must be noted, however, that in the fifth and sixth centuries the Kingdoms of Scotland and England did not yet exist, and this region called *Yr Hen Ogledd* (The Old North), was inhabited by native Britons who spoke Cumbric, a Brythonic language nearly identical to Old Welsh. Culturally and linguistically, the Britons living in this area at that time would have been considered compatriots with those living in what is now Wales. Under ever-increasing pressure from the Anglo-Saxons, these northern Britons were eventually forced to retreat from their homeland, but they took with them their tales, histories, annals, king-lists, genealogies and poetry, which continued to be transmitted over the passing centuries. Although the oldest surviving manuscript of Welsh poetry, *The Black Book of Carmarthen*, dates to the mid-thirteenth century, the poems contained in it and other manuscripts are often far older. Some, including the Myrddin poems, allude to battles and events from the Early Medieval, that period of time following the withdrawal of the Romans from Britain which was formerly called the "Dark Ages."

Geoffrey of Monmouth (Galfridus Monemutensis) had established Caerfyrddin (Carmarthen) in southwestern Wales as Merlin's birthplace in his wildly popular circa 1136 book, *Historia Regum Britanniae* (The History of the Kings of Britain). In *Vita Merlini* (Life of Merlin), written some fourteen years later, Geoffrey moves Merlin's story back to its northern origins, seemingly after having gained additional information about his protagonist by way of these Welsh Myrddin poems.

In what is considered to be the oldest poem, *Yr Afallennau* (The Apple Trees), Myrddin, who has lost his reason during the Battle of Arfderydd, has been become a wild man of the woods, living as an outcast in the Caledonian wilderness. Guilt-ridden and relentlessly pursued by his enemies, he addresses an apple tree as he bemoans his present bleak existence, contrasting it with his earlier days when he had worn a torque of gold. His reference to wearing a torque into battle gives the poem an archaic feel, harkening back to a time before the coming of the Romans, when Iron Age Britons had worn these ornate Celtic neck rings as a symbol of their status and prestige. It is an indication, perhaps, that the Britons living north of Hadrian's Wall may have retained some of their earlier customs and traditions.

In *Yr Oianau* (The Greetings), another poem from the *The Black Book of Carmarthen*, each stanza begins with Myrddin's salutation to a little pig, which has become his sole companion in the wilderness. He warns the pigling to avoid mountain tops and to burrow only in hidden places in the woodlands, lest it be forced to flee from the hunting dogs of the men who are tracking them. (Interestingly, Geoffrey makes Merlin's animal companion a wolf). In the poem, Myrddin pitifully complains to the pigling of his wretched and hopeless state: "Snow up to my hips…Icicles in my hair…Since the Battle of Arfderydd I care not, Were the sky to fall and the sea to overflow…"

In addition to the Myrddin poems, Geoffrey was also clearly influenced by two prose tales which had persisted in the north about a certain Lailoken, a hairy and naked madman who communes with beasts in the forests of Caledonia after losing his reason during a horrific and costly battle. Although the battle is not named, the description of its location in the first tale, *Lailoken and Kentigern*, makes it clear that it is Arfderydd, and the story too closely parallels that of Myrddin's for him to be anyone else. Tellingly, in the Welsh poem *Cyfoesi Myrddin a Gwenddydd ei Chwaer* (The Conversation of Myrddin and his Sister Gwenddydd), Gwenddydd (Ganieda) sometimes addresses her brother as "Llallogan,"which is a parallel Welsh form of Lailoken. Elements that Geoffrey used from the second tale, *Lailoken and Meldred*, include a prophetic madman being held in captivity by a king, the prisoner's unexpected laughter which leads to his release, and the later fulfillment of his seemingly impossible prophecy of a triple-death.

In using these newfound sources for his Merlin "sequel," however, Geoffrey creates a chronological difficulty for himself. In *Vita Merlini*, Geoffrey has his protagonist fighting in the actual circa 573 Battle of Arfderydd and interacting with such historical late-sixth-century figures as the bard Taliesin and Rhydderch (Rodarch), King of Strathclyde. Yet in his earlier book, *Historia Regum Britanniae*, Geoffrey depicts Merlin prophesying to the mid-fifth-century King Vortigern. Geoffrey tries, rather unconvincingly, to reconcile this problem by portraying Merlin as being extremely elderly by the end of *Vita Merlini*. One of Geoffrey's fiercest critics, Giraldus Cambrensis (Gerald of Wales), an acerbic churchman who lived a generation or so after Geoffrey, was quick to pounce on this anachronism. He concluded that there must have been two Merlins: Merlinus Ambrosius from Carmarthen, the son of an incubus, who prophesied to Vortigern and Merlinus Celidonius from Scotland, the prophetic wild man of the woods who lived in the time of King Arthur (although putting Arthur in a late-sixth-century context would have been equally anachronistic).

For Geoffrey, however, there is only one Merlin. In the opening pages of *Vita Merlini*, Geoffrey states that Merlin, famous throughout the world as prophet and king of the proud Demetae in southwest Wales, had traveled north to fight on the side of Kings Peredur and Rodarch against the savage marauder Gwenddolau. Later in the book, Merlin's identity as Merlinus Ambrosius from the *Historia* is confirmed beyond a doubt when he reminisces with his sister Ganieda about the predictions he had made to King Vortigern as they stood together beside the drained pool from which two battling dragons had emerged.

While Gerald of Wales was certainly not being unreasonable in questioning Merlin's supernatural longevity and in offering a possible alternative explanation, his vitriolic attacks upon Geoffrey are much less palatable, particularly in light of his frequent borrowings from Geoffrey's works for his own books. The most notorious of Gerald's harangues comes from his book, *The Journey Through Wales*. In it, Gerald relates that when he was in Caerleon, he learned of a man who was much plagued by demons. When these harrassing spirits became too much for the man to bear, Saint John's Gospel was placed on his lap, and the demons vanished, flying away like so many birds. But when the Gospel was removed and the *Historia Regum Britanniae* by Geoffrey of Monmouth was put there in its place, the evil spirits immediately returned, alighting not only on the man's body but all over the book as well and, as Gerald assures his readers, staying longer and being more vexatious than ever.

While more recent critics do not typically invoke demons when evaluating the historical accuracy of *Historia Regum Brittaniae,* they can be almost as scathing in their judgments. Yet, in Geoffrey's defense, he himself had never called his book a history, but had, in fact, titled it *De Gestis Britonum* (On the Deeds of the Britons). This title is, perhaps, more indicative of what Geoffrey's aspirations may have been: the creation of an epic-poem for the Britons much as Virgil had done for the Romans and Homer for the Greeks. Geoffrey, who makes numerous allusions to classical literature in his works and to Virgil's *Aeneid* in particular, may have similarly intended to bestow a foundational origin story myth upon the British people. As Geoffrey himself says in the coda to *Vita Merlini*:

"We have brought the song to an end. Therefore, you Britons, give a laurel wreath to Geoffrey of Monmouth. For, indeed, he is your Geoffrey, and he once sang of your battles and of your leaders, and he wrote a little book called *The Deeds of the Britons*, deeds now celebrated throughout the world."

Only because of Geoffrey of Monmouth's epic artistry to guide the way have I been able to create my own version of the enduring tales of the legendary King Arthur, his trusted advisor Merlin, and Merlin's equally sagacious sister Ganieda.